Gold Among the Trees

By

Peter King

This is a work of fiction.

Published by The Elite Lizzard Publishing Company 2023

~<u>Prologue</u>~

Meredith, 9th Viscount Hantington or Merry to his friends, put down his cup of breakfast tea and absently reached for the last slice of buttered toast before picking up another morning paper. Just as he start reading, the phone rang.

"Good morning, Meredith." The Permanent Secretary for the Treasury interrupted Merry's morning routine. "I hope I'm not disturbing you." Before Merry could answer, the PS went on "What have you heard about movements of assets out of Hong Kong? We can't follow some of the transactions, and that's causing disquiet among the upper echelons."

"Why?"

"They're worried those assets might not be suitable"

"You mean proceeds of crime? Why ask me?"

"Give it a thought, will you?"

"Hold on! That's really outside my field."

"You've a reputation for pulling rabbits out of hats. Don't ruin your reputation." And the call ended.

Merry just sighed, but after a few moments he reached for the phone and muttered "I think I know whom to call."

1.

Peter Holroyd swivelled his chair and looked content-edly out of the window. Under a bright and cloudless sky, he could see the upper arc of the London Eye and the tops of the Parliament buildings above the trees of the park across the road. Just inside the park, summer blossoms ornamented flower beds nestling between green swathes of tended grass. Absent any sign of the office buildings visible in other parts of the city that supposedly testified to superior architecture, this view gave him a comfortable feeling of permanence and stability. *A perfect day for a walk in the park,* he thought contentedly. Just then his phone rang.

"Peter, old boy," Merry's voice floated down the line. "Not disturbing you, am I?"

I hope not, Holroyd thought. "Oh, Merry. No, not at all. What can I do for you?"

"I wondered if you would be free to have dinner tomor-row evening."

"That's awfully decent of you Merry. May I ask, why this generous offer?"

"I have a project that is right up your alley. How does dinner at the Athenaeum, sound?"

Holroyd paused before answering.

"This isn't like last time, is it?"

"Whatever do you mean?"

"Last time we had dinner there I ended up getting shot

3

at, and finally, landed in a Chinese jail before being escorted out of the country."

"I say! That's not entirely fair. You ended up quite nicely, as I recall and no thanks from you." Merry tried to sound hurt but failed.

Dinner at the Athenaeum was a delightful idea, but Holroyd was married now and would have to ask Pearl before accepting. In any case, he wasn't about to place himself in danger again and risk leaving Pearl alone.

"Merry, as you know I'm married again and we're just settling into our new domestic arrangements."

"Why not bring her along as well?"

"That's a great idea. Pearl will enjoy the experience, but I'll have to confirm it with her." And with that the call ended.

Holroyd sat back. He and Merry had gone to school together after which Merry had gone into the Civil Service and was now quite senior, while Holroyd had landed in academia. *What does Merry have up his sleeve this time? He only calls when he wants something and when he does whatever he wants it's usually to be found at the end of a very greasy and very rancorous bargepole. Last time, I ended up in the company of more bodies than a plague pit, not to mention the assassination and kidnap attempts on me personally. But to be fair, by working for Merry I met my wife, in the end was given recognitions by both China and Britain for my contributions and received my university tenure. Still, I'm not sure the cost was quite worth it.* "I won't go through anything like that again, not for all the tea in China. I'm very comfortable as matters now stand," he muttered to himself.

He looked around his flat. Heavy dark green velvet drapes framed the large Georgian style windows through which sunlight sometimes streamed from morning to afternoon, mellowed by the foliage of trees in front of the house. On the cream-coloured walls of his study-cum-living-room gilded sconces in which small electric light bulbs replacing the original wax candles provided a soft light.

Shelves filled to overflowing with books stood against one wall, and carpets and scattered rugs in clashing hues and different patterns covered the floor. His desk that had belonged to his great grandfather was built of solid wood and had brass or maybe gilt handles on the drawers. His Georgian silver tea set gleamed on a Chippendale sideboard above which to one side hung an 18th Century American Eagle Mirror, and to the other an early version of Constable's the Hay Wain. Holroyd was particularly fond of this painting although he suspected it might be a fake. His own expertise was in Ming and Qing maritime travels not early 19th Century English paintings.

Anyone looking at him would see a middle-aged man with a wrinkled face and a mournful expression wearing rather thick-lensed glasses on a head bearing only a distant memory of hair. Perhaps five feet eight inches, his body inclined to paunchiness. He generally wore an open necked cotton shirt that had seen better days, and now hinted at a frayed collar while his tweed jacket sported old-fashioned leather patches at the elbows, and his trousers showed no sign of ever having supported a crease. In these days of designer T-shirts, jeans, and hoodies, Professor Peter Holroyd was most definitely out of tune.

Holroyd liked the quiet routine of his academic life and

preferred the company of books to most people. He oved seclusion and abhorred social occasions with their meaningless exchanges of small talk, family news, and tales of holidays in ghastly tourist traps or wildernesses best left to mother nature. The parameters of professionalism still dictated his social life although that was changing in subtle ways since his marriage to Pearl.

He had met Pearl, or Shao Yao to give her Chinese name, when she was working as the deputy librarian in the Chinese provincial town of Fujinhaizhou. He had been smitten at first sight, but circumstances at the time did not permit him to pursue his desire. He was able to return to China and marry her only after his task there had been completed. Once safely back in England, Holroyd looked forward to a blissfully happy future. And now the invitation from Merry. He was not sure how Pearl would react.

She was curious but also excited at the prospect of dining in such an august place. Relieved, Holroyd rang Merry and confirmed they would be there.

***

Arriving at the Athenaeum, Holroyd had explained to Pearl that the Athenaeum included fifty-two Nobel prize winners among its membership of men of letters, philosophers, artists, and other disciplines.

On entering the lobby with its parquet floor, Holroyd pointed to the gilded statue of Pallas Athena, still gleaming pristinely from the top of the stairs as it did before Victoria was crowned Queen.

Pearl looked at the general décor, "Peter! This isn't

welcoming! In China, our old buildings mix tradition and art to help you adopt a good spirit. Here, I almost feel as if I've been told to report to my ancestors to explain my behaviour.[1]"

Holroyd laughed. "There are many buildings in England that are very similar and are testimonials to a lot of history and even greatness. But I can see how one might feel that way."

"Well, then I should do some research to learn the history and how greatness is judged." Pearl answered with seriousness. Holroyd just smiled.

On learning his identity, the club porter led them to the wood-panelled bar where several elderly couples were chatting, and some lone individuals sitting in wing-back leather chairs that had supported the bottoms of members during Victoria's heyday were hiding behind newspapers. Merry was sitting in a corner behind a small table surrounded by more modern chairs. On seeing them enter, he stood up and greeted them warmly and led them to his corner. Pearl looked at the painted portraits hanging on the walls, mostly depicting elderly grandees with mutton-chop whiskers, and wearing the ecclesiastical garb of bishops in the Anglican Church.

"Peter! Look at those pictures. Those men don't look very happy," she whispered.

Before Holroyd could find a suitable answer, Merry interrupted with "Drinks, Pearl? Peter?"

Once settled with glasses in their hands, and after some

---

[1] Chinese traditions include the QingMing Festival or going to the tombs of ancestors both to tend the site and for some people report on their actions to the departed (and maybe get back praise, advice, or reproach as suits the report).

small talk, Merry came to the point. "Peter, I have a small problem and I think you would enjoy helping out on this one."

"Hang on, Merry! That opening sounds awfully familiar, and I have to tell you that once bitten, twice shy."

"Oh, no! This is right up your alley. It's a pure research project and I assure you there's no danger involved. It has to do with a ship sailing from China."

Holroyd admired the sparkles reflecting the lights as he twirled his cut crystal glass. "That doesn't sound very interesting."

"It may not be, but we want to be certain it isn't." Merry paused to take a swallow and went on to explain how matters weren't very certain in Hong Kong right now. Many Hong Kong people were making moves to get out while they could, and were moving capital to other countries such as Canada.

"That's hardly surprising," Holroyd's commented. "So, what's your interest?"

"We, and other countries, are concerned that such capital flows are all above board. We try and keep an eye on what's going on so that we don't end up with someone who is escaping with ill-gotten gains."

"Ill-gotten gains? That's not my field at all."

Merry took another swallow and went on to explain the big problem of cash being moved around by the Asian Drug cartels. Law enforcement was doing its best to monitor and eventually step in to stop it, but often the description of the cash transfer was screened by deceptive, but plausible labels, such as proceeds from the sale of goods or property. It was often difficult to get behind that screen. Hong Kong was one of the places being watched.

"I'm following you. But to be honest, it's not something I'm interested in." Merry ignored Holroyd's reaction.

"Now, here is where it gets a bit strange. One of the people we are watching has started to look for a ship."

"That's not so strange, is it? It should be easy enough just to call up a ship broker. I'm sure that any man worth a few pounds would have connections."

"Yes, but that's not where the inquiries are being made. From what we've been told, requests for information have gone to the National Archives in Hong Kong, Taiwan, and Beijing as well as a couple of libraries including the Bodleian."

"Oh! Now that is strange." Holroyd suddenly became curious. "Have you learned the nature of the inquiries?"

"We got a general idea but no specifics. They're asking about a ship sailing from South China to the East during the middle of the 17th Century."

"Pardon? You're telling me that one of the people who is or might be trying to get out of Hong Kong today is searching for a ship that's over 300 years old? The only reason I can think of is that it carried a cargo that might be worth recovering today. But why would that have anything to do with trying to move capital out of Hong Kong?"

"That's the question I want you to answer. It's possible that somehow this search for a ship is a cover for a new method of moving capital. Personally, I can't see how it could be possible, but supposedly wiser heads than mine want it looked at. I thought you would be the person to approach."

"That's decent of you and you are right, it's something I'd love to do. But as you know, I'm busy here and I don't have the resources to undertake the sort of research this would require."

"Yes, I thought of that. I've taken the liberty of suggesting a visiting professorship for you at a university on Vancouver Island with a research grant that should cover what you need. They've agreed subject to your acceptance."

"Why would you choose a university on Vancouver Island? As far as I know, they have no expertise in Ming or Qing Dynasty voyages."

"Well, the inquiry specifies to the East, and I don't know where to the East a Chinese ship would go. I thought you'd find it easier to be close to China without going there."

"There are places closer to China than Canada's West Coast," Holroyd pointed out.

"But they don't speak English or Chinese in those places, do they?" Holroyd had no immediate response.

Merry went on. "I was thinking, it could give you a base from which to follow up on the claims of that fellow Gavin Menzies and his book…what was it called again?"

"1421. But you must know that his claims have little to do with the North American West Coast. Besides which his claims have been challenged on various grounds not the least of which a great deal of circumstantial evidence flawed by questionable scholarship."

"But you aren't quite convinced they are fake, are you?" Merry looked at Holroyd with a grin and reached for his drink.

"No. Just because evidence is circumstantial does not mean it's not valid, and demanding a standard of scholarship has its weaknesses," Holroyd responded.

"How so?" Merry sat back and looked at Holroyd expectantly.

"Well, standards of scholarship have been used to support opinions that subsequently were proved false." Holroyd paused for a moment. "For example, academics claimed for years in scholarly peer reviewed publications that the statues on Easter Island could not have been put there by people from Latin America because they could not have travelled there. A similar claim was that the pyramids of Latin America could not have been influenced by the ancient Egyptians because, again, there was no means for the ancients by which to have crossed the Atlantic Ocean. Then after the War, Thor Heyerdahl built crafts based on ancient designs and by making the voyages showed that the academics were wrong in using lack of transport as an excuse not to consider those influences. Furthermore, recent examinations of thousands of years old Egyptian mummies revealed traces of coffee and cocaine, which as far as we know could only have come from the Americas. That suggests transatlantic trade existed long before Columbus."

"What are you saying then?" Merry asked puzzled.

"Proving that something was possible advances the possibility that something could have happened although it does not prove it did happen, but it certainly destroys any claim that it could not have happened."

"Following that logic, it would be feasible for the ship in question to have sailed much further East than Asia. There aren't many places east of Asia until the west coast of North America. So, it's possible such a ship could have reached North America," Merry observed.

"Indeed, it's possible."

"And if you were on location on the West Coast out there you might be able to find some evidence that this Chinese ship reached there," Merry artlessly raised the idea.

"Yes, it might." Holroyd seemed to be tempted, but paused.

"So, will you take the challenge?" Merry leaning forward looked intensely at Holroyd and Holroyd sensed he was being enticed to accept.

"I'd love to. It's very generous of you," Holroyd accepted.

"*Shenme*?" Pearl gasped before switching to English "What?"

Startled, Holroyd backtracked "I can't give you an answer right now. It's not as if I'm footloose and fancy free anymore," he sensed the cat was out of the bag.

"Yes. Well do let me know. Shall we go and dine?"

***

Pearl refused to talk on the way home. Once inside the

door, she complained.

"How could you accept? We've only started to settle down."

"Yes, I know, *qinaide*, but it's a wonderful opportunity for me."

"Oh, yes! An opportunity for you!" Pearl's voice rose. "Is that all you think about? What about us? What about me? You don't love me at all!" Before Holroyd could mount a defence, Pearl went on relentlessly, "You have already achieved so much. What more opportunity do you need?"

"Sweetheart! It's not about me, it's about my work," Holroyd said.

"What's the difference?"

"I can further knowledge about how Chinese were able to do so much more travelling and exploring than the West ever could at that time." Pearl stopped as she considered this approach.

"Oh! You mean you will show how clever and advanced the Chinese were?" Her voice lowered as she explored a potential profit.

"Yes, dear."

Her face brightened for a moment, but then she returned to consider her own position and in a forlorn voice pointed out, "But I will be alone here in a strange country and with no friends."

"You have met some of my colleagues here and they will be your friends," Holroyd pointed out.

"Old stuffy men who have never left England but have fixed ideas about the World and no sense of art or music," she scoffed.

"Now that's not fair."

"Yes, it is. And with the winter coming I will be forced to sit here alone in the dark not able to go out because of the cold and the rain."

"Why not come with me? I am sure we can arrange it."

"You want me to go to a place that is full of wolves, wild bears, and covered with snow and ice most of the year?" Pearl looked at him stonily.

"But the West Coast isn't..." Holroyd was stopped by the look on Pearls' face and understood that was not a good idea to pursue that argument and considered a new defence. He suddenly had an idea that he thought would please her.

"While I am away, you could invite your mother to come and visit."

"That's a lovely idea. She will enjoy that so much." Her face brightened and Pearl gave in, but Holroyd suddenly remembering how often Chinese mothers-in-law liked to rule the home even if they were only invited guests and wondered if he had secured a Pyrrhic victory.

2.

The flight from London had been tiring and the flight from Vancouver to Victoria had been decidedly bumpy and uncomfortable. The long taxi ride from the airport to the university hadn't done much to improve Holroyd's feelings of weariness. However, he was warmly greeted at the university and taken to his university provided quarters.

The apartment was modern and functional. The windows of his sitting room afforded him a view of distant mountains and even a glimpse of the sea. The rooms were tastefully painted and hung with prints of paintings depicting forests and seascapes, and the furniture was contemporary Scandinavian. But the place lacked personality. Here, his desk was spartan with only his laptop and a couple of folders containing his lecture notes. To be candid, he missed the personal touches of his London flat.

Holroyd felt jet-lagged, and sleep deprived. Not even the prospect of the coming year cheered him up right now. At least the autumn weather promised to be pleasant.

He unpacked the rest of his things wondering why he had brought formal evening attire to go with the thick woolen clothing he thought would be necessary for the winter. If the winter clothing wasn't enough, he could buy one of those artic coats and snow boots if needed ... maybe colourful ones so Pearl would also have them. But perhaps he wouldn't need to.

Even though he was tired he switched on the television and watched the local news. The COVID epidemic was still raging; there had been a mass shooting on the East Coast, a gang warfare had broken out over drugs in Vancouver, and several hundred more children's graves had been found at a former Residential School site. *Oh! How lovely and reassuring to learn all that.* After the news, there was a sitcom that he found incomprehensible and switching the TV off, he sat back thinking about his quest.

He knew in the mid 16th Century the Spanish established a transpacific trade route between Manila and Acapulco, in part bringing Chinese trade goods to send on to Europe. However, he could not recall any report of a Chinese ship sailing eastwards beyond the Philippines at that time. Other than to neighbouring Asian countries, where and why would a 17th century Chinese ship sail further eastward?

In China, the 17th Century brought in the destruction of the Ming Dynasty and the installation of the Qing. Those events were accompanied by unrest as the people had respected the Ming and were not happy with the new regime. But why would anyone today be interested in a ship that sailed from China to the East at that time?

Interest in ships' movements is and was generated by who or what was being transported and for what reason. *I can only guess what personage, cargo, or reason from that time could possibly be linked to the current movement of capital out of Hong Kong. But perhaps Merry is right and working on his request could answer if a Chinese ship came here far earlier than people think.* The thought was exciting.

He stopped, stood up, and went to shower before going to bed when he remembered he had lectures to prepare. He decided he could safely postpone that to the morning.

3.

Getting up the next morning as he went to prepare his breakfast, Holroyd noticed an envelope had been slipped under the front door. He bent down, retrieved, and opened it to see an invitation written in Copper Plate script. He read 'Dean Joseph Hummersdorf, PhD, cordially invites you to attend a reception, held in honour of Peter Holroyd PhD.' The time was for the same evening and Holroyd was requested to reply. Holroyd was irritated at the short notice, but dutifully responded he was honoured to accept the invitation. Absent were dress instructions and Holroyd realized he would have to decide for himself how to dress.

On thinking about the formality of the invitation and reflecting on his impressions from England of how deans behaved, he decided Black Tie was appropriate and he gloomily decided he would dress accordingly. He hated these occasions, but the situation demanded he attend.

Arriving at the dean's house a maid led him through to the garden from where came sounds of laughter and the smell of roasting seafood and vegetables on the grill. His entrance was announced by the maid, and everyone turned to look at him in silent amazement. He, in turn, looked over at the guests many of whom were dressed in open-necked sports shirts and slacks. A few wore T shirts, shorts, and sneakers. No one moved and Holroyd wondered what to do or say.

Finally, a beefy individual in a well-worn T-shirt monogrammed with the words 'Save the Whales' came over with a can of beer in one hand and the other stretched out in greeting.

"Hello, Doctor Holroyd. I'm Jim Dodson, Mayor of this city. I guess our host forgot to tell you, we like informality, but that aside, welcome to our community. Take off your Jacket and tie, open that shirt, roll up your sleeves and come in to meet the rest of the group. Care for a beer?"

Chagrined by his clearly inappropriate dress. Holroyd mumbled a greeting, and accepted a can of beer. He took a sip and grimaced at the cold and weak brew.

"Isn't that better?" asked Dodson and grasped him by the elbow to steer him to the crowd that had now resumed their former gaiety.

"Peter! Glad you could make it." Hummersdorf came over.

Holroyd, still preferring the old Imperial system of measurements, judged the man was perhaps five feet three inches tall, thin, with pinched features and slicked down black hair. He wore a faded green polo shirt and checkered slacks, the colour of which possibly included khaki. "I do apologize for the short notice, but today was the only available cay unless we waited until later in the year. Sorry I wasn't at the door to greet you, but I was busy at the grill and didn't notice your arrival, but I see Jim here filled in for me. Let me take you round and introduce you."

Holroyd was escorted to meet dignitaries and faculty members and promptly forgot their names. He met a First Nations lecturer and was told there was another who unfortunately could not be present. On asking, Holroyd learned there were some First Nation students attending the university although integration with the other students was sometimes difficult. Further questions about the nature of the problem were met with polite evasions, and Holroyd decided this was not the time or place to pursue the matter.

One young man who greeted Holroyd cheerfully was introduced as Hummersdorf's son Rodney. He was dressed in a well-worn T-shirt and jeans that seemed to sport more holes than material, but overall gave an impression of a sunny disposition.

Introductions over, Holroyd was left to circulate as best he could. As everyone knew everyone else, he found it awkward to get into conversations, and his naturally reticent English background didn't help, but the others tried to include him. However, he found most of the groups deep in discussion on academic or social topics of which he had little knowledge and soon drifted away to try find a group in which he could join the conversation.

Dodson reappeared at his elbow and led him over to a group of women. "Jane, meet Peter Holroyd. Peter, this is my other half, Jane."

Holroyd found himself introduced to a large overweight woman incongruously dressed in a checked shirt, pink shorts, and sandals. "Welcome to Canada. How do you like it so far?" She gave a friendly smile.

Holroyd smiled and mumbled that he liked what he saw.

"It's a great place if you like hunting, fishing, and hockey. But coming from England, you might find it a bit boring."

"I'm sure I won't be bored. I can always find something to do."

Holroyd wasn't quite sure how to continue and almost desperately looked around the garden.

The patio was bordered on one side by a well-manicured lawn, itself bordered by flowers and leafy plants he did not recognize. A stand of Rhododendrons behind which could be seen trees marked the edge of the property opposite the house. "It's a lovely garden."

"Yes, it's nice, and when the Rhododendrons are in bloom it's magnificent. Too bad you missed them, but you'll probably catch them next Spring."

"Is the dean the gardener?"

"I think it's Ron. Joe isn't one for flowers. But, come on over and get something to eat. The sea food is all local and we have some of the best salmon in Canada." With that he was taken around to exchange more friendly but meaningless platitudes all the while drinking beer and eating a variety of seafood dishes and an occasional hamburger. It was precisely the sort of social gathering Holroyd disliked, but he knew he was duty bound to participate and pretend he enjoyed the hospitality.

As the occasion dragged on, Holroyd stood to one side, wondering when and how he could decently take his leave. He felt an itch on his neck and another on his exposed arm. Just what was missing! Insects! *I wonder if they're the type to carry disease.* And from then on, the party lost more of its attraction.

"I can't let you stand there at a party held in your honour without introducing myself."

A well-built tall individual who almost towered over Holroyd came up to him, hand outstretched. "Ron Manning."

"Pleased to meet you."

"I hope so!" Manning grinned. "But you seem a little lost."

"Yes, a little. It's never easy for me to meet so many people I don't know."

"Oh! Don't worry, you'll be part of the community in no time. Just take it easy. It's not like England where people maintain formality for decades. We don't worry about your social background so much; we accept you for who you are and how you join in."

"That's very encouraging, thank you. May I ask what you do?"

"I work at the Naval Armaments Depot. I keep the Navy supplied with things that go bang."

"If you're not in academics, how is it you are here?" Holroyd asked curiously.

"Oh, Joe and I are partners."

"Joe?"

"Yep, your host the dean."

"You mean, you two have a business together?"

"No way. We're married," Manning laughed. Holroyd who hadn't quite got used to such modern developments asked, "How does that work out for you?"

Manning smiled and replied "Hey! This is Canada. If it's not hockey we don't worry about which team you play on."

"Ah!" Holroyd nodded.

"Tell me about your work." Manning changed topics.

Holroyd talked about his work and was delighted to find Manning listening attentively. Manning replied by saying that his hobby was native societies and their histories. "Did you know, for instance, there's proof that people survived the ice age here?"

"I had no idea."

"Occasionally, people come across ruins or artefacts that don't fit the common beliefs about how this region was settled. Several First Nation Bands have oral traditions that testify to events that go back centuries, if not millennia."

"And you have studied these traditions?"

"Studied would be an exaggeration, but followed many of them, yes."

"Would you be open to discussing these traditions with me? I have a sense we might find some common ground. You see, I want to find out if any Chinese or other Asian ships came here during the 16th or 17th Centuries, and perhaps there's mention of such a visit among the traditions." Manning thought for a moment.

"Don't believe I ever heard of such visits, but let's keep in touch. Oh, hey! More food is ready. C'mon over and grab something before it's all gone." Grasping Holroyd by the elbow he led him to the food table. As Holroyd took a salmon sandwich, a voice drew Holroyd's attention.

"So, you're the one who insists the Chinese discovered America." A hand touched Holroyd's arm. "Paul van Vervoort, Anthropology."

Holroyd turned to see a thin man with a bloated face looking at him with slightly unfocused eyes.

"Complete nonsense of course. There's no evidence for it. Surprised your paper got accepted."

"Pardon?"

"Oh, c'mon. You are way off track so why pretend otherwise? It's all unsupported conclusions and wild assumptions. Not scholarly at all." He took a hefty swallow from his beer. "You're just another fraud." And with that he staggered drunkenly.

"What was that?" Holroyd was completely stunned. Not only was the attack unexpected, but it was also taking place at what should have been a celebratory occasion. Before he could frame a response, Vervoort continued. "What is so unfair, is that while you get your lies published, and my papers are challenged, I'm the one who gets shot down." Vervoort took another hefty swallow some of which dribbled down his chin. "Whose arse have you been kissing?"

Holroyd felt a rising wave of outrage and fury. He was just about to make a cutting reply when Manning reappeared.

"Ah! I see you have met our resident anthropology expert. Hi Paul."

Vervoort mumbled something and took another gulp but dribbled much of it down his shirt and without commenting on the mishap, Manning continued, "I'm sure you two will have lots in common to talk about."

"I don't see that happening," Vervoort slurred and veered away.

"Do I sense a disagreement here?" Manning asked.

"Yes, to say the least," Holroyd answered. "I hope he isn't always like that."

"I can't say. Depends on whether he feels you're going to undermine his own work."

"Has he any interest whether the Chinese came here first?" asked Holroyd. "If he does, maybe he and I can exchange ideas. But from his comments, I somehow doubt it."

"No idea. Paul follows all sorts of research. But you might want to watch your back with him. It's best not to get on his wrong side."

Holroyd watched as Vervoort weaved his way through the garden. *Just what I need. A Faculty member ready to scotch my work even before I've begun.* He noted a youth drinking from a can of beer and standing by himself and wearing clothing that Holroyd thought as a mix of Grunge and Goth.

"Who is that young man? He doesn't seem to fit in here."

"That's Paul's son, Mark." Something in Manning's tone suggested disapproval and Holroyd turned to him: "Troubled lad hangs around in some gang that got hauled in for selling drugs and a liking for strong drink," Manning explained.

Holroyd turned away and mingled with the guests again trying to mix in. Despite the general friendliness, he felt uncomfortable. As soon as he felt he could decently slip away, he did so.

4.

"Good morning, class." Holroyd put his briefcase on the desk. "Welcome to this course on 16th and 17th Century maritime voyages here on Canada's West Coast."

He looked at the students in the lecture hall that could easily seat 300 people. He noted that it was only about a quarter full for the first lecture and briefly wondered if this was a sign that students today had no interest in his subject or disbelieved there could be anything worth listening to.

I suspect, Holroyd thought, *most of the students sitting here are just curious to see me rather than to learn about my field. Oh well, let's see how many turn up for the second lecture.*

"Now, I expect most of you assume I will be lecturing on the voyages of Europeans and Indigenous people here, but that's not where I will be going. I know nothing about such activities." He paused expecting some reaction at this admission. There being none, he continued, "In fact, for the purposes of this course, I consider such activities to be irrelevant or at best, immaterial." There was a stir of surprise.

"Excuse me, Professor, but are you dismissing the activities of First Nations as irrelevant or immaterial?" Several students sat up showing signs of interest.

"For the purposes of this course, yes. There is no evidence that Indigenous people engaged in any maritime travel other than for coastal purposes such as fishing, war, or trade. However, that does not necessarily apply to civilizations further south such as Central and South America." The admission was met with complete silence.

"Any other questions? If not, let's proceed."

"Proceed with what?" asked a feminine voice. "I don't know about any others here, but I'm not about to sit here listening to more Imperialist Colonial Bullshit." Many students agreed and several students stood up gathering their books preparing to leave the hall. Holroyd was stunned by the reaction.

"Sit down," he shouted in an uncharacteristically thunderous voice. All movement stopped and everyone looked at him.

"I said sit down. You will do me the courtesy of hearing my next comments after which, if you still so wish, you may leave." Some students remained motionless looking at him, others sat down. Holroyd took a deep breath and in a voice that resembled his lecturing tone he repeated. "Resume your seats if you please." Slowly the class settled back.

"In this course my focus is on 16th and 17th Century Transpacific contacts and communications between people from Asia and Europeans on the West Coast of the Americas."

"But Europeans did not get to the West coast until the 16t^h Century and then only by the Spanish and much further South. The West Coast of Canada wasn't visited by Europeans until the 17th or 18th centuries," one student said.

"James Cook came here in about 1750," another student pointed out.

Holroyd looked up and smiled. "Yes, that is so. But, why do you think the exploration of the West Coast was a European achievement? Please note I do not say discovery. That feat most definitely lies with Indigenous people." There were some appreciative chuckles.

"But to whom are you referring then?" a male voice asked "Aztecs? Incas?"

"Maybe, though a far as I know they were not Asian civilizations. Furthermore, I am not aware either civilization engaged in northward travels. No! I suggest Asians and in particular the Chinese were the first foreigners to come here." There was a stunned silence.

"Bullshit. The Chinese couldn't have. That would mean they had developed a navy equal to European navies, and there's no proof of that," a female commented in a manner that could be heard around the room.

"If you are so certain of that, then there is no point in you attending this course and you should leave to enroll in a course that you feel will be more educational. The door is right over there." He stopped and waited. Students looked at each other uncertainly and several including the girl who had first raised an objection got up and left. Once the class settled down, Holroyd started his lecture.

"We will be looking at what we know about Chinese naval capabilities, and activities. We will consider how prevailing winds and currents might have influenced the flat-bottomed ships to see if such influences could have supported transoceanic voyages, even if such voyage was unintentional. We will look at instruments and knowledge of astronomy to see if these sailors could have navigated safely. We will then consider what is missing in deciding if transoceanic voyages from China to the West Coast could have taken place. We will examine whether, if they were capable of so doing, they reached the West Coast of Canada. We will compare those findings to European navies of the same era, to conclude why the Europeans were such latecomers." He paused. "Oh, yes! Let me emphasise here and now that the Europeans were latecomers when it came to transoceanic voyages." There was a rustle of anticipation in the class.

Holroyd continued. "In this class, you will be asked to form teams, do research, and write essays on topics that will be handed to you. Our purpose to look for evidence that a Ming or Qing Dynasty ship ever came here." He paused. "I want you to form teams who will work together on the projects I will be assigning. I will be meeting with each team separately to discuss the progress of your assignments." He paused again. "Any questions? If not, please hand in your team lists by next week." The bell rang and students gathered their books and left the hall. As Holroyd packed his briefcase, a woman entered and asked him to come to the Dean's Office.

He was escorted into an office that was spacious and airy. Large windows afforded a view over the campus lawns beyond which the blue waters of the sea could be seen framed by trees that grew along the campus roads. Paintings of what appeared to be local landscapes hung on two paneled walls while a full bookshelf covered the third. A couch and two armchairs flanked a small coffee table to one side while a large desk dominated the rest of the room. The desk was carefully arranged with an intercom, a laptop, and a framed photograph facing away from any visitor's view. Two uncomfortable looking armchairs faced the desk. Dean Hummersdorf rose from behind the desk.

Hummersdorf today wore a bespoke light grey business suit, a pinkish shirt that was almost covered by a dazzlingly bright red and yellow tie. Pale green socks peeped out between his trousers and his highly polished black shoes. A pair of glasses hung on a beaded chain around his neck. Holroyd was not impressed.

"Please be seated, Doctor Holroyd," Hummersdorf commanded, indicating one of the chairs and sitting himself down behind the desk. "I'm sorry we have to meet again, especially under such an unfortunate circumstance."

"Pardon? I don't understand to what circumstance you refer."

"I just had an uncomfortable session with one of your students who's complaining you are dismissing First Nations as irrelevant and immaterial. I'm pretty sure those were her words."

"Are you serious? Some student takes my words out of context and gets into a snit, and you haul me over the coals?" Holroyd couldn't believe what he was hearing.

"What's a snit? Do you find this funny?" Hummersdorf frowned. "I assure you this is not the time for jokes." Holroyd said nothing. Hummersdorf looked at him in silence.

"Well, this time, I won't take any action. You are a respected academic, but you are new to Canada. You may therefore not appreciate the sensitivities of the First Nations that influence many of our activities. That having been said, I trust I will not have to deal with a repetition in the future."

Holroyd was completely taken aback. "Are you giving

me a formal warning?"

"Let's just say we had a talk, eh?" Holroyd was sorely tempted to reply, but decided discretion might be the better part of valour.

"Is there anything else?" he asked acidly.

"No, not at all. Good day."

Well, I've been put on notice, thought Holroyd as he walked out the Dean's Office. *Not quite the welcome I expected. What was it Dorothy said? Oh yes! This isn't Kansas anymore. I wonder what else can go wrong.*

5.

Alan Eddy or He-who-talks-with-Eagles to give him his native name, gazed over the calm waters of the cove. The sun was rising into a cloudless summer sky giving a pink hue to the snowy tops of mountains across the bay. Their reflections danced in the smooth waters decorating them with delicate rose and white patterns. The morning's peace implied the onset of another glorious day, but Eddy felt a sultriness in the air that threatened rain probably by late afternoon or early evening.

On the side of the bay closest to him, the rocks waited for the sealions and seagulls that would soon be sunning themselves while squabbling over the best places to occupy.

At the beach's edge, a sluggish sea supported strands of kelp waving in some submerged current. Sometimes a sea otter would poke its head above the surface and survey the surroundings before diving down again. Occasionally a small wave would ripple over the sand in a manner that suggested a loving kiss on the rocks and pebbles or an apology for the intrusion of the sea on land.

Behind him, the tops of totem poles were silhouetted against the brightening sky. The totem poles stood majestically, or if shifted by wind and soil erosion, leaned crookedly towards the nearby trees. Lovingly carved to remember the deeds of past village notables, the carvings represented bears, wolves, killer whales, otters, and eagles.

Impassively, the carvings looked out imposingly over the waters, gazed upward towards the sky, or downward to grounds that no longer supported them. Wherever their gaze, they protected the village and its heritage. Eddy looked back at them. *What stories of glory and honour would you tell me if you could talk?*

It was quiet as befits the village memorial ground, although occasional puffs of wind whispered through the giant trees acknowledging the homage these ancient growths were paying to the sanctity of the area.

Eddy sat on a large rock separated from its arboreal kin at the water's edge, and silently communed with his surroundings. He would come to sit on the same rock and try to reach out to the spirits of nature and of his ancestors. He would lay a fresh salmon on a nearby rock as an offering to his brother the Eagle and watch to see if the offering was accepted. The ritual gave him comfort and many times he had returned home convinced the spirits had given him guidance in some form. He did this as often as he could to escape from his legal office and the interminable and often fractious arguments over indigenous rights.

He had missed performing the ritual for several weeks and was eager to make amends today. So far, he had followed his custom, but the offer had not been accepted. Suddenly, the sealions started barking out in the bay but Eddy could not see far enough to know what had excited them. For a few minutes longer nothing else disturbed the silence in the cove until two scavenging western gulls dived at the offering and began squabbling for the morsel. After dividing the spoils, they flew off in different directions and silence returned.

"I have not forgotten you, my brother! See! I have returned to you," he called, but there was no reply. Only the rising sun climbed higher to illuminate the trees and the totem poles. No further ripples from the sea or turbulences from fish or sea otters disturbed the waters, and no further squawking seagulls or barking seals broke the new silence. No sounds came from the forest behind him, and the morning hum of insects had not yet started; it was a silence Eddy could hear. The spirits of his ancestors and of the woods were refusing to communicate. He sat there for a long time before getting off the rock.

He cast one last look around the cove before walking back along the footpath that led to his village. As he did so, he increased his pace noting sudden rain clouds gathering. "Just what I need, getting soaked at the end of a frustrating day. What is my brother telling me? Something is not right. I must talk to the shaman."

6.

In the Band village near the university, a woman was asking questions of an elderly couple in one of the houses that lined what was euphemistically called the main street. No one knew her real name or where exactly she had come from, but she was well known as Elisa in the First Nations communities for her work. Looking at her casually, no one would have guessed she completed her law degree with honours at the University of British Columbia, was a master of *jiujitsu*, and had collected a vast file on abuses suffered by the indigenous people. That file was probably the most comprehensive outside the one held by the Federal Department of Indian and Northern Affairs.

Elisa looked at the elderly couple across the Formica topped kitchen table.

"You really want to know what it was like for me in the residential schools?" she asked softly. "It was hell." The couple waited expectantly. After a moment, Elisa went on.

"I was forcibly removed from my parents and put into a Roman Catholic Church school run by nuns. The idea was that we should lose our heritage and our culture, a policy that was actively supported by successive Canadian governments.

We were dressed in western clothing, had our hair cut short, and punished if we used our native language.

Each day we followed the same routines of classes, cleaning, with breaks for meals and finally sleep. We ate tasteless food that barely kept us alive, and then not always. If we fell sick, we might recover depending on whether anyone cared to help us get better. Several of the children were raped. If we complained we were punished. If we failed to follow the rules, we were punished. Punishments included being locked up in small spaces, getting beaten, no food, and extra work. Although some nuns cared about us and tried to make our lives bearable, few were successful. If we died, we were hurriedly and secretly buried in unmarked graves."

The report was greeted by silence.

"It wasn't unusual," Elisa continued. "I've heard that story in almost all the reservations I've visited, and many times in several of them." She paused. "I decided I would work to make sure no other children would ever go through such an experience. And I want to bring the abuses to the notice of people who can do something about them and make the abusers pay for what they did."

"I hope you'll succeed, but what brings you to our village?" asked the man.

"I believe one of the abusers is here somewhere. If I can find him, I want to bring him to justice. I am asking around to see if there was any hint of such a man." Elisa answered.

"I haven't heard of anyone, but if we can help in any way ..." the old man did not complete his sentence. Elisa nodded and got up, put on a cheap transparent raincoat over her sweat suit and tucked the pant legs into gum boots. Thanking her hosts, she walked into the evening rain that had become a downpour. Ignoring the inadequate rain hat that came with the coat, she left her braided black hanging loosely over her shoulders.

As she walked down the main road, she noted the

broken windows and doors of many of the houses, and some houses that had only plastic tarpaulins stretched over the roof. Abandoned detritus littered the front of many of the houses and almost all the houses could have used repairs and coats of paint. Clean water and a working sewage disposal system was beyond this settlement. An assessment of the surroundings that would have been depressing at the best of times was exacerbated by the oncoming darkness and the rain.

A slurred voice called out from the lit porch of one of the houses. "Hey! Wanna have fun?" Looking towards the source of the question Elisa noted three teenaged boys ogling her. She sighed recognising yet another sign of the social pathology that was so common on many reservations. It was a situation she had encountered several times and each time she relied on her position as an elder matriarch to face and defuse the situation. She went up to them, looked them over, noting a smell of glue, alcohol, and unwashed bodies.

"Now then, haven't you got better manners than that?"

"C'm here," the tallest of the three reached out for her. One of the boys was groping his belt trying to drop his pants in anticipation, the last one was lying on the floor giggling.

"Don't do that. Go home right now." Recognising the boys, Elisa tried to calm the situation, but the first boy did not heed her command. One hand still holding her, he pulled out a knife saying, "I said, c'm here bitch or else I'm gonna do you well and good."

"I don't think so."

The boy lunged at her, but she had moved to one side,

knocked the knife away and planted her elbow in his face. She heard something break just as the second lad with pants open, but now with a large hunting knife in one hand, lurched from behind. Twisting to meet him, Elisa kicked him in the groin, and he dropped the knife as he sank to the ground confused by the pain that was seeping through his drug fuelled brain. She noticed the third boy was still giggling on the floor and thought with some compassion. He's *probably lost in a dream world and unaware of what is happening around him.*

Suddenly the scene was lit by the lights of an approaching car. The car stopped and the Band Policeman got out. Approaching the group and noting the conditions of the three youths he asked. "Hi Elisa! What's going on here? Anyone seriously hurt?" He turned back to Elisa. "Seems these boys are a bit the worse for wear. How about you?"

"Nothing that won't pass, but I'd say there will be some sore heads tomorrow." Elisa sounded confident. The policeman nodded "If you're OK, I'll ship these guys to a safer place." Elisa thanked the officer and started on her way back to her house. As she was about to open the door, her cell phone beeped. Looking at it, she frowned noting the message came from an unknown number. *Who is this from? Just as I was about to go home, someone wants to meet me near the village gate.*

She thought for a moment, thinking over going to a meeting in these miserable conditions with an unknown person. *It's not the first time an unknown caller wants to meet me, but a meeting could be dangerous. Still, that's what I trained for in the gym and, anyway, it goes with the task, and wouldn't be the first time I've taken a risk. I'd better meet that person, or else I might never learn what he wants to tell me.*

Accepting the risk, she texted an affirmative, put her phone back in her pocket, and walked towards her car. It was an old Dodge that had seen better days, but it still served her well and anyway, she couldn't afford to buy a new one just yet.

To her annoyance, the car wouldn't start, and she regretted not having had the car serviced earlier. She looked out at the weather, debating whether to cancel or go; and finally resigned herself to walking in the rain. It was only a short distance from the village to the proposed meeting place quite near the burial grounds. "This had better be worth it." She muttered.

From a darkened porch nearby, two youths took another swig from a shared bottle as they watched her slamming the car's door and walking away. As soon as she disappeared around a corner, they ran over to the vehicle, put back the previously removed distributor cap and drove off on their joy ride.

***

As Elisa walked towards her meeting, a car was on the road leading to Eddy's village. There was little traffic, but darkness was setting in, and the road was slick with rain. The weather had turned increasingly bad with gusts of wind driving the rain across the windshield with enough force to rock the car, and temporarily overcome the efforts of the windshield wipers to clear the vision ahead. The driver was unfamiliar with the area and drove slowly peering into the darkness ahead. Much as he wanted to drive faster, he had no desire to hit some nocturnal animal or, worse yet, skid off the road into a ditch from which it might be difficult to get out.

"OK, let's get this show on the road," he muttered. He pulled over to the side of the road, stopped, and forgetting to switch on his flashers, reached for his road map. *Still a way to go* and he swore loudly. "Should I abandon or go there in this miserable weather?" he muttered to himself.

A gust of wind shook the car and a sheet of rain again reduced visibility to a few feet. "Dammit, I've come too far to quit now." He reached for his cell phone and sent a text message: 'Ready to meet now.' and posted a location.

Another car came up from behind, its lights momentarily blinding his vision. As it passed, he noted it was an RCMP cruiser which stopped and backed down to park in front of him. An officer got out, the rain shining off his rain gear, and shone his torch over the car. He approached to driver's side and motioned for the window to be lowered. He shone his torch at the driver and swept the inside of the car.

"Good evening, sir. Any problems?"

"None at all, officer."

"May I ask why you stopped, sir?"

"Yes. I needed to send a text message, so I stopped to do so safely."

"I see. Well, sir, you've stopped on a dark road with limited visibility but have failed to turn on your flashers to warn other drivers."

"Oh! My goodness! So, I have. I am sorry." He reached down and turned his flashers on.

"Thank you, sir. May I see your license, and registration, sir?"

"Of course." The driver took off his gloves, reached over to the glove compartment, and rummaged to find the documents among several other items. Just as he handed them over, another car came up from behind driving at a great speed, but jammed on its brakes as the policeman and the cruiser became visible. The car began to slip on the wet pavement and glanced off the cruiser before veering on up the road at high speed.

"Bloody idiot!" The constable handed back the documents without examining them, and with a distracted and hasty "Please drive carefully," dashed to his car and drove off to catch the disappearing speeder.

Relieved at the departure of the policeman, the driver turned off his flashers, put his gloves back on, and drove to a turnoff that led to the location he had chosen.

By the time he arrived, the rain had slackened but the wind showed no signs of calming. He parked a short distance away to reduce any chance of it being seen, and putting on a rainslicker, a waterproof hat, another pair of gloves, and a pair of gum boots he exited the car. He checked again to see if it would not be seen by a casual passer-by and grabbing a powerful flashlight started walking. Other than trees swaying in the wind he saw little beyond the cone of light delivered by his torch.

The howls of the wind whipped the branches into some arcane frenzy, and he shivered superstitiously afraid malevolent spirits might be lurking in the darkness. He trudged towards the meeting point.

About half an hour after his meeting, the driver returned to his car , took off the rain gear, and drove home. On the way, he stopped at a small river, took off his gloves to strip a cell phone of its battery, lowered the window, and threw the parts as far as he could into the dark waters. Once done, he closed the window and putting his gloves back on, drove home.

7

Manning called. "Hi Peter. I wonder if you'd care to stop by. It's informal, so don't bother to dress up," he chuckled "I have beer, but feel free to bring whatever suits you. Oh! Joe won't be here. He's tied up with a faculty meeting or something." Holroyd clad in an open necked shirt and baggy flannels, brought a bottle of Okanagan wine.

Manning led him to the patio and with a brief excuse vanished into the kitchen. Holroyd observed that this house reflected the personality of the occupants. A few framed photographs on the mantel piece showed Manning in Naval uniform and on the wall hung pictures of ships next to ship's crests mounted on wooden plaques. *So, Manning has also been in the Navy. Perhaps we can swap yarns.* But there was an underlying femininity in the furnishings that gave testimony to softer tastes.

Lace doylies covered the arm rests on an overstuffed sofa and couple of armchairs, and plants hung in macrame baskets in front of a large picture window. A display case in one of the corners held a collection of exquisite porcelain figurines of scantily clad males and females. The paintings hanging opposite the display case echoed the ones he had seen hanging in Hummersdorf's office, and Holroyd wondered who had influenced whom in collecting art and furnishing the flat.

Manning came back with a tray on which there were two cans of beer, a glass and Holroyd's wine, and a plate of nachos.

"I thought it best to give you a heads-up. When your appointment was announced, Paul hinted he has no time for you and will do his best to see you get discredited."

"Really?" Holroyd was stunned. "Why on earth would he take that position?"

"Paul submitted a paper on the history of Asian people moving towards North America. It was rejected and he went on a rampage accusing someone at UBC of bias against him." He paused. "A full investigation was launched, the accusation was dismissed, and he got reprimanded. To cap it all, he went through a messy divorce and his son is keeping bad company. He's been bitter ever since, and from what I hear, hasn't been coping too well."

"I can understand that, but why choose me? We've had no contact before I came here."

"I can only guess. He might have seen your appointment as a threat to his own position, or he is jealous of you. After all, you come with high credentials."

"Well, thank you for the warning. I'll be on my guard."

Sitting comfortably on the patio, they change the subject and discussed politics, exchanged Navy experiences, and Manning gave an outline of what to see and do in the region. He went on. "Something that might be of interest in your search. Some Junior Rangers wandering through the forests near Anyox, a former mining town that disappeared some fifty years ago, stumbled on the graves of WWI volunteers. The site was totally overgrown with vegetation, and they only discovered it when one of the kids tripped over a headstone. Couldn't believe what they found, but there's a happy ending. The Rangers now tend the site and hold a Remembrance Day ceremony there every year. They have to trek in because otherwise the site is inaccessible.”

“Amazing! I suppose there could be other sites like that one.”

“Yes. But searching for one could be dicey because so many lands around here are tribal, and many of the Bands don’t take kindly to trespassers, especially if anyone goes near a village burial site.”

“Tell me more about these burial sites.”

Manning went on to explain that burial customs varied between Bands and even between villages.

“Burial sites would be found on land that had been set aside for the purpose. The sites didn’t always mean a place where people were buried. Often the body was cremated, and the ashes might be scattered on land or at sea. In some cases, however, the remains might be boxed and put on top of a totem pole. Not everyone got a totem pole. The person had to have been outstanding in some way, like an exceptional shaman or warrior and so most people didn’t qualify.

“Some poles like the ones Emily Carr painted, were erected to commemorate a special event or to acknowledge the spirits. Those poles had many meanings, but were specifically carved as part of the Band heritage. You can see how such a place would be seen as sacred.”

“Yes.” Holroyd again nodded his understanding.

“Interesting! I’ve never seen an Indian burial ground,” Holroyd said.

"Well, if you do want to visit one, you'd better get permission from the Band. Generally, the Bands aren't too keen on people traipsing through the sites like a bunch of gawking tourists. And in this province, the First Nations have a lot of influence, if not power."

"I got a right dressing down from the dean because some student got all hot under the collar that I was dismissing the Indians here."

"Oh, yes! Joe told me about that. He's sensitive about anything that refers to First Nations. By the way, we don't refer to them as Indians anymore. The correct term is First Nations."

"Thanks. But what's the problem?"

"A couple of problems. First, do you know anything about the history of the First Nations here?"

"No."

"Ah!" Manning took a swallow and went on to explain that when the English won the Seven Years War, George III in 1763 issued what is called the Royal Proclamation, by which Canada was politically organised. Part of the document reserved a large area in the North American interior for the exclusive use of Indigenous peoples. With regards to Aboriginal rights, the proclamation states explicitly that Indigenous people reserved all lands not ceded by them, or purchased from them by representatives of the Crown. Those lands encompass most of what is now Canada.

"During the 19th and 20th Centuries, First Nations signed a series of treaties that set out the relationships with the Crown. However, complicating the issue was the establishment of the Residential School System in the mid 19th Century. The intent was to assimilate First Nations into the mainstream by systematically eradicating any Indigenous culture. For years First Nations accused the schools of horrific abuses, but no one listened. Only recently, the demolition of one of the school buildings revealed a mass grave with hundreds of children's skeletons. Similar graves have since been found and it's become a major issue."

"That's terrible. How could this have happened?"

"Culpable deniability all over the place." Holroyd sat silent thinking about atrocities that had taken place in other parts of the Empire.

"You mentioned a couple of problems. What's the other one?" Holroyd resumed his questioning.

"Oh! Yes! Much of the University is on unceded land claimed by the local Band. There's a kind of agreement under which the University respects Band rights and the Band allows the University to stay. It's not written anywhere and it's fragile. There's a Band member on the Board of the University."

"Not written down! You mean the University occupies lands without some form of signed contract?"

"Exactly so."

Holroyd's curiosity rose further. "How can such an agreement be enforced?"

"Oh! First Nations' oral traditions have the same legal standing as a written agreement."

"That must be unique to Canada," Holroyd observed.

"I'm not sure about that. I believe other courts such as in Australia and New Zealand have adopted the same position." Holroyd sat silent thinking over the ramifications of such a legal position.

"You mentioned fragile? How?"

"If the Band thinks the University is disrespecting the Band rights, they could force the University to make amends. Joe thinks your comments could be taken as disrespect." He paused. "It's particularly sensitive now because the University wants to expand and has requested the use of more land. So far, there's been no response, and some of the University's Board are getting anxious."

"Oh! Well, I hope I can calm any fears with time," Holroyd said.

"It's not quite that simple. You may not have time. The University needs the Band's agreement sooner than later. There's a major donor somewhere in Asia who's offered to fund a new and cutting-edge laboratory complex, but he won't wait forever. He recently hinted that he may decide to go elsewhere if nothing happens soon."

"I see. I can sympathise with the dean." Holroyd sat silent for a moment before continuing "I have a question. I'm here to see if I can find any evidence of early Chinese visits to these coasts, some proof of a visit. Something left behind." Holroyd looked abstractedly at the sky as if to marshal his thoughts and took a sip of wine.

"That's pretty broad."

Holroyd settled back and explained how a ship leaving China could end up on the West Coast. The crew would land to try to replenish stores, particularly water and maybe meat and vegetables, cereals because they would be familiar with those. They would probably also fish. They might additionally try and careen the ship's bottom. At the same time, they would want to see if there are locals to contact for trade. But all that takes time. So, they might build a few huts and live ashore while all this is happening. They might also put up a marker to mark their visit.

"You mean a sort of 'Kilroy was here'?" asked Manning.

"Yes, that sort of thing."

"Ok! Go on." Manning waited.

Holroyd continued by explaining it would be unlikely they would clean up the site by demolishing the huts and collecting any garbage. Someone passing the site later might find a marker, some ruined huts, perhaps some discarded utensils, and infrastructure.

"I can follow that. But failing a marker, how would this later visitor know who had actually been there? I mean from what you describe, things like that could have been left behind at any time," Manning said.

Just then a couple of hummingbirds hovered over a bed of golden day lilies and Holroyd watched fascinated by their behaviours as they darted from bloom to bloom seeking nectar. Manning followed Holroyd's gaze, before remarking "Beautiful, aren't they?" He then resumed his questioning.

"So how would you know who had left the things?"

"Well, utensils, such as cooking pots, pieces of pottery such as porcelain, or tools, perhaps even some rags can be distinctive enough to give a clue. How, for instance would a piece of Ming pottery have landed on the West Coast, if not brought here by some Chinese?"

"Perhaps brought here by some European settlers? Maybe the Spanish came up this far, or maybe the Russians came down through Alaska and had some pottery with them?" Manning suggested.

"Possibly, and if so, it sheds light on who was here but doesn't address if the Chinese did. Mind you, you do add to the possibility of a Chinese visit because like the Russians and some Japanese fisherman, a Chinese ship might crawl up along the Aleutian Islands and down the Alaska coast."

"Sounds possible." Manning unconvinced shook his head. "You might find it useful to visit the museums one of which is more a private collection and it's on the mainland. I know the owner and can arrange for you to see the collection. Take the Ferry. It's much more convenient and you get to enjoy the scenery." Holroyd nodded.

"Let's suppose you are right this far," Manning mused "How would you go about finding places a ship might have stopped? The West Coast is huge and we're talking one ship."

"I'm hoping that we can narrow down where to search by making some reasonable assumptions. I'm thinking that before landing, the ship might explore the coast to see if there are signs of habitation. Such signs might include buildings, smoke, offshore fishermen. Finding such a sign, I would expect the ship to put in to see what's there."

"Not too many villages built on the shoreline round here. Too vulnerable to attacks from the neighbours. On the other hand, there are many totem poles on or near the shore-line," Manning said.

"Seeing a pole and recognizing it to be manmade could be a reason for the ship to put in."

"There are quite a few such places up and down the coast. Big task to explore all of them. It would cost a fortune to finance such a search and I don't think you'd get much support from the University."

"I have some funds available, and I was thinking of sending the students out to do some exploring. Make it a class project. Do you think that might be possible?"

"Don't know how Joe will answer that. But otherwise? Possible? Yes, but I doubt you'll have much success." Holroyd heard the doubt in Manning's voice.

"I tend to agree, but who knows? I won't find anything unless I go look."

"Good luck, then. And you had better first get everyone to agree and make damn sure no one does anything that might violate Band lands, particularly lands that are burial sites." He got up. "Care for a refill?"

Refusing the offer, Holroyd returned to his apartment to find a parcel had been delivered.

8.

Halfway around the world, Wang Lin Fei sat in his office overlooking the Hong Kong harbour and answered his office intercom.

"The Chancellor of the Canadian University is on the line," his secretary announced.

"Put him through."

"Chancellor! How good of you to call. How may I be of service?"

"Good day, Mr. Wang! I just wanted to bring you up to date on the University's plans for the proposed research facility that will be built with your generous support."

"Please do so."

"We have obtained the necessary regulatory approvals for the design of the building, and we are negotiating the land deal with the local First Nations Band. But I wanted to seek your approval for a proposal that the Board of Governors has put forward."

"Indeed?" Wang Fei Lin's tone conveyed his interest.

"The Board seeks your approval that you would al ow us to name the facility in your name."

"That is most generous of you, Chancellor. I shall be very happy to accept when the day comes." He paused. "Do you have any target date for the opening?"

"I'm afraid not."

"Ah! I see." There was a pause. "I'm sure, Chancellor, that you can understand that I am hoping for the honour of opening a facility precedes the honour of my meeting my ancestors."

"Yes indeed. But did you say *a* facility?" The 'a' was stressed for emphasis.

"Yes, I did. I am sure you would be as disappointed as I would be, if such a facility were to be located elsewhere." Wang made no attempt to hide his threat.

"Oh, I am confident you will be with us in person." The Chancellor moved swiftly to reassure the generous benefactor.

"I can only hope your confidence is not misplaced. I am not prepared to wait to the point where I might not have a choice which event to attend."

There was a silence at the other end.

"Thank you for your call, Chancellor. I wish you good day." Wang closed the call.

9

Holroyd was surprised that mail had arrived so soon after his arrival in Canada, but opened the parcel to find a scanned copy of The Dong Xi Yang Kao or 'Study of the Eastern and Western Seas (东西洋考) that Andersen, his favourite London bookseller, had sent by courier. The book was a systematic account of maritime activity in the South China Sea out of the port of Quanzhou written in 1617. Holroyd had almost lost his life searching for a copy on an earlier occasion, but circumstances now gave him a chance to study it. Specifically, he hoped to find further evidence that early Chinese sailors could have reached the West Coast of what is now Canada.

Holroyd believed such a voyage was possible, but few academics agreed with him. Holroyd had studied their objections and concluded there was no basis for rejecting the possibility. He noted a report that a researcher had been given access to the only known copy of the *Cronica Universalis* written by a Dominican Monk Galvano Fiamma between 1339 and 1345 and had discovered therein a reference to a land to the West of Iceland, that is , North America.

'*So much for academic certainties; here's another nail in the coffin that Columbus discovered America,*' he muttered to himself. Furthermore, some academics really take the biscuit when they dismissed the possibility that the fourth Century Irish priest Saint Brendan, had reached Labrador in a craft made of leather. That view crashed spectacularly when Tim Severin successfully replicated the voyage.

Holroyd had applied the lessons of modern-day adventurers to the notion that Ming and early Qing Dynasty Chinese sailors had also completed voyages many academics deemed unlikely if not impossible. But views of what had been deemed impossible had been challenged by researchers who now asserted other explorers and not Columbus had discovered America. Noting that Mayans, Incas, and Aztecs among other civilisations were living quite happily in America before the arrival of Columbus, Holroyd found the notion of a European discovery laughable but the results of those 'discoveries' were anything but laughable[2].

He liked how Menzies had applied his navigational expertise to examine how winds and currents could influence the trajectory of ocean going Chinese flat-bottomed vessels. Holroyd followed suit. He noted that a vessel leaving China and ignoring wind patterns could have reached the West Coast of Canada by drifting alone though winds would play a decisive role.

One academic, Derek Hayes, had reported that The Kuroshio Current tends to push Asian ships northeast into the westerlies thus reinforcing movement towards North America. Records of unlucky Japanese fishermen being blown to North America supported Hayes' finding.

"Given this evidence, Chinese sailors could have reached the West Coast during the Ming Dynasty even if proof has yet to be found," he muttered.

In addition to the Dong Xi Yang Kao, Holroyd found a

-----

[2] *The Catholic Church in issuing the Papal Bulls Dum Diversas (1452), Romanus Pontifex (1454), and Inter caetera (1493), set the scene for the enslavement of indigenous people in the (then) non-Christian territories.*

separate envelope that he was about to open when the phone rang. Annoyed, he put the envelope on the table, not noticing that it slipped off the table to land invisible under his chair.

Pearl called to ask if he was excited at the prospect of starting the lectures, and if there was snow. Holroyd assured her all was satisfactory and there was no snow yet.

"Oh! That is great!"

"How are things with you at home?"

"Mother has come to visit, and I am very happy she is here," Pearl said.

"Wonderful. Give her my best wishes."

"I will. We have been very busy. Mother has been improving the house."

Alarmed, Holroyd sat up. "Improving the house?"

Pearl had very fixed ideas about how a household should be managed, but he had clearly failed to consider that his mother-in-law also had her own ideas about the living arrangements and habits of a respected professor. To his unease, it seemed the women were rearranging his home.

"What has she done?"

"Oh! We gave away so many old clothes that we found."

"Old clothes? Whose old clothes?" Holroyd now became worried.

"There were some clothes from your first wife, and some children's clothes, as well as a few of your unfashionable worn clothes."

Holroyd's heart missed a beat. "My wife's and my daughter's clothes? You gave them away?" His voice caught. Keeping their clothing had been irrational, especially now that he was married again. But he wasn't prepared for this abrupt separation. "And my old clothes?"

"Of course! Why keep them?"

"I liked my old clothes!" Holroyd began to wonder what else in his life had been changed while he was away. "What else has she done?"

"She has recovered the old couch and chair in the study, and she has moved some of the paintings into a cupboard."

"What? Why?" *Is the Constable in a cupboard? What possessed the women? Why did I ever suggest her mother to come visit? Is she about to be a permanent fixture?* A shiver of horror and dismay went up his spine.

"The Feng Shui man told us they are too old fashioned and bring no peace or joy into the home." Pearl went on remorselessly.

"Feng Shui?"

"Oh! Yes! Mother asked for professional help to make sure it is done right."

"Anything else?" Holroyd asked.

"No, that is all now. But the Feng Shui man told us to make more change."

"Oh!" was all Holroyd could manage.

Clearly Pearl had accepted this new regime. Only his love for Pearl compensated for what he suddenly realised was an unexpected series of unfortunate events. Now he wondered if the opportunity to come to Canada as a visiting professor was worth the cost. Strangely, the womenfolk had not objected once he accepted the position to leave. Only later did he realise that conjugal separations for reasons of work were an accepted feature of modern Chinese life and of course gave the wives unsupervised freedom to rearrange the home.

"Oh! And there is more good news. My nephew will be coming to visit us."

"Which one?" Holroyd asked, curious which of the many nephews was in question.

"The second son of my eldest brother's third wife. He is in second year university at Fujinhaizhou and is studying to become an engineer. He is very clever and doing very well. He is very tall and plays basketball and badminton. He came first in the school championships, and he will be going to the Provincial competition after he returns to China."

"That's excellent!" Holroyd commented.

"Many girls like him because he is very handsome. He won an English-speaking competition and was on local television." He could hear the pride in her voice. "His parents are sending him here as a reward."

"Oh, my! When will he be arriving?"

"Very recently! I am so excited." Pearl's joy was clear.

"Recently? Oh! You mean soon."

"Yes? I am wrong?" He sensed a plaintive tone in her

question, and hastily changed the subject.

"What will you be doing with him?"

"We will go to China town, and then go to the Tower of London, St. Paul's and Westminster Cathedrals."

"That's nice," Holroyd went on. "I have some other suggestions you might enjoy. Take the boat cruise up the Thames to Hampton Court and Kew Gardens. Those places are very beautiful. Lots of flowers and trees."

"Oh! How nice. Hapten Court and the gardens of Q." Holroyd smiled at the mispronunciations.

"Who was Q? Was he a famous general?" Pearl asked. "Or perhaps an administrator with a garden like the Humble Administrator's Garden in Suzhou?"

"No love!" Holroyd could not help laughing. "Kew is a place. There have been rich men's houses and gardens there for over eight hundred years. It's one of the best places in the world for flowers and trees."

"Then we will go there. We can take pictures of ourselves to send to our family in China. They will be very pleased." Pearl almost purred in anticipation of the face she would gain at home. With that the conversation ended. Holroyd was not too sure he was optimistic about his flat in London, but hoped the nephew's visit might distract from the renovations for a while. *Good luck with that.*

10.

Holroyd spent the weekend in Vancouver. He followed Manning's suggestion and took the bus and ferry service even though the trip lasts over six hours. Catching the first ferry, he still had time to visit the exhibition that afternoon.

On arrival, he booked into a hotel before setting out to visit the private collection Manning had spoken about. He arrived at the door and pressed the intercom to announce his arrival, but surprisingly there was no immediate reply. While he waited, he turned to view the estate.

The house was a three-story building built of granite blocks with incongruously small windows. It was set back and separated from the street by a wall that bounded a beautiful garden that extended from the front to continue along both sides of the building. Bushes and trees framed flower beds and manicured lawns. And yet, despite the beauty, Holroyd felt as if he was standing in front of a fortress rather than a family home. *This was built with money but with little taste. Why such a massive structure?*

Finally, the door was opened and on introducing himself he was admitted by an impeccably dressed young man to a superb collection of West Coast art. *This is as good as the collection of Chinese art I saw in Fujinhaizhou! However, this one is hardly likely to have been gathered by theft or black-market purchases.*

He admired silver pendants, bracelets, and other items of jewelry intricately carved to represent the animals and birds of the West Coast. But also, there were exhibits that clearly were not from the West Coast or even North America.

In one display case he saw examples of Columbian pottery, in another wooden African Masks glared out at him, and further down Inca *quipos* or beaded strings had been laid out with an explanation of what they represented. In another case he saw an exquisite, but misshapen example of gold filigree inlaid with gems of different colours next to a distorted gold object surrounding a large red gem that might have been a ruby.

This looks different from everything else. That piece almost looks like a part of a hairpin from Chinese Imperial times and the other piece looks like a ring from the Renaissance period in Spain or Italy. They don't fit the collection of native arts. I wonder if they arrived on an old Chinese ship. If so, is this is a clue to the ship I'm looking for?

He looked around to see if he could ask anyone. Just as he was resigning himself to be disappointed a door behind one of the display cases opened and three men came out.

One was the young man who had welcomed him, but because they had their backs to him Holroyd could not see who the other two men were. They were slim, well dressed, and had the black hair that Holroyd recognised as Asian. He could not hear what was being said, but the body language suggested there was some sort of argument whereby the young man seemed to be refusing a request. Finally, the group broke up and the two men turned to leave, but as they did so, one man glanced back into the exhibit hall and looked at Holroyd.

Holroyd had an impression the man was Chinese, but they left before he could be certain. *Probably tourists also come to see the collection*. Thinking no more about it, Holroyd approached the young man who was about to re-enter the room.

"Excuse me. Are you the curator here?"

"Yes. Can I help you?"

"I wonder if you could give me some information about two of the exhibits." Holroyd indicated the two gold items. "These two items don't seem to fit into this magnificent collection of native arts." Holroyd indicated the two gold items.

"Why do you think that, Professor?"

"Well, they are both made of gold and inlaid with gems, but I see no other such items in the collection. And the workmanship is very different from everything else. I wonder where these pieces come from." Holroyd looked at the curator.

"Offhand, I don't know. Let me get the catalogue and check." The curator disappeared, but returned with an iPad and started scrolling down. "Oh! There's not much here. They are listed as gold items inlaid with gems circa 1600 AD."

"AD?" Holroyd smiled. "I haven't heard that used for quite some time. I thought the current politically correct nomenclature was BCE or even BP." The supervisor looked confused.

"Don't worry! Probably before your time."

"I'm sorry, Professor, but that's all there is."

"Might there be a record filed away that would give further details?" Holroyd persisted.

"Perhaps you could give me what details you are thinking of. Then I can go and look."

"I'm interested in finding out how these items came to

be part of the collection. Did the owner find them or buy them?"

"Professor! This is a highly respected collection responsibly gathered over many, many years. How else would an item be on display?"

"Oh! Please don't misunderstand me. I am in no way suggesting that there are items of, shall we say, questionable provenance."

"Then what is your interest?"

"Where the items originated and how did they end up here?" Holroyd waited.

"Perhaps the owner purchased them on one of his trips."

"That's possible of course. But look at them. Why buy pieces that are in such conditions? I mean if the owner can afford to buy items of quality as all the other exhibits clearly are, why buy something that is so out of shape? Why not buy something that's in good shape?"

The curator had no immediate answer. "Let me check with the owner. But that may take some time as he is traveling and doesn't always answer my calls. I'll let you know."

"Who is the owner?"

"Mr. O'Mallory."

With that, Holroyd thanked him, passed over a business card, and continued to admire the rest of the collection, without seeing anything else that aroused his curiosity.

Returning to his hotel, he Googled O'Mallory and found several entries among which only one appeared to be the most likely. This O'Mallory was described as a retired businessman resident in Victoria and now engaged in several philanthropic activities, mainly focused on Indigenous culture. Among his activities was listed his support of museums with a short paragraph that his private collection was kept in the old family mansion located in Vancouver. Nothing was said of his business or of family origins. *Not much that helps me.*

Over supper, he started to think again about the two gold pieces. *They seem so out of place and unlike all the other exhibits have no explanation about their origins or how they had been acquired.* He decided to return and have another look at them the next day.

The phone woke him at 2 am, "Professor Holroyd? O'Mallory here. I'm sorry to call at this hour, but I'm told you expressed interest in a couple of exhibits in my collection. You want to know where they come from. Right?"

Not yet fully awake, Holroyd fumbled for the light on the bedside table "Oh! Yes indeed." *What's so urgent that you had to call me at this hour? Why not have your man pass on the information, or send an email?* "Just a moment, please, I want to find my notebook and a pen." He got out of bed and went over to the desk before picking up the phone again. "Right, you were saying?"

"I'm not quite sure of the origins myself. In fact, I've often wondered about them. You pointed out some anomalies that I too had noticed, so I'd be pleased if you could offer some suggestions."

"I'll be only too happy to do so if I can."

"All I can tell you is that they are family heirlooms going back about a hundred years or more. The earliest record we have is that they were bequeathed by one of my grandmothers who married an American trader who then settled around the time that Victoria was founded. The family always assumed he left trading and became one of the successful gold miners."

"Assumed? Are there no family records?"

"We lost most of our family records in a fire around the turn of the Century."

"That's regrettable. But a fire might explain why the items are so damaged."

"Yes."

"I'm sorry I can't be more helpful."

"Not at all! And thank you for the phone call."

Holroyd was now fully awake and decided to follow up on what he had learned from the phone call. Given the two curious pieces of jewelry were supposed to have come from one of O'Mallory's ancestors who married a rich trader around the time of the founding of Victoria, Holroyd decided to look up trading in Victoria around the 1850's.

When in 1858 gold was discovered on the Fraser River, the activity at the rose from supporting a mere fifty residents to providing for some 30,000 people passing through Victoria on their way to the gold fields. With the establishment of the city in 1864, the settlement outgrew the Hudson Bay Company's post, which was demolished, and the land sold off. *I wonder if any HBC trader could have become rich enough by trading to acquire such items of gold, and if so, how? On the other hand, he might have joined the gold rush and struck it lucky enough to have bought the items or acquired them in a personal trade with someone.*

"I'm not getting anywhere." With that, he shut his laptop and returned to his slumber.

The next morning after breakfast he went back to the exhibition. On entering the exhibition hall, he saw quite a few people wandering through the exhibits. A young couple that could be students were looking carefully at the African exhibits; a family of Asians admonishing their three boisterous children to behave looked around as if to decide what next to admire; and a well-dressed young Asian man sauntered casually past several display cases before heading towards the case containing the gold artifacts. *Busy place today*, thought Holroyd as he entered.

Suddenly, there was the sound of breaking glass. Holroyd turned toward the sound and came face to face with the young man who roughly pushed Holroyd aside, before running out to the street. Holroyd rushed to the front door to see if he could catch the fleeing man but was too late.

Holroyd re-entered the hall and saw that the display case containing the two gold items had been smashed and the items had been taken. The other visitors were standing around the case chattering volubly, and the curator was running out of his office only to stop and stare at the empty case with dismay.

The police finally arrived. Holroyd heard the witnesses give their reports, but other than he was Asian, there was no consensus on the man's appearance. When it was Holroyd's turn to give his statement, he reported what he had seen.

"I am puzzled though." He added. "Why was there no alarm? I would think the place was fully protected. And there was one thing that I wonder about, though it may be purely unrelated. I saw the curator have an argument with two people I think were Asians. I just wonder if there's a connection." The officer nodded, wrote it down, and thanked Holroyd, before going back to the curator.

Holroyd overheard the curator admit that the alarm system had been turned off during the open hours; and the CCTV cameras were temporarily under repair. As to the two Asian men, the curator just gave a summary of the discussion that had focused on the provenance of the two items, and if they were for sale, which they were not.

Once the police had left, the curator informed everyone that the exhibition was closed and asked everyone to leave. As the other visitors trooped out, Holroyd went over to the curator.

"Would I be correct in saying the two items have no known historical significance?" The curator looked at him with surprise.

"As far as I am aware, yes."

"And the value of the gold and gems would not be worth very much either?"

"Probably not that much. I would estimate perhaps a couple of thousand dollars."

"If I am right, then I am curious about the theft. I mean this was such a brazen act, in full view of anyone present, and I would have thought there are items that would have been much more attractive for a thief." Holroyd waited for an answer.

"Now that you raise it, I am curious, too. In all my time here, those items have been the subject of curiosity by only yourself and two other visitors that were here yesterday at the time you were here."

"Do you know who they were?" Holroyd asked.

"No. I got a message from someone leaving no name, but supposedly a friend of Mr. O'Mallory telling me they would be calling. I had no qualms admitting them as I knew you would be visiting at the same time." He stopped. "Now that I come to think of it, the caller did not specifically mention Mr. O'Mallory, he just said the owner had recommended he should stop by."

"Did you confirm that with Mr. O'Mallory."

The curator shifted uncomfortably. "No. It did not occur to me to do so."

"Pity. You might have avoided the theft if you'd troubled to check if the caller was lying."

The curator said nothing, and Holroyd left to return to the Island.

11.

Holroyd thought about the provenance of the stolen items when the front doorbell rang. Surprised, Holroyd went to the door wondering who would be calling. Two RCMP officers stood outside. They were dressed in dark blue trousers with a vertical yellow stripe down the side. One wore a white pressed shirt denoting an inspector's rank and the other a pressed grey shirt denoting a non-commissioned officer. Their belts and boots positively shone.

"Good morning, sir! Professor Holroyd, is it? Inspector Tomlinson and Sergeant Alvarez." Tomlinson introduced themselves. Holroyd stood aside and motioned them into his sitting room. Taking off their field service caps, they entered and took their places on the indicated sofa and looked around. Holroyd was embarrassed by the impressions they might have of the scattering of papers and files on the desk and on the coffee table, but neither officer gave a sign of noticing anything amiss.

"Excuse us arriving unannounced, but we were told you might be able to help us with an ongoing investigation." Tomlinson opened the briefcase he had been carrying and extracted a file folder. From the folder he took two photographs, looked at them, and handed them to Holroyd. Each was a colour photograph of what appeared to be a *yuanbao*[3] but taken from two different angles. The first showed the object in its entirety.

---

[3] *A Chinese gold ingot used during Imperial times*

"That's a picture of a *yuanbao,* but they haven't been in common use for at least 100 years."

"Yes sir. It is. Have you seen one of these before, Professor?"

"Not in real life, no."

"Not surprising, because it would not usually be available to the public, at least not any this big. I say 'usually' because this example appeared on a market that is most definitely not open to the public at large."

"I take it you don't refer to an official market, such as a bullion dealer or a bank, so I assume you mean the black market?"

"Yes."

"I'm not an expert in such matters, so may I ask what how you think I might be able to help you?"

"What can you tell us about the second picture? It's this stamp, sir. Looks Chinese but from when or where we couldn't find out," Tomlinson stated.

The second photograph showed the imprint of a Chinese Chop that Holroyd was unable to recognize off hand.

Holroyd looked at the photograph again. "That does not look like something I remember having seen. But no question that it's a chop."

"Chop?"

"Like a seal that is used on Western official documents. This one is Chinese and fairly old at that. But again, it's not something I've really studied. I think there are Chinese professors on faculty who would be more knowledgeable."

"Yes, sir. We tried to meet with them. Professor Yue is in China and unable to get back right now, and Professor Li was unable to give us any help, but suggested you might have some thoughts. Another source also recommended you to us."

"Recommended by whom?"

"I believe it was a Mr. Hantington. Do you know him, sir?"

"Yes. And by the way, it's Viscount Hantington."

"I see."

"So, may I ask why His Lordship recommended me?"

"He didn't give us much information other than you had been of great help to the British and Chinese governments in recovering ancient Chinese documents and treasures."

"That little adventure included identifying documents but not any of the treasures. However, since you've come this far, let me ask you where you got this ingot?"

"Our American colleagues passed it over to us and asked for our help." Tomlinson paused as if to allow Holroyd to comment, but Holroyd said nothing.

"There's an additional matter that puzzles us." Alvarez looked at Tomlinson who nodded and then faced Holroyd.

"It's a matter of identifying or dating this gold." Holroyd looked up with a puzzled frown.

"Dating?

"Yes, sir. We can't date when this gold was cast." Holroyd nodded to indicate he followed so far.

"However, we noted a small nick or cut in which we found lodged some carbon fibre." He pulled out another photograph that showed an enlargement of one edge of the ingot in which a cut could be seen and a minute piece of what appeared to be cloth.

"If the fibre had been in the gold before refining, it would have disappeared during the melting, so this fibre lodged in the nick since the casting. We dated the fibre only to find its date was about 300 years ago."

"Are you saying this ingot was wrapped in cloth that was 300 years old?" Holroyd was astonished.

"Yes, sir!"

Holroyd felt a surge of excitement. *Could this have been brought here on a Chinese ship centuries ago? If so, that would support my theory of an early Chinese visit, but where did it come from, when did it arrive, and why?*

"So, it's reasonable to think the ingot is also that old. But then how did it get here?"

"Exactly so, sir. As you can imagine, gold today is not wrapped or stored in 300-year-old material, at least not by any gold dealers we know of." Holroyd nodded.

"We think that one explanation is that the ingot was wrapped and put into a container centuries ago. As you can readily see, such an explanation opens a whole new raft of questions as to where, when, and by whom, the gold was stored like that. And of course, how it found its way to a market in North America." The two police officers looked at Holroyd who shifted in his chair but remained silent.

"If it's part of some ancient, buried treasure, the location becomes important because there are laws that govern keeping it," Alvarez commented.

Holroyd sat up and again looking at the photograph observed, "If the Americans asked you to help out, that would suggest they aren't sure who has jurisdiction."

"Exactly."

"And how am I able to help?" Holroyd asked.

"If it's a three-hundred-year-old piece of Chinese gold, could you perhaps suggest how it might have arrived in North America? Arrived by means other than someone smuggled it in," Tomlinson asked.

"Looks like an interesting challenge, gentlemen."

"Yes, sir. Do you have any immediate questions?"

"Oh! Many! But none that I could ask usefully right now," Holroyd answered briskly.

"Then we'll take our leave, sir. Thank you for your time, and I am sure we will be in touch."

After the departure of the policemen, Holroyd sat down at his desk, thinking furiously. He was torn between wondering about the yuanbao, pursuing his quest, and preparing for a scheduled tutorial with some of his students. Finally, he decided the tutorial took precedence at this moment. *But perhaps I can get the students to help in my quest.*

12

Holroyd consulted the list of teams and picked one at random with which to meet first. The team listed six boys and girls with Annie Bright Star, as the team leader.

They met in his apartment and settled down around the table. Holroyd placed plates of cookies on the table and offered soft drinks, coffee, or tea.

"Welcome everyone." Holroyd opened the meeting. "Your assignment is to examine if Ming and early Qing Dynasty ships might have been the first foreigners to visit this part of the World." He saw to his satisfaction the students were listening attentively.

"Can you give an example?" One boy asked.

"How about a sign like Ching Chong's take out, established 1650?" the other boy offered and was rewarded by some laughter.

"Unlikely," Holroyd remarked drily. "But let me show you some examples." He got up and flashed up his computer to retrieve a file. He found what he was looking for and flashed a picture on the screen. The team gathered round him.

"This picture appears in Menzies's Book '1421' and shows what are called the Bimini stones, the Bimini Road, or the Bimini Wall, and is described as an underwater rock formation about 300 feet long." The picture was of submerged stones, rectangular in shape, and lying in a straight line. "This is from the Bahamas." The class looked at it carefully.

"Various explanations have been put forward as to the origins, some more preposterous than others including the possibility that they are evidence of the lost city of Atlantis. Menzies, however, offered a reasoned theory that they represent a slipway used to repair or career ships that have been at sea for an extended period."

"Professor, why are people arguing about what these stones mean?"

"Most of the arguments have been put forward by academics who have little, if any, knowledge of navigation, how flat-bottomed ships performed, or how ships crews would maintain their ships. Often, theories were put out based on European sailing experience. As Menzies points out, such experiences don't always apply to flat bottomed ships such as the Chinese junks."

"Other than the Bimini stones, is there any other proof that Chinese sailors could have reached Atlantic shores?" asked another student.

"One suggested proof is finding inscribed stones such as the *Shutesbury Stone* in Massachusetts and the *Pedra do Letreiro* in the Cape Verde Islands." Holroyd flashed a photograph of the Cape Verde item.

"Is that writing on the stone?" asked a girl.

"Yes, but we're not sure if it's Chinese or some other script."

"Wouldn't a stone marker like that be eroded after so long? Would the writing still be readable?"

"I think that would depend on the environment and the stone used. Remember, some very old, chiseled monuments look like new, as for instance in Rome, Greece, and Egypt. Others don't last long at all."

"Even if any inscription is still readable how would we find such a marker? Anyone have a suggestion?" Holroyd asked.

"Everything around here gets covered in moss or other growth," one of the girls remarked.

A lively discussion followed until Holroyd took control and explained how such proof could be found using the Anyox Find as an example.

"What's the Anyox Find?"

Holroyd reported what he had been told.

"Given the Anyox Find, one proof would be a site that has evidence of human occupation." He paused before explaining what and why such a find would support evidence of a previous visit.

Annie put up her hand. "Professor, couldn't the search be narrowed by looking at existing sites that meet your criteria? I mean couldn't we find places visible from the sea that have been settled for years and might have such evidence? Such a place might be on or near the shoreline."

"Excellent, Annie."

"I know of four such sites near here, including my own village. Do you think I could ask the elders to do some exploring?"

"That's a good suggestion, Annie. Go ahead and choose a site to do a write up. The write up should include a physical description of the place complete with a detailed map and photographs showing what's visible from the sea. Then write up a history of the place such as when it was settled and anything that could be of historical note. You can include oral histories, stories, and any memorabilia that villagers may have." He paused. "Any questions so far?" There were none.

"Do not break any local rules about where you can go to take pictures but do include a description of those rules in your write up," he instructed.

"Talk about looking for a needle in a haystack," muttered a boy.

"That's what history is partially about," Holroyd chided. He explained how evaluation of old sites and any artefacts found there gave clues of the past, added to which were records and or memories to give some context.

He pointed to the discoveries of Pompei, Troy, Ur of the Chaldees, and the lost civilizations in Central America.

"For years, the siege of Troy as described by Homer in the Iliad and the travels of Odysseus in the Odyssey, were considered nothing more than magnificent pieces of literature. Then came along the German archeologist Heinrich Schliemann who believed Homer's tales were in fact historically based. He found the remains of fortifications in the place he believed to have been Troy and he found gold jewelry including what is now accepted as Priam's gold, thus proving that Troy did exist, and Homer's Iliad was more than just a tale."

"Why were these tales not believed earlier?"

"Many archeologists and historians refuse to accept oral traditions or ancient writings as fact, and instead rely on physical evidence to prove what may have taken place. There are many academics, on the other hand, who will refuse to consider as fact anything that is outside of their own experience or beliefs. Darwin's theory of evolution was fiercely attacked despite the evidence because the so-called experts of the time believed the Bible was accurate. There are many today that continue to discredit facts on that basis."

"Who is right?" one student asked.

"Do you mean right on the basis of facts or on the basis of beliefs?"

"Are they so different?"

"Good question. You could argue that a fact has been wrongly interpreted, such as did Schliemann's really find Troy or some other forgotten place, and did the gold belong to Priam or someone else? On the other hand, you could assert that beliefs based on the Bible are accurate. There have been archeological finds to support the Bible. Personally, I think the truth is a mix of both the physical proofs that are found and the traditions that have yet to be supported by new discoveries."

"Is it worth it?"

"Is what worth it?" Holroyd responded.

"Is it worth spending all that time and money to dig up history?"

"I leave the answer to you, but ask you why you are in this class?" Holroyd paused and the questioner laughed. "Got it."

"Right. Any further questions? If not, you have your as-signments." And the meeting ended. The students filed out chatting excitedly, and Holroyd cleared the coffee cups and cookie dishes.

13.

Annie's team stood at the edge of the forest that enclosed the Band burial grounds. "Listen everyone, please. We're here to look for something that shouldn't be here but shows that someone was here, like a marker or something people might have used but left behind."

"Like what?"

"I dunno exactly. The professor said perhaps a stone marker or some old tools or pottery."

"What are we supposed to do if we find something?"

"Do not touch it or disturb it. We're supposed to take pictures and report back to the professor."

"Better make sure we take notes where we found whatever it is so we can find it again in all this forest." One of the boys commented.

"Normally, only Band members are allowed here, but I was given special permission for you to come along." Annie continued. "Remember to respect the sacredness of the place and don't disturb the spirits. Don't smoke, eat, drink, or make loud noises. Don't leave anything behind when we leave. If you break any of these rules, I'm going to be in deep shit. And if I am, I promise none of you will be far behind. All clear?" The others nodded.

Quietly the group moved along a darkened well-trodden path. Occasional shafts of sunlight pierced the gloom to illuminate ferns and other growths struggling to survive. At one point, the group reached a small, almost hidden track that meandered and finally petered out under the undergrowth.

"Hey, we shouldn't go down this way!" Annie called out.

"Why not?" One boy asked.

"It's not allowed," Annie answered.

"Why?"

"It's a special place and no one is to go there."

"What's so special? All I see is trees and more trees," the boy asked.

"Perhaps there's a ghost waiting to grab our souls. Ooooooooooo." And he gave a loud ghostly wail.

"Stop that! It's not funny!" Annie mixed anger at his disrespectful behaviour with a tinge of fear that it might be true.

"C'mon Annie. This is an adventure!" The boy responded.

"Yes, and it's what the Professor asked us to do," one of the girls pointed out.

Annie hesitated. "I dunno . . ."

"Who's going to know?" The boy insisted.

"We're only gonna look. We won't be doing any damage or leave anything behind," the girl added.

"Don't be a spoil sport, and anyway we won't be staying long."

"Oh!" Annie hesitated and then as curiosity gained the upper hand. "Okay!"

Everyone trod carefully, unsure of hidden burrows or exposed roots that could cause a misstep or fall. As the group moved deeper into the forest one of the girls tripped and fell heavily. The boy next to her moved over to help, but stopped and pointed at the ground.

"Hey, what's that?" he asked.

Sticking out from earth that had been the dislodged when the girl fell was what looked like the sole and part of a boot.

"That looks like a boot. That's strange! Why would a boot be there?" Using his hands, he cleared away some of the dirt.

"Oh! Fuck! There's a leg in there." He recoiled from digging further.

"Eeeeew," another girl exclaimed in horror and disgust.

Annie went over to have a look, "let's see."

"Oh! My God!" Yet another student exclaimed almost hysterically.

"Dig some more. No! Wait! Let me dig." More body parts became visible. "Hey, it looks like it's a complete body." He dug a little further and then stopped. Lying face down in a shallow grave was a fully clothed woman. Her head was bare so that her black braids could be seen clearly, and she was clothed in rain gear. She lay with her head a bit to one side and her arms neatly placed along her body.

"Who is that?" the girl whimpered.

"Let's see." And the boy started to continue removing dirt before reaching to turn the head.

"No! Don't touch her. Everyone, stop!" Annie spoke and then used her cell phone to call for help and give a short but animated report.

The class stepped back from the grisly find and stood or sat around wondering who it might be. Some spoke in subdued voices and recording the find on their cell phones. The fun and curiosity with which they had entered the forest was gone.

The Band policeman accompanied by several villagers arrived within a few minutes. The Policeman looked around. "Everyone, my name is Armstrong, and I am the Band police-man. Stand back please while I see who this is." He removed more dirt to inspect the body. As more of the earth was swept aside, Annie suddenly gave a scream as she recognised the clothing.

"Those look like Elisa's clothes. Oh, please God! No!"

Armstrong turned to look more closely at the body. "Oh hell! Yes, it is." He used his hands to scrape away more earth around the body. "Everyone, listen up. We don't know how this woman died and until we do know, this is a police crime scene. I'm cordoning the area off." He stopped and following police procedure when a murder is discovered on Band lands, he called in the RCMP. Once the call was completed, he faced the students.

"All of you need to give statements of what exactly hap-pened here today, including why you are on village lands in a place you should not be." He pointed at one of the villagers and said, "Samson here will take them down."

No one moved.

Armstrong faced the students. "I said give your statements now and then get away from here, before I start getting annoyed."

He looked at Annie. "Annie, what do you know about this?"

"I don't know how she came to be here. The last I saw of her was when she stopped by our house and had a long talk with my parents."

"Ok. Tell your parents I'll be dropping by. In the meantime, everyone, give me your statements and then everyone except my team leave." Still, no one moved.

"I said, get on with it! NOW!"

"Keep your shirt on, we're cooperating," the boy who had found the body muttered. Armstrong glared at the boy who hastily stepped back. Samson pulled out a notebook and a pen from a shirt pocket and started taking statements. Once everyone had been interviewed, and the students, except for Annie, left for home chattering quietly among themselves, Armstrong turned back to Annie.

"You were in charge, and you're from the village, so you know you're not supposed to be here. So why were you here?"

"Our prof at the University asked us to go look for anything that showed outsiders have been here."

"What prof?"

"Holroyd. But I asked my uncle if we could get permission to go look and he agreed."

"Even though this is a forbidden place?"

"Yes." Armstrong remained silent before asking "What more can you tell me about the last time you saw Elisa?"

"I didn't hear what they talked about."

"What time did she arrive and what time did she leave?"

"She arrived in the early evening and stayed for about a couple of hours."

"How was she dressed when she left?"

"I suppose the same way as when she arrived. But I dunno. I only heard her leave. I didn't see her leave."

"Ok, Annie. You can go home now, but I will be talking to you again." Annie left and Armstrong turned to his fellow workers. "Until the Mounties get here, I want two of you to stay here and make sure nothing is touched, I'm going over to meet Annie's parents."

His announcement was met with an initial silence before the villagers started arguing among themselves. Finally, one the villagers stepped forward. "Eliza was one of ours. We're taking her back for proper treatment."

"Don't do it! You'll get into trouble," Armstrong warned.

"Shut up about trouble. We all know what trouble means ... damned white men pushing us aside, and we've had enough of that to know how to deal with it." Murmurs of agreement came from the villagers as they moved to take charge.

"Stop, right now." Armstrong barked and stepped forward. "No one touches her until the police forensics team has done its job."

"And if someone does?"

"He'll be spending the next few weeks in jail for interfering in a murder case." This announcement was met with a mixture of resentment and acquiescence.

***

The RCMP arrived in response to the Band's call that a murder victim had been found on Band lands. Accompanying the forensics team were Sergeant Alvarez and Constable Brayden.

Sergeant Alvarez was slim and just tall enough to have been accepted into the force. His black hair and dark complexion testified to his Spanish ancestry. In contrast, Brayden was tall, blue eyed, and fair haired and could have modelled as an American University Quarterback. Whereas Alvarez gave an impression of quiet efficiency, Brayden exuded self-confidence and a swagger that sometimes indicated a tendency to bully his inferiors.

"Did anyone move her?" asked forensic team leader.

"No," Armstrong answered.

"Did you take any photographs or notes about the site?"

"Some, but I expect you'll want to take more."

Brayden joined in the conversation "Jeeesus!!!! This was a murder site, and you didn't make full notes or take enough photographs? Who told you to do that?"

"No one."

Alvarez moved forward as if to get between the two men and to defuse what appeared to be an escalating confrontation, but before he could do so, Brayden continued. "And just who do you think you are?"

"I am the Band policeman, and my name is Armstrong, though my proper name is He-who-follows-the-Thunderbird."

"Some policemen you are! You failed to follow even the most basic rules of murder investigation."

"Hold it! Don't tell me what to do. This is tribal land, and she was a First Nation woman. I was waiting for the forensics team before I did anything more, but until they come, we have our own rules, too." Armstrong bristled.

"Then you don't need us," retorted Brayden and Alvarez moved in quickly.

"Hold it, Constable. You're way out of line here. Armstrong works with us and gets the same respect as any of our men would. Get on with your inspection and leave the rest to me." He turned to Armstrong. "We'll deal with him later."

Armstrong assumed a mollified tone. "Good! What is he? Acts the insolent little prick but looks as if he's still wet behind the ears. What's he doing on our murder site?" Alvarez did not acknowledge the observation but asked.

"How was she found?"

"Some university kids tripped over her."

"What university kids? Was this a student trip to party out here, but it went wrong?"

"No. They were given an assignment to look for old artifacts to prove a foreign ship may have landed here."

"Given by whom?"

"Their professor at the University."

"Does this prof have a name?"

"Holroyd." Alvarez looked at Armstrong.

"We've met with him on another matter. So why would he send his students to look here?" Armstrong reported what he had been told about Holroyd's quest.

"We'll have to talk to him again. Now, about Elisa. What do you know about her?" Armstrong reported what he knew.

"Have the next of kin been informed?"

"No! I'm trying to find them. Nobody here has any knowledge, so I'm calling around to see if anyone knows. I'll be including any leads to friends and co-workers."

Alvarez nodded, satisfied that steps were being taken.

"Anything on her last movements?"

"We know she arrived here and met with some of the locals, but I'll have to check if they know where she was before that."

"How did she arrive?"

"She drove here."

"Have you checked her car?"

"It's missing. When she was nowhere to be seen, everyone assumed she had driven off without notifying us."

"We'll put out a notice to look for it. We'll need license plate and description."

"It's an old red Dodge and the licence is..." he opened a notebook and gave the details.

Suddenly, Alvarez heard Brayden announced loudly. "I think we should do some digging in an area of, say ten feet radius from where these remains were found. You men, there! Grab a shovel each and start digging." The leader of the forensics team jumped up.

"Hold it, Constable. That's not proper procedure!"

"It's our case!"

"Hold it, Brayden. Forensics are in control now, and they know what to do." Alvarez broke in and turned to the forensics leader. "We won't dig where you are working."

Brayden was angry but turned to the men. "Start from ten feet from the grave in all directions."

"Make it at least thirty yards and I won't argue." The forensics team leader was not happy, but deciding a jurisdictional argument now was not appropriate, shrugged his shoulders and went back to his work.

From the angry expressions on some of the faces, the villagers were not happy at the prospect of digging in the area nor of the presence of the federal officers.

"These are our lands and sacred to us. You don't tell us to dig without Band permission."

"You're right, but this is a murder scene, and I am suspending that rule in this case," Armstrong stepped in.

"Why so big an area?" One of the men asked.

"Because I told you to." Brayden assumed an authoritative pose and glared at the man.

"Just what do you think you're gonna find by all this extra digging?" asked another villager angrily.

"Look, just do as you're told," Brayden retorted. "It's a federal matter now, and I want this whole area examined."

Armstrong glared at Brayden, furious at his attitude and looked for help from the forensics team leader.

"Perhaps the constable has a point. But I don't see the harm as long as there's no interference in our area of work."

Brayden frowned at being challenged, but changed to a smug grin at the support he got from his colleague. "C'mon, don't stand there like a bunch of idle spectators, grab a spade and start digging."

"That brings us into the sacred grounds."

"Stop wasting time! Just get on with it," Brayden seemed to be fraying at the edges. Several grumbles could be heard from among the digging detail, but they started picking up shovels and a couple of pickaxes.

"How deep do you want to go?"

"As deep as it takes until we find something or hit rock."

"And if we find nothing?"

"Then we find nothing. Let's cross that bridge when we get to it."

"Our people are going love this," came the sarcastic comment.

"Just do it." Brayden seeing Armstrong's by now furious face, added "Please" as an afterthought.

For a while, the sounds of insects going about their business were added to the muted conversations of the forensics team and of picks and shovels attacking the earth.

"Hey!" came a shout from one of the diggers. "Lookee here!"

"Looks like a piece of old metal." The other workman clustered around to have a look. "Looks old. What's it doing here?"

"Careful now! Clear away the dirt without damaging what's there."

At last, the rusted remains of a sword became visible with the skeletal remains of an arm stretched towards the hilt. "Hey! Armstrong, come and look at this."

Armstrong stepped forward to see what the man had found. "Ok everyone, stand back! Let me look." Armstrong knelt by the find and carefully removed more dirt away revealing more remains and tattered rags of cloth and a few metal buckles. The skull showed signs of fractures and an arrowhead lay next to one thigh bone. Band members were standing around watching and Brayden left what he was doing and joined them. Armstrong called Alvarez over.

"From the sword and the scraps of clothing and pieces of metal, I'd say this doesn't look like it was a native," Brayden voiced authoritatively.

Several people bridled at his use of the word native. Pushing Brayden aside, Alvarez bent down and took a piece of cloth from the body and put it into a plastic bag. He stood up and called the forensics team.

"Hey guys! Looks like we found another one." The team leader came over. He looked at the remains.

"That looks old. I'll take some preliminary samples, but at first guess I'd say this is a job for a forensic anthropologist." Alvarez looked at the remains.

"I think you're right." Armstrong admitted and turned to the villagers. "Ok! Stop digging, but put someone to watch over the place." He turned to the forensics team leader. "When do you think your expert can be here?"

"I'll give them a call, but I don't see the need for hurry," objected the team leader. "I doubt it's urgent to discover how this person died, or whoever was the killer. I mean, look at what's there. I'd guess that's been lying there for a very long time, so a few days more won't change much. But we will take photographs and record whatever else is there. The rest can wait."

"Would it be OK to get in touch with the university to see if they can recommend someone?" Armstrong asked.

"Hold it! You heard what the man said. This is a federal matter so back off." Brayden growled.

"Let us do a preliminary examination," The forensic leader interjected. "If the remains are as old as it looks like they might be, I don't see the harm. As I said, this is not likely to be a crime for us to solve." Armstrong nodded.

"This then, is another avenue to explore, and I don't think the elders will be happy about it," Armstrong observed. Then a thought struck him. *I wonder if this has anything to do with the task that professor gave his students? I'll ask Annie, and then get in touch with this Holroyd. Meanwhile, I'll go and visit Annie's parents.*

***

Annie's parents were sitting on their porch enjoying the late afternoon sun. George, Annie's father, was drinking from a can of beer and his wife, Mary, dozed with a piece of unfinished sewing on her lap. The peaceful scene was interrupted by Armstrong's arrival. Mary woke with a start while George glanced at the visitor with a mixture of curiosity and irritation at the interruption.

"Now what?" George growled as Mary put down her sewing. Armstrong stood at the foot of the porch.

"Hello, George. How are you, Mary? I'm here following up on Annie's report Elisa had visited you shortly before she disappeared. Why was she here?" Armstrong asked. "Did you know her?"

"First time we met her."

"So, what did Elisa talk to you about?"

"She told us there had been one of the teachers at her school, a lay brother, who had systematically abused the children, including herself. He then disappeared and she thought he might be near here."

"Did she say who?" Armstrong asked.

"No."

"Did she say if there had been any complaints at the time of the incident to the authorities about this guy?"

"She complained to the principal, who was a member of some Catholic order, but he had refused to act. She then went to the diocese, but they ignored her. The local police sided with the Church and did nothing. However, there was one RCMP officer who believed her and followed up."

"What happened?"

"Nothing. His superiors said they had investigated the case but found nothing to support her accusations. He was transferred out shortly after that."

"That was it?" Armstrong ran a hand through his hair and persisted.

"Yes."

Armstrong changed his line of questioning. "Did she say what she was going to do next or where she might be going?"

"No."

"Did you see anything unusual that night?"

"Some of the kids were out on the street. One group was high on alcohol or drugs, maybe both." Armstrong remembered he had seen Elisa with those drunken kids and realised he might be the last person to have seen her alive. Mary continued

"Then there were Maggie's two boys together running down the street, but I couldn't see where to. Maggie was asking us about them because she hasn't seen them for days. It's not like them to be gone so long. She is getting worried they may be in trouble."

"Ok, I'll speak to her. But back to Elisa. You don't remember anything else?"

"No."

As he left, Armstrong decided he should make some enquiries with the RCMP to see what might be in their files about Elisa and her chase of school abusers. *And just why did that Professor, Holroyd suggest his students go looking in that place? Did he know anything about Elisa or her work, or was there another reason?*

14.

Johnny Otter sat against a tree halfway between the pits where the bodies had been found with his hunting rifle lying on the ground next to him. All around was an impenetrable darkness that would last until Moonrise. It was peaceful but Johnny could hear the whispers of desultory puffs of wind among the trees and the scurrying of nocturnal animals in the undergrowth. An occasional flapping of wings testified to an owl on the hunt; a sudden splash meant a fish was after some juicy morsel that was on the surface or maybe just an insect flying too low for its own good.

Johnny was at one with his surroundings. *Why am I sitting watch over where the bodies were found? What's it to us? It's not as if either of them was from the village, and why was she killed? Now that I think of it, she was probably killed by a bunch of those white fuckers. It's been like that since they first came here.* He paused. *Who's going to come here now that she's dead? And who would be interested in a skeleton that's been here for a very long time?*

He gazed up at the sky where a half moon was peeping in and out from among scudding clouds. He appreciated the contrasts of the bright clouds on top and the darkness underneath. *Why did those kids wander around here? Why were they sent here?* Suddenly he heard a twig snapping and he sat up to listen intently. *That's not natural.* He stood up, reached for his gun, and peered into the darkness.

"Who's there?" *That's a dumb question as if anyone is going to reply.*

He thought he heard a rustle and another twig snapped behind him, before he felt a blow to the head, and fell unconscious. His relief found him tied to the tree with his face caked with dried blood from a scalp wound. His rifle was missing.

"What the hell happened to you?"

"I got sandbagged."

"Who would want to do that?" His relief untied Johnny and looked around the area. As far as he could determine nothing had changed. The earth had only been disturbed where the bodies had been dug up.

"Nothing new has been disturbed so what's behind the attack?"

"Maybe poachers?"

"What's there to poach?"

"Yeah! There's no salmon here and anything else isn't worth poaching."

"Any tracks around?"

"Yeah! Lots, but probably from those schoolkids and the cops. I don't see anything different." He looked down at Johnny.

"You ok to walk, or should I send for help?"

"Give me a swig of your water and I'll walk, but come with me just in case. Someone's gonna pay for this." Together they made their way to the village.

"You sure you haven't been drinking again?" Armstrong looked at Johnny.

"Never drink when I go into the woods," Johnny muttered.

"I didn't see any bottle," Johnny's relief ventured.

"Ok! Let's go over it again," Johnny repeated what had happened while Armstrong listened and asked several questions to make sure the report was consistent.

"Right! OK, let's go back there and see what we can find."

"Nothing! There's nothing to be found," Johnny muttered but by now was suffering from a headache and feeling very weak. Seeing Johnny's condition, Armstrong told him to go to the hospital and have his wound looked at, while he and the relief made their way to the pit.

On arrival, they looked around, but as prophesized by Johnny they saw nothing that helped to understand the attack.

"I wonder what we're missing." Armstrong wondered. "I don't see how Johnny was the target. So, what were the attackers after? I think there's a link to the victims, but I can't think what it might be."

"You mean whoever attacked Johnny might have had something to do with Elisa?"

"Maybe. Or maybe with the skeleton, though I can't see how."

"Let's get back to the village. I want a watch on this place now but by two people and they better be armed."

"Tchah!" the relief spat onto the ground.

15.

Holroyd was shocked by the phone call.

"Professor, we found Elisa's body and the police are here questioning everyone. They want to know why we were wandering around in the village burial grounds," Annie was almost hysterical.

"Now calm down, Annie, and tell me exactly what happened." Holroyd tried to be as soothing as he could, and Annie gave him the details.

"That's terrible! But you and the class are not responsible. You were carrying out your assignment and from what you've told me, you had the village's permission to go into that area. It's just bad luck that there was a body there," Holroyd answered.

"My uncle gave me permission to go looking but we went into an area that was forbidden. The Band policeman thinks I have something to do with it."

"That's ridiculous. What's his name? I'll get in touch with him and clear things up."

"Armstrong."

"Thanks. Another question. Did your uncle have the authority to give you permission?"

"I don't know."

"And just why did you go into that forbidden area?"

"I thought we might find something, and I didn't think it would matter," Annie was almost crying.

“I see.” Holroyd sat silent before resuming “There’s not much that can be done right now. We’ll just have to wait and see how this plays out. Meanwhile, try not to worry. I’m sure it will all work out.” And with that he hung up. *I wish I felt more confident, but I’d better let the dean know before he hears it from others.*

16.

Dean Hummersdorf was not happy as he tried to react to the deluge of bad news coming at him from all sides. Holroyd had called with the news of the find and the media could be expected to clamour for information.

Donors were expressing unease over the reported developments and demanded assurances Hummersdorf could not give. Faculty members were seeking reassurances that everything was under control. Parents were phoning to ask about the safety of their offspring. The Board of Governors wanted to call a meeting wanting to know how this would influence negotiations with the Band. The Band elders were furious at the incursion of white people into their lands and the desecration of their burial site demanded an immediate meeting.

Hummersdorf could see no escape and was unsure to whom he could turn to for advice or help or, preferably blame. He set about scheduling the meetings starting with the Band Chiefs.

The meeting was held in the Board room at a large rectangular polished wood table surrounded by modern leather chairs. Band council members sat at three sides of the table while Hummersdorf, flanked by a stenographer sat on the fourth side.

"We are very disappointed," the Band Chief opened his remarks once the introductions and preliminaries had been dispensed with. "We agreed to allow the University to build on our lands with the understanding that our traditions would be respected. Now, they have been violated." There was silence.

The Chief went on. "Some of your students trespassed on the Band burial grounds. Furthermore, they found the body of a murdered First Nations woman there."

"Yes, I learned about that only a short while ago. The discovery of a murdered woman is terrible. I trust you are not implying that anyone at the University is responsible for her death." Hummersdorf answered.

"We are implying nothing," another member of the Band delegation offered.

"I'm sorry. I didn't catch your name or your role."

"My name is Alan Eddy, and I am the Band lawyer."

Hummersdorf sat back.

"How was this allowed to happen?" the Chief asked.

"It was not allowed," Hummersdorf interjected.

"But it happened."

"So, it seems," Hummersdorf shifted nervously in his chair.

"Seems?" The Chief's disbelief was patently obvious.

"I don't have all the details as yet and . . ." Hummersdorf got no further.

"We do. I think we would move ahead faster if you accepted our word." Eddy paused. "Unless you are suggesting we are making all this up."

"I'm not suggesting anything. I'm merely pointing out I don't have the full story."

"We've just given it to you."

"Er, well, ..." Hummersdorf floundered.

"Then let's move on. How do you propose to ensure it never happens again?"

Hummersdorf assumed what he hoped would be a position of strength. "I can hardly offer any suggestions until I have all the facts."

"Here we go again," one of the Band elders remarked.

"What's that supposed to mean?" Hummersdorf was beginning to bluster.

"It means we're not getting anywhere and might as well leave now."

"Dean, we do not want to be unreasonable," the Chief announced. "Given you have nothing to suggest at this time, we'll adjourn until you have some worthwhile proposals to discuss." Hummersdorf looked like a condemned man getting a last-minute reprieve.

"Until that time, we require that no-one from the University enters the Band lands and most definitely does not conduct any excavations. We may require more, and if we do, we will notify you. Do you follow?" Hummersdorf nodded.

"Should anyone again trespass on our lands we will arrest and charge them. Furthermore, any such trespass could result in a reconsideration of the original agreement we have with the University," the Chief continued ruthlessly.

Hummersdorf started as if stung. "What? What do you mean by reconsideration?"

"I'll just remind you that the university sits on our lands only by our grace."

Hummersdorf blanched as he realized the import of what he had just heard.

"Oh!" He took out a lavender handkerchief from his pocket to wipe his brow. "Let me just say that on behalf of the University I apologise for any actions by any of our students, faculty, or anyone else that may have caused offense. And, while I regret that you feel it necessary to make demands because of anything that may have happened, I will comply."

"Nothing! Just empty words! Just what you might expect from a two-faced white weakling," an elder was heard in the background.

"There he goes again. Won't admit they fucked up," another elder grunted. The Chief looked at Eddy who nodded and the meeting broke up.

Outside the meeting room, the Band delegation stood together to exchange opinions on the outcome. Hummersdorf came out and went over to Eddy.

"I wonder if I might have your card."

"Of course."

"Oh! Thank you! I'd like to ask you unofficially how we should proceed."

Eddy looked surprised. "I thought it was made that pretty clear in there."

"Oh! No! I'm referring to our discussions for expanding the University on Band grounds."

Eddy could not believe what he heard. "Could you repeat that?"

"I'm asking about the expansion discussions."

"Given recent events, I'd be of the opinion there are no discussions." He turned away leaving Hummersdorf aghast.

***

Once back in his office, Hummersdorf collapsed into his chair and addressed the wall, "What next? How the hell am I going to explain this mess to the Board? More to the point how can I avoid getting blamed?" He thought over what little he knew. There were questions he needed to know how to answer. *Who authorized the students to go over Band lands?* He picked up the phone, dialed a number, and proceeded to ask questions.

Holroyd! Of course!

He sat back thinking how to put all the blame on the visiting professor. But how to set that up? He picked up the phone and spoke at length. When the call was done, he sat back with a degree of satisfaction. *Now to start cutting that ass down to size.* The phone rang.

The Board's Secretary's voice, absent the usual niceties, informed him the Board of Governors would be meeting next day and he was requested to attend.

"I'm not sure I'm free. I'll check my schedule and get back to you," Hummersdorf prevaricated.

"I don't think you fully understand, Dean. The meeting has not been called at your convenience. Whatever you may have on your schedule will have to be rescheduled."

"But . . ."

"Let me give you a heads up. The president received a complaint from the Band elders and is furious. The Board members are very concerned what this may mean for the University's plans." She paused. "I'd suggest you be well prepared if you value your position." Hummersdorf went cold.

"Very well! I'll be there." He slumped in his chair and his tone suggested resignation mixed with fear. *What now?* He sat back before making a couple of further calls before asking his secretary to have Professor Holroyd come to his office immediately.

"I think you know why I've called you in," Hummersdorf fired off as Holroyd entered.

"Not really."

"Then let me summarize it for you. You disregarded my warnings and sent your class off onto Band lands without getting the necessary permissions or authorizations. Consequentially, you have riled the elders and derailed expansion negotiations, and maybe even jeopardized the future of this University." Hummersdorf paused, furious, but savouring the moment.

"What?"

"Oh! Don't pretend you have no idea what I'm talking about." He stopped. "I'd say that's a pretty impressive set of achievements considering how long you've been here." He stopped and looked at Holroyd. "However, I doubt you will be here much longer. The Board is meeting tomorrow morning and I'm recommending you be fired effective immediately. The sooner you disappear, the happier I will be."

"You can't do that," Holroyd burst out furiously, but also suddenly feeling very insecure. He got no further.

"I think you underrate what I can or cannot do and overrate your importance."

"My importance?" Holroyd was taken aback. "I wouldn't claim to be important, but I think my work speaks for itself."

"Ah yes, your work! A wild goose chase to prove your belief that Zheng He was the first foreigner to visit these shores. A belief based on a discredited examination of Zheng He's voyages by a pretentious naval officer with no academic background worth mentioning," Hummersdorf commented derisively.

"I'm not claiming Zheng He was the first foreigner to come here. That honour I believe probably belongs to one of his admirals, Zhou Man."

"And what makes you believe that?"

"First, while it is possible to prove something did happen, proving something did not happen usually depends on proving an alternative that did happen. I have found nothing to suggest an alternative for Zhou Man's voyages. Menzies demonstrates how Zhou Man could have sailed, but he falls short when it comes to evidence. However, because the Waldseemüller map of 1507 shows the eastern American and Asian seaboards with some accuracy someone, either European or Chinese, did go there. The western seaboards of the Americas as shown are reasonably accurate, so either Waldseemüller got some, even if incomplete information, or he just guessed. Given the importance of map making at that time,

I doubt he guessed. I'm trying to find out how such accuracy was determined and by whom." He paused.

"Admittedly, I saw a report that an Australian professor claimed Menzies had misinterpreted the Waldseemüller map, but in his article dismissing Menzies' claims, he refers to an analysis by a respected mariner, Phil Rivers. Rivers examined Menzies' claims and cast doubts on Menzies' claims concerning the American Northwest Coast because certain features are not mentioned on maps of that era. I think explanations for such a discrepancy are possible and as such leave Menzies's claims in the realms of possibilities."

"So, you think you know better than so many respected authorities on the subject?" Hummersdorf snorted derisively.

"Almost all of them dismissed Menzies for lack of proof or corroboration. Admittedly, Menzies made some claims that should be verifiable, but as far as I know, whereas some research does suggest Menzies overreached himself not all the claims have been dismissed. None have conclusively dismissed the sailing capabilities of those Chinese ships and failing that, the possibility of a ship arriving here remains unanswered." He paused. "No, I don't know better than them, but I have questions, and answers to which should prove or disprove my hypothesis about who arrived here first."

"But if there are sufficient unsubstantiated claims, it is reasonable to accept the whole work is worthless."

"I could point out the Bible could be said to meet that criterion."

"Don't you dare to blaspheme!" Hummersdorf jumped out of his chair building a head of steam, but then calmed down. "Anyway, I don't see how your opinions could possibly be significant."

"How do you know what's significant in my field?"

"I may not, but I have an independent evaluation that I trust." He stopped. "Let me say I trust that evaluation more than I do yours."

"Did you listen to yourself?" Holroyd looked at Hummersdorf with amazement. He paused. "Have you read Menzies' book?"

"No, and I have no intention of bothering myself with bogus claims that have no support among academics."

"You might want to change your mind. Many academics have had to eat crow when their assertions proved false. If I remember rightly, Nate Silver noted that only about 3% of academic findings could be replicated accurately." He took a deep breath to compose himself and said, "This is outrageous."

"Oh! Outrageous or not the matter is out of your hands. There's a meeting of the Board of Governors at which I will be making my recommendations that I am confident the Board will accept. You, on the other hand might want to consider where your future lies."

Once outside the Dean's Office, Holroyd found he was trembling. Once again, his academic career looked as if it was about to go down in flames. *What the hell have I done to deserve this? Who is this independent source who can bring my work into question?* An uncharacteristic wave of frustration mixed with self-pity washed over him. He walked slowly toward his apartment. He was not happy as he entered his rooms.

To be sure Holroyd conceded he had tasked his students to do some exploration and had not cleared it with the dean, but to say he had done so without permission of the Band was wrong. He had warned his students and Annie had told him she had received permission from her uncle.

Clearly the dean was not his friend and Holroyd wondered if his quest was now in jeopardy. "Not the position I had hoped for when I came here," he muttered to himself.

***

The Board met and discussed developments on the reservation. Hummersdorf appeared before the Board and asked what he had done so far to diffuse the concerns expressed by the Chiefs.

"I asked the responsible faculty member to give me what he knew." Hummersdorf assumed a position of authority.

"Did that differ from what the Chiefs told you?"

"Oh! Most definitely! He claimed no knowledge or responsibility for what happened."

"Do you believe him?"

"I did at first. I like to support faculty members if there are problems. Since then, however, I've developed doubts."

"How so?" Asked one Board member.

"His story differs from what the chiefs told me. I believe the chiefs."

"That's very nice of you," derisively commented the village representative, "but what are you going to do about this mess? And, more to the point, how will you prevent another violation?" Before Hummersdorf could reply another voice interrupted.

"Just who are we talking about?"

"Peter Holroyd." Hummersdorf's tone conveyed his displeasure of the name.

"Holroyd? Are you serious? That man has come with the highest recommendations from his university, and even the British Government. I suggest you should be very sure of any initiatives you may consider."

"I assure you that I will do nothing before I am certain, and I will then advise the Board to get direction."

"Do you have any idea why Holroyd has adopted his position?" asked a woman member.

"Holroyd has a bee in his bonnet about the Chinese being the first foreigner to arrive here. I believe he will go to any lengths to prove his idea."

"What is your opinion on that?"

"From what I have been told, it's an idea that lacks even the smallest justification."

"Have you discussed the matter with him?"

"Not yet, no. I intend to do so as soon as I can but have been distracted by current events that I believe to have priority." Hummersdorf shifted nervously.

"That's understandable. Anything you wish to add?" the president asked.

"Yes, I've just been advised that his academic claims may not withstand scrutiny." There was a stunned silence at this revelation.

"Are you saying the man's a liar and a fake?" A woman member seated next to the president broke the silence and asked.

"Much as I hate to admit the possibility, yes I am beginning to think so."

There was complete silence, before the president sighed.

"That would be very unfortunate if it were found to be true. You're certain of the advice you've been given?"

"Oh! Yes!"

"Would it stand up in court?"

"Perhaps not in a criminal or civil court, but I think it probably would before an academic tribunal."

"Is this a formal accusation? I mean, are you recommending immediate disciplinary action?"

"Immediate? I don't think so. Perhaps later."

"I think the members here support your actions so far," Interrupted the president. "However, I would suggest you meet with Holroyd sooner than later. I am sure the Board will support you when you have come to a decision."

"What's our next step?" a member asked.

"At this point we should sit back until we know more," the president advised. "And Dean, I suggest you advise Holroyd to be less visible on and off campus for a while, until the dust has settled. I'll talk to the elders again to make sure we're all singing from the same scoresheet." The meeting adjourned.

Hummersdorf returned to his office. He picked up the phone.

"Holroyd? Hummersdorf here. The Board has taken notice of your conduct and is ordering you to stop any further trips to the Band lands. You're very lucky because no disciplinary action will be taken against you." He paused dramatically. "For now." And hung up.

He opened his diary to write up his notes of the board meeting when the phone rang, and Manning called to tell Hummersdorf that the body they found up on the reservation was Elisa's.

"What? Who?"

"Elisa! You remember she had a research grant with your ex-wife to examine abuses in the Residential schools."

Hummersdorf felt an apprehensive shiver. He knew some of those histories and had heard of many more; if her death was in any way linked to any of those histories, he might find himself drawn into the investigations and did not relish the idea at all. He had his own secrets that if they ever came to light would end his career and maybe even send him to prison. Hummersdorf felt dizzy and grasped the edge of his desk to steady himself.

"You know, I'm getting fed up with that fucking troublemaker."

"Who are you talking about, Joe?"

"Holroyd."

"Oh! Calm down. Holroyd's just a harmless academic. He hasn't been here long enough to become a troublemaker."

Hummersdorf saw red. "That shows how little you know! You have no idea what he managed to stir up at his university and then in China." His voice rose, "We should never have invited him to come here," he almost screamed. "I'll get that bastard if that's the last thing I do." He slammed the receiver down, but doing so did nothing to calm his emotions.

"Dean! Is everything OK? I heard shouting." The door had opened, and his secretary stood looking at him with concern.

He controlled his voice "I'm fine, thank you. Now please make sure I'm not disturbed again."

Next, reluctantly, he tried to call his ex-wife to find out what she remembered of Elisa's work. It was not a call he wanted to make. He remembered her reaction on discovering his sexuality had caused wounds that would probably never completely heal, and their divorce had been acrimonious. To his relief, she did not pick up the phone, so he left a message.

***

Holroyd was stunned. He poured himself a drink. A feeling of Déja Vu swept over him as he remembered the stab in the back he had received at his English university just before he had taken on a previous task for Merry. Once again, he was on the defensive when all he had done was to pursue his professorial duties.

17.

Holroyd looked up from his computer where he was researching ancient Chinese sea voyages when the phone rang.

"Professor Holroyd? My name is Armstrong. I just want you to tell me why your students were wandering all over the tribal lands."

"Oh yes. I was about to call you." Holroyd explained the reason he had assigned the task to his students.

"Did you tell them to get Band permission?"

"Perhaps not is so many words, but yes," Holroyd said.

"I see. Does your project have anything to do with the old remains we found nearby?"

"Not as far as I know. Can you tell me more?" Holroyd asked and Armstrong gave a short description of the find.

"That sounds very interesting. It might have some link to my quest, but I can't say for sure until I know much more." Armstrong thanked him and ended the call.

Holroyd sat back thinking when there was a knock on the door. Holroyd opened it to see the two RCMP Officers.

"Professor Holroyd? We have some more questions to ask you. May we come in?"

"Yes, of course, Inspector." Once seated, Tomlinson opened the meeting.

"I believe you have been informed about the body your students found."

"Yes, terrible!"

"Just why did you send your students there?" Holroyd explained how he was looking for evidence to support his theory.

"No other reason, sir?"

"No. Why?"

"Something has come to our attention." Holroyd waited expectantly.

"You will remember that we found a remnant of cloth in the gold ingot that was passed on to us."

"Yes, and I think you determined the remnant was over 300 years old."

"Yes, would it surprise you to learn that the skeletal remains we found near the murdered woman was about 300 years old?" Holroyd sat up as if stung.

Tomlinson continued "Our forensics people tell us it's from the same period and the origin is Southeast Asia. Or more precisely South China."

"I see, and just what do you want from me?"

"We hope you can give us an explanation."

Holroyd was puzzled. "Pardon? An explanation of what?"
"What you knew about the skeleton, the cloth, and the ingot."

"I have no idea."

"I see, sir." Tomlinson paused. "I find it too much of a coincidence that you send your students to search an area reportedly to find proof that a Chinese ship was the first foreign visitor. Then, in the area they are searching, they find evidence of that someone came here probably from China and possibly at the same time when the ingot got wrapped in cloth. Possibly, the person brough the ingot with him."

"Him? Are you sure the person was a male?"

"Yes, sir. I doubt many females at the time went around armed with swords." Tomlinson paused. "Is there anything you might want to tell us?"

"No Inspector, my expertise is ancient cartography and maritime voyages."

"We are well aware of your background. But at the same time, we have some questions about it."

"Pardon? What is there to question?"

"We know your performance at your university was questioned and that consequently you took some leave. We also know that while on that leave you got involved with criminals engaged in stealing valuable artifacts."

"But you must also know I was fully exonerated in all those activities," Holroyd protested. "Anyway, my quest here is to find proof that the first foreign ship to these shores was a Chinese ship."

"Yes, we have all that information, but you were hardly exonerated. You were reinstated by intercession from the government. In doing so, it's possible they glossed over some of your activities." He paused to let that sink in, and then continued, "However, that's not our concern. What is our concern is you maintain you are pursuing a quest for which we have reliable information has no basis."

"Let me guess, the reliable information comes Professor van Vervoort."

"Why would you assume that?" Alvarez asked.

"For some reason, he has it in for me."

"And what reason might that be, sir?" Tomlinson asked softly.

"You'll have to ask him," Holroyd answered dismissively but Tomlinson looked at Holroyd with doubt.

"Is there anything else, gentlemen? If not, perhaps I can get on with my work."

"Yes, there is." Tomlinson leaned forward. "Seeing as how this fabric is centuries old and comes from across the Pacific, it must have come by sea."

"I see your point," Holroyd nodded.

"Given that you claim to be an expert on ancient Chinese maritime voyages, perhaps you concluded the ingot we asked you about came here by sea from China. Perhaps you even had some information about such a voyage. That could explain why you sent your students into that area after we showed you the ingot." Tomlinson paused for Holroyd's reaction.

"That's a ridiculous suggestion." Holroyd began to feel very uncomfortable.

"Ridiculous or not, we think it's plausible. But other than trespassing on tribal grounds, it would not be a criminal act were it not for the murder." Tomlinson paused. "What can you tell us about that?"

"Nothing at all. I knew nothing until one of my students called me to tell me about it. I don't see how you could think I had anything to do with it."

"Perhaps you went up there to look around after we showed you the ingot and the woman saw you. Perhaps there was an argument, and she was killed to make sure there would be no report of your visit."

"That is the most fantastic idea I have ever heard. I'm surprised you even brought it up."

"Surprised or not, sir, we will get back to you." The officers left.

Holroyd sat trembling with worry thinking over the meeting. Somehow the police suspected him of murdering Elisa to cover up a possible visit to the site looking for what? More ingots? *How am I going to prove I never went there?* He got up and poured himself a strong drink and then another.

Somewhat calmer, he changed his line of thoughts and realised that his search would be made easier if the skeleton is that of an Asian, who might have arrived on a Chinese ship.

If, on the other hand, he was a European, he might have been a passenger on a Chinese ship, but more probably on a European one. Holroyd wondered who will conduct the examination of the remains and when his origins will be determined. *I'll have to follow that up.*

***

In response to a call from Armstrong, Tomlinson and Alvarez went over to Armstrong's small cubicle that served as his office and listened to Armstrong's report of the meeting with Annie's parents.

"So, the only fact that she passed on was that a former abuser assumed a different name and may now be teaching here or near here?" asked Tomlinson.

"Or maybe working in some other trade," Armstrong amended.

"And there was an RCMP investigation that went nowhere?" Asked Tomlinson.

"Yes."

"So, you think that Elisa's death may be linked to this search?"

"Yes," Armstrong said.

"I agree it's possible, but it doesn't give us much to go on. If I understand correctly, this abuser left Elisa's school some ten or fifteen years ago. That's a long interval and gives someone a lot of time to disappear completely," he mused. "We wouldn't know about him unless he does something to attract official or local notice."

"I want to follow it up and would appreciate your help."

"We'll look into it, but to be honest, I'm not very hopeful."

"I expected as much," Armstrong let his bitterness surface.

"Look, we are terribly understaffed here at this detachment, and as you can imagine, finding the murderer is just one of our priorities. I can only promise we will do our best to get to your request as soon as we can. But there is another matter you should know." And he gave his reasoning that the students might have been sent there because Holroyd knew something that so far, he had not admitted.

"The fact that an ingot is involved could indicate there's more gold to be found there or nearby. If that is even suspected, I can see a public frenzy if people start hunting along those lines. We've got an ongoing investigation here and we don't need speculation or amateur sleuths getting in our way. Nor do I want any interested parties to run scared when they realise we're trying to find the origins and owners of the gold."

"You think Holroyd might go public?" asked Armstrong.

"I don't know. From what the Brits told us, it's unlikely. On the other hand, look at how he's supposed to have disobeyed the University and got the chiefs all riled up. Maybe our good professor isn't quite as trustworthy as he's been made out to be. Time will tell."

Once outside again, Alvarez turned to Tomlinson. "Who do you want to follow up on this abuser?"

"Give it to ...what's his name? Oh, yes! Brayden."

"Not sure he'd be the best man for the job," Alvarez observed.

"Unless you can suggest someone who isn't up to his neck on other jobs, he'll have to do."

Alvarez just shrugged.

***

Brayden relished the limelight. Here he was just weeks out from the RCMP training depot at Regina, and already assigned to a murder case. His troop of cadets had benefitted from an accelerated program that reduced the normal 26-week course and on completion he had been assigned to the Victoria Detachment. True, he hadn't exactly shone during the training program: in fact, he had scraped through at the bottom of the list of successful candidates despite which he had been sent to one of the most sought-after units.

On arrival, he was assigned a field coach who would supervise him during a six-month Field Training Program. Unfortunately, his field coach was away on sick leave and with a local manpower shortage no new coach had been assigned yet. None-the-less, he had been sent to help investigate the discovery of Elisa's body. How lucky can he be?

18.

Holroyd pondered what his next move would be when the doorbell rang.

"Good evening, Professor." The campus policeman greeted him and then turned to introduce another man. "This is Inspector Hollingsworth from the Vancouver Police who wants to ask you a few questions. May we come in?" *Oh Hell! I forgot to get back to them.* Holroyd stood aside as the two men entered and invited them to sit.

"Thank you for allowing me to meet with you, Professor. We did try to get hold of you earlier, but we're here now." The policemen sat down, and Hollingsworth took out a notebook. "As I think we told you, it's about the robbery you witnessed at the O'Mallory Collection. Just a few questions if you don't mind." No, Holroyd did not mind.

"Might I see your passport, Professor?" Holroyd retrieved it from his desk and passed it over to the inspector who copied down the details in his book. Satisfied he had made the entries correctly; he handed the document back.

"What led you to go to the museum?"

Holroyd told the inspector of his evening with Manning and how the latter had suggested he would benefit from a visit there, even going so far as to arrange an introduction.

"So, you went there on the Saturday morning. Other than this suggestion, did you have any specific reason to go there? Wanting to see something of which you were aware?"

"No."

"But you did see something that caused you to ask the curator about it," Hollingsworth persisted, and Holroyd realised the Inspector was waiting to see if he was going to lie.

"Yes, two items of gold, but both in rather bad shape."

"What was your interest in them?"

Holroyd explained why he thought them curious.

"And that was all?"

"Yes."

"But then you went back on the Sunday morning. Why was that?" Holroyd explained that he had received a call from O'Mallory in the middle of the night voicing the same questions as Holroyd. So, Holroyd had decided he should have another and closer look at them.

"So, you looked at these items, asked about them, and returned the next day just as someone decides to steal them. Could of course be coincidental, but I don't like coincidences because that's what they rarely turn out to be."

Holroyd remained speechless and he felt a trickle of cold sweat running down his back.

"Did you know or recognise any of the other visitors at the exhibition?"

"No." Holroyd watched as the inspector made another note.

"Let's focus next on this young man that committed the theft. You said that he pushed you out of the way to give him enough time to escape. Is that correct?" Holroyd nodded.

"But you could not give a description of the man."

"Other than he was Asian, that's correct."

"I see." The inspector paused. "Tell me about your duties here."

Holroyd complied.

"I don't quite see how your duties and interests would lead you to want to visit an exhibition of native art. Bit outside your field isn't it?"

"I suppose so, but I've just arrived from England as you can see. It's my first visit to Canada so visiting a museum is one way to learn about this part of the world. I trust that's not illegal." His attempt at jocularity fell flat.

"Not if that is the real reason for your visit." The inspector paused. "Is there anything you might want to add?"

Holroyd didn't think there was. He shook his head.

"I understand you've become involved in finding a body up on the reservation."

"Not directly, no! But my students went there." Hollingsworth looked at him and Holroyd suddenly felt nervous as if he was being studied as a possible suspect.

"You seem to be leading not only a busy but an interesting life here," Hollingsworth said after a moment. "A life that's much more interesting than I would have expected from an academic."

Holroyd said nothing.

"You see, I begin to wonder why all these happenings

have you as a common element."

"Other than I was present at the events, I car see no other linkage."

"Well, sir, perhaps you can't or won't see the linkage and I hope you are correct there is none." Hollingsworth paused meaningfully.

"Now wait a moment, Inspector. Are you suggesting I have something to do with either or both events? That's preposterous." Holroyd assumed an indignant tone and leaned forward forcefully almost coming out of his chair.

Hollingsworth unfazed looked at Holroyd coolly. "Yes, sir. It may well be, but we are in the early stages of our inquiries." He shut his notebook with a snap. "Thank you for your time, Professor. But please don't leave the area without letting us know." With that he got up and left, leaving Holroyd more worried than he was before the visit.

19.

Arriving at the site, van Vervoort noted the cordoned off area within which Elisa's body had been discovered and went over to the recently disturbed earth where the skeleton had been revealed. He directed his assistants to start sifting the earth around the remains while he hunkered down and looked at the skeleton itself.

"You don't look like anything I've seen from around here," he muttered. "The natives usually don't leave skeletons lying around. Let me clear away a little more and see what else is there." Carefully, he scraped away more of the dirt and came across a bone. Gingerly he took it out and brushed away more dirt. "Now just who were you and where did you come from?" He scraped away further finding more bones and some mostly rotten fabric although he noted some gold threads.

He reached for the fabric, but it came apart in his hands revealing a gleam embedded in the remains. Carefully, he extracted the object that had caught his attention and realized it was gold. *Oh! wow! This can't have come from here.* He looked up to make sure no one could see what he had found or if he found anything else. He took a hold of the object, but was unprepared for what he saw. He sat back considering his find. *This most definitely is not indigenous.*

There, in his hand, lay a crucifix of gold inlaid with enamel and gems and attached to a gold chain. The figure of Christ on the Cross wore a crown and a skirt or robe that reached to his knees. His hands were opened so that the nails in his palms could be clearly seen. His ribs stood out and his face conveyed his suffering and the agony of his execution. *This looks like a Thirteenth or Fourteenth Century crucifix, like one I saw in the Metropolitan Museum of New York. How did that get here?* He placed the object into his bag and rummaged further only to find a badly twisted lump of gold embedding a highly polished stone. Not sure of the significance of either object he put them both in his bag and stood up.

"I'm done for the day," he told his team of helpers. "But you carry on to see what you might find. Meanwhile, collect all the bones, put them in a box, but make sure you label the box with the place and date where they were found. When that's done, send the box to the university museum for further examination."

"Any luck yourself, Professor?"

"No! At least not yet. But it's early yet so who knows." With that he left the site and returned to his car.

Before starting the engine, he examined the crucifix again. *That's clearly European and, by the look of it, it probably belonged to some Catholic priest or, because those things didn't come cheap, more likely to an abbot or bishop. That being the case, that's a Catholic Bishop lying there with the crucifix perhaps part of his regalia. But if that is true, then what is he doing there? I'll have to figure out the reason, but it can wait because what this find proves is that the Catholics came here and probably were the first.*

"Gotcha, Holroyd!" He shouted and looked around to make sure no one was in earshot. "I'm going to announce this find and get the credit." *Finally, I'll get vindicated.* He smiled all the way home.

***

Holroyd looked at the poster inviting everyone to a presentation by Professor Paul van Vervoort on his recent findings proving the first foreign visitors here had been Europeans.

How is he going to prove that? Holroyd decided he had better attend.

To his surprise, the Lecture Hall was quite full, and he recognized several of his students among the audience. On the dais, van Vervoort sporting a very smug smile was flanked by Dean Hummersdorf, the Mayor, the Chaplain, and two people he did not recognize. Hummersdorf stood up and reached the lectern.

"Ladies and Gentlemen, please take your seats so we can begin." He then went on to introduce van Vervoort in glowing terms as a distinguished member of the faculty, and an acknowledged expert on discoveries and settlements on the Northwest Coast of America. He consulted his notes before continuing.

"The question has long been debated of who the first foreign visitors to these shores were. We have heard theories the first ones came from the south of America from what is now California, or even further south from Mexico or Central America." He paused dramatically before raising his voice. "Someone here asserted that the honour belongs to Asians." He paused before adding disdainfully, "Even though there is no proof to support those suggestions." Several chuckles went through the hall. "However, as we will now hear from Professor van Vervoort the question finally can be answered." He turned to van Vervoort.

"Professor, the floor is yours." And he sat down to a smattering of applause.

"It's an honour to be able to present to you my findings and the answer to a question that has bugged us for so long," van Vervoort began before launching into his report of being asked to investigate the findings of the skeleton and what he had discovered. He showed slides of the bones, the wood and fabric remnants focusing on the gold thread.

"Based on the find of these items, I can confidently state that a western person was lying there with personal objects of value. We have examined the bones and conclude the deceased died in the middle of the 17th Century and was a male in his early to mid-forties who lived a protected life. What I mean by that is, he did not perform continued hard labour or suffer from malnutrition." He paused to take a sip of water.

"There is some evidence of parasitic invasions that appear to be of tropical origins. The likely origin is Central America where, by the time of the death of this individual, the Spanish had already established a thriving colony." He paused to survey the audience. Satisfied everyone was following him with interest, he consulted is notes and went on.

"Among the personal items I found these." He showed a photograph of the badly twisted gold with its jewel and the crucifix. There were gasps from the audience.

"The gold and stone are probably all that remains of a signet ring. That being so, the person was of a high social rank." He paused to let the audience consider his words before continuing.

"The crucifix is without a doubt a medieval crucifix of European origin. Such religious items were not cheaply produced. So, who would have had this object in his possession?" He let the audience think to whom the crucifix might have belonged. After pausing he proclaimed, "I conclude that its owner was a Catholic prelate probably an Abbot or a Bishop." There was total silence in the Hall.

"Now, you may wonder what a Catholic prelate was doing here. There are no previous reports that any Catholics ever came to these shores much before the 18th or 19th Century, but obviously this person and these objects came here much earlier." He paused for a dramatic moment.

"So, what is the likely explanation for these objects? To answer that, let's pause for a moment to step back and consider what was happening in the North Pacific area." He changed the slide to show a map of the North Pacific ocean with the Philippines on the left side, Central America in the centre, and Europe to the right.

"The Spanish had established colonies in Mexico and the Philippines and conducted rich trade, whereby Asian goods moved through Manila to Acapulco and then onwards to Europe." He used a pointer to the routes that were taken.

"Sea travel was notoriously unsafe because of weather and …" he paused for effect, "piracy." He paused again, "Rich trade routes attract pirates and the Manila to Mexico route was no exception. Indeed, piracy proved to be a problem that continues even now." He took a sip of water.

"I suggest that our prelate was travelling on one of the ships carrying cargo that included a vast treasure from Manila to Acapulco. However, the ship was captured by pirates who then arrived here probably driven ashore by a storm. I submit the ship was damaged to the extent that repairs were necessary. While the crew was repairing the ship our prelate managed to escape but was recaptured and killed." He paused again to look over the by now rapt audience.

"But then why was he left here unless the pirates had more pressing business to attend to such as finishing repairs? In hurrying to complete their task, the pirates just left the dead man to rot without a decent burial." He stopped to take a sip of water.

"I suggest that the ship's damage was enough to threaten its seaworthiness and the pirates decided as a safety measure to bury their loot. That being so, I conclude there has to be more loot than just these items and I am proposing that a full-scale excavation take place to find the rest."

There was a moment's silence before a voice from the back asked. "Excuse me Professor, but are you telling us that there is treasure buried on the reservation?"

"Yes, that is what I am telling you."

Other voices joined in.

"Wow! He's telling us there's pirate gold among the trees! I thought it's usually hidden in caves or in sunken vessels," one person remarked.

"Seems not this time," came the reply. Turning to van Vervoort, he asked "How much do you think might be out there?"

"Given the reported sizes of pirate loots maybe a ton or more."

"What would such a loot be worth today?"

"Well, a ton is 32,000 ounces and gold today is worth around $2,000 an ounce, so the intrinsic value could be around $64 million. The historic value could of course be …" The rest was lost as there was a sudden stir and when Holroyd looked around, he saw several people hurrying out of the hall. van Vervoort was looking at Holroyd with a triumphant grin. Holroyd was appalled.

"You stupid incompetent jackass!" Holroyd jumped to his feet and yelled at van Vervoort. "Have you any idea what you have just done?"

"Oh, indeed I have! I have proved that you are nothing but a blowhard charlatan," van Vervoort shouted back.

Holroyd was both thunderstruck and aghast. How could any credible academic propose such a scenario with so many holes in it? The location of the find was fact, as was the finding of the crucifix and probably its authenticity. But to suggest that it was part of a pirate loot was stretching it beyond any reasonable belief. And to add injury to this specious, but spurious claim, he had opened the door to what would probably turn out to be a crisis if not a disaster.

That bloody fool! Based on what I can only describe as blatantly dishonest research leading to a preposterous conclusion, he has just opened the site to treasure hunters. This will not go down well. He stood there watching as audience members milled around van Vervoort in what could only be described as rapturous adulation.

"I think this lays your ideas well and truly to rest." Dean Hummersdorf appeared at his side clearly gloating at the prospect of Holroyd's fall from grace. "Perhaps you might want to reconsider your position here. No one appreciates a discredited academic at an institution of learning and certainly not this one."

Holroyd turned to him.

"I quite agree with you. No one does. However, I am far from reconsidering my position although others may have to do so." He faced the dean mustering a show of bravado. "In fact, I suspect quite a few people will be wiping egg off their respective faces."

"I'm sure you will be leading the pack." Hummersdorf spat back. "I wouldn't be too sure about a pack though. I predict you will be alone when it comes to that point." On that note, Hummersdorf disappeared into the crowd around van Vervoort while Holroyd left the Hall furious, but dispirited.

As he exited the hall, Holroyd muttered "They have no idea of what's likely to happen."

***

Hummersdorf was terrified. He was alone in the flat as Ron was away on a business trip. He had been woken at two a.m. and roughly hauled out of bed. Now he sat on a living room chair in his red silk pajamas and blue fluffy dressing gown facing two masked men.

"Who are you? How dare you attack me like this?" Hummersdorf summoned whatever courage he could.

"Who we are is immaterial."

"There's nothing of value here for you to steal."

"Now, there you are wrong when you claim there is nothing here to steal," one of the masked men replied.

"What do you mean I am wrong about anything worth stealing. Look around you."

"Looking around is not the issue."

"Then what do you want?"

"Yes! That is very much the issue."

"I don't understand," Hummersdorf whined.

"Let me make it simple for you. What is your colleague not telling us about the treasure he says is buried near where that woman was found?"

"You'd better ask him."

"Surprisingly, he is nowhere to be found. We know how close you are to your colleague, so perhaps you know where he is."

"What?" Hummersdorf was surprised. "I have no idea."

"That is a shame, but you are here. So, I hope we can avoid unpleasantness and you will tell us what we want to know."

"But I don't know anything more than what he told us at his lecture."

"Come now. You want us to believe you two have not exchanged information about the treasure?"

"Yes."

"I do not believe you."

"That's your problem. And even if I knew anything more about the treasure, why should I tell you?" Hummersdorf tried to be defiant.

"Because the consequences of not telling us could be very unpleasant for you."

"You wouldn't dare!"

"Do not underestimate what I would or would not dare. There is much in your life that I am sure would make interesting reading to your colleagues and perhaps even the authorities."

Hummersdorf suddenly felt very afraid, and a trickle of cold sweat ran down his back. His voice began to tremble.

"But I don't know anything." Hummersdorf's voice trembled piteously.

"Perhaps we can see if you have any ideas."

Hummersdorf's bladder let go and he began to cry.

"*Ayee! Zhen exin.*" The man behind Hummersdorf spat on to the carpet and changed to English "What a disgusting sight. No dignity here."

The leader stood silently looking at Hummersdorf considering the next move. Finally, he said, "What do you know?"

"I don't know anything," Hummersdorf wailed. "If you want to know more go see that troublemaker, Holroyd. He's the one who has the answers."

"Yes, we will ask questions of this Mr. Holroyd," the leader said. "Meanwhile, we will leave you to reconsider your position. I need not point out that any reference to our meeting would hardly benefit you as people might ask what it is you know that would be of interest to us. Any pretense of ignorance would hardly be accepted given your public support of your colleague and his claims of a vast treasure waiting to be recovered."

Hummersdorf sat there trying to regain his composure and a sense of relief that the meeting was over, but the leader was not finished.

"Do not for a moment hope we will not pursue this matter with you." And the men departed leaving Hummersdorf with a feeling or dread. Still trembling, he got up to pour himself a stiff drink. *What has Paul got me into? It all started with that damned Holroyd.*

Throwing his glass at the wall with as much force as he could, he screamed, "Holroyd! You bastard! I'll get you for this even if it's the last thing I do." He ignored the stains on the wall and carpet and the overpowering smell of urine as he went to shower and change his clothes. He did not get back to sleep.

20.

"Did you hear about the lecture at the University?" Alvarez entered Tomlinson's office.

"Nope. What of it?" Tomlinson continued to leaf through a file on his desk.

"That expert prof we asked to look at the skeleton near where Elisa was found claims there is treasure somewhere near there."

Tomlinson stopped and looked up. "How does he come to that conclusion?"

"He found a medieval crucifix," Alvarez replied.

"How come we didn't find it?"

"The forensic team was busy with Elisa's grave and the decision was made not to disturb the skeleton until a forensic anthropologist arrived."

"I see. Who was our man on the spot when that decision was made?"

"I was, but the forensic team leader all but recommended we could do that. It seems our people didn't think there would be any urgency about a 300-year-old death and have more pressing priorities at the moment."

"I might have guessed. So, who engaged this expert? What's his name?"

"I sent Brayden to contact the university. He came up with van Vervoort and the Band policeman had no problems with that."

"Figures. Did van Vervoort report the find together with anything else he may have found?"

"Not yet."

"Get over there and find out why not. He'd better have a good reason, or we may have to charge him with theft." Alvarez acknowledged the order and Tomlinson continued

"How does he support that there's treasure?"

"I have no idea, but that's what he claimed," Alvarez admitted, "Holroyd went ape."

"How so?

"Claimed van Vervoort's claim on the provenance of the treasure was so much bullshit."

"So, he doesn't believe there's treasure?" Tomlinson paused "Or is Holroyd worried that van Vervoort has revealed what Holroyd wanted to keep hidden and so stopped Holroyd from getting the treasure himself?"

"Can't answer that now."

"Did van Vervoort say anything else?"

"He did say the treasure is buried on the reservation."

"He said what?" Tomlinson sat up as if a wasp had stung him. Alvarez repeated what he had said.

"Jeezus! That means there will probably be treasure hunters all over the site. The Band will go bananas over that. Better get on the blower and warn them. This could end up like Oka all over again." Tomlinson sighed and then continued "How does that fit with what we know?"

"Maybe it does." Alvarez assumed a look of superiority.

"How's that?"

"If van Vervoort is right, we might have an answer to the ingot."

"Sounds possible." Tomlinson mused. "I wonder if the good professor found anything else that he's not telling us about. And how does that tie in with the woman's body?"

"Maybe there's no connection. But maybe Elisa stumbled on someone looking for whatever may still be there, and they killed her to keep her quiet?"

"Perhaps! It seems too circumstantial to me. I think there is a link, but I have no idea what it could be."

***

The Band Council had been hastily summoned after learning of van Vervoort's lecture. "I don't like it," the chief grumbled. "There are too many things over which we have no influence, let alone control." Murmurs of agreement came from around the table. "How dare the University come on our lands and do a dig without our agreement?"

"It's not quite like that. My niece asked if she and her classmates could wander around for a class project to see if there was anything of historical interest to be found," Annie's uncle said.

"Then how come they found a body on our Burial grounds?" The chief looked around the council table before turning to Armstrong.

140

Armstrong gave an account of events and added, "But we don't know if there's treasure, there's only that professor's word for that."

There was a moment's silence until an elder said, "This treasure is going to give us a lot of grief. I don't like it."

"I agree. I think we'll be facing crowds now that they think there's treasure to be found," grumbled a member.

"Who started all this? Was it that guy who said there's treasure on our lands?" asked an elder.

"No. One of Annie's profs called Holroyd or some such gave them an assignment to go searching on our lands," Annie's father answered.

"Why would he do that? Did he think or know there is treasure buried somewhere here?" asked another Council member.

"Maybe. Whatever his reasons, let's make sure neither he nor his students never come near here again," the chief observed, and then turned to Eddy, "Alan, where do we stand legally?"

Eddy explained that while the treasure could be found on unceded or unsold village lands, who can claim the find isn't clear. Not all the rights under the Royal Proclamation or existing treaties had been settled. The rights of ownership of buried treasure has never been tested, although ingoing treaty negotiations could eventually resolve the matter.

"Our ancestors should never have agreed to negotiate with these white bastards," grumbled a council member. "They never live up to their promises and look at the messes we're in now." There were murmurs of agreement.

"It's too late now, so we've got to make the best of it," Eddy remarked.

"Is there any chance there's more there?"

"That professor who found the crucifix claims there's more to be found. But, given they found the crucifix and nothing else, I think it's unlikely." Eddy paused. "That raises a question in my mind. What will we do if and when we get a horde of treasure seekers wanting to dig around where the body was found?" He turned to Armstrong.

"You're the Band's policeman, what do you think?"

"I don't think we can do much by ourselves, but we can get help from the federal government. After all, given Elisa was murdered, the site is under federal control."

"Does that mean the Army could be called in?" asked another member.

"Possibly."

"Here we go again. Another standoff with the feds. It's getting out of hand," grumbled yet another member.

"It occurs to me that there may not be any treasure to be found, but that does not mean there never was anything to be found." Eddy spoke up.

"What do you mean?"

"Perhaps there was a truck load of treasure down there, but over the years people recovered most of it."

"And we never knew about it? Seems far-fetched to me."

"Perhaps we did. I think that other professor, Holroyd, has some ideas about that. I'll talk to him again." The Chief nodded his agreement.

"If this treasure was recovered, there should be some record of it," the chief went on. "Perhaps there's some mention in the oral traditions. Shaman, do you remember any oral tradition that suggests something like that happening?"

"I don't, but I may know someone who might."

***

The shaman found Muuuskvaviiit or Old John as he was locally known, sitting in his rocker on the porch outside his shack. Rumoured to be in his dotage and fast becoming senile (if he was not already there) John was the repository of much Oral Tradition. A great deal of that tradition was unknown to the shaman to his embarrassment, but he was fortunate that Old John was still alive.

The shaman greeted the old man and ceremoniously proffered tobacco and salmon cured in the traditional way.

"Welcome, my old friend. Much time has passed since we last met." Old John greeted his visitor.

"I am happy I have been able to see you again."

"Your happiness may not last long. I am getting old and preparing for my departure."

"Not too soon, I hope."

"We shall see." And the old man gave a cackle that served for a laugh. "And what brings you here?"

"I seek to tap your knowledge."

"About what?"

"The treasure that was found on our lands."

"Oh! That!" the old man grinned.

"What do you know about it?"

"Not much! It was only a story my grandfather passed on to me. As far as I know, there was never any support for the story. But very few knew of it." He looked at the shaman with a sly smile. "I dare say, you don't."

"Please tell me."

Old John explained that it was supposed to have happened long before the wars of the Nine Tribes and before the arrival of the white men. "Mostly those wars were about territory, but also about capturing slaves and stealing food. My grandmother was stolen from that group down the coast that is now extinct. She was a wise woman and she bore many children including my father." The old man wandered off into further reminiscences.

"Yes, yes, but what of the treasure?" The shaman gently stopped Old John's reminiscences to focus on the pressing matter.

"What treasure?"

"The one that was found on our lands."

"Oh! That's only a story. I never believed it."

"But what was the story?"

"A treasure was buried somewhere near my village."

"Your village? Not my village?" the shaman asked confused.

"I just told you. That's the trouble with you youngsters …. never listen to your elders. But you'll learn one of these days."

"But about which village are you talking?"

"Our village, of course. What other village could we be talking about?"

"When was this treasure buried? By whom? How?" The shaman was becoming insistent.

"I'm tired now. I want to take a nap." The old man's voice became querulous and even childlike. "Go away, please."

"I will. Can I come back so you can finish the story?"

"Maybe. Go now." And the old man started to nod off.

Frustrated, but realising he would not get any further, the shaman returned and reported what he had been told.

"We must get his story and record it," Eddy insisted. "It may be the best proof we can get."

21

"Alvarez, where are Elisa's effects?" Tomlinson searched through the file on Elisa's death.

"Hang on." Tomlinson heard the rustle of paper as Alvarez went through his file. "I don't see anything on that. Could just be shoddy paperwork, but I'll follow up on that."

"Did you not already do a follow up?"

"No, I left that to the constable." Alvarez admitted shamedly realising he had failed to see whether it had been done, Tomlinson gave an audible sigh of exasperation.

"Get a hold of the constable who went up there with you. He's got some questions to answer." And Tomlinson hung up. "Bloody Hell!" was all he could muster.

Constable Brayden could not believe he was about to discuss his find with the inspector! Obviously, he believed he had caught the eye of his seniors and that presaged a bright future.

"Come in Constable. Bring me up to date on the Elisa case." Brayden thought Tomlinson's tone was perhaps a little brusque given the significance of the matter. Brayden recounted the sequence of events.

"That's all in your written report," remarked Tomlinson. "I want to hear what's not in your report."

"I don't follow, Inspector."

Tomlinson consulted the file on his desk. "You reported you and Sergeant Alvarez were sent to investigate a reported murder." Tomlinson looked up. "Did you check if there were any signs that suggested how she might have died?"

"No. Anyway, isn't that the job of the pathologists?" Tomlinson said nothing.

"Next question. Did you examine the body to check for her personal effects?"

"Yes, but I didn't find anything."

"Did that not seem suspicious to you?" Brayden did not reply. Tomlinson then asked, "Did you follow up on that?"

"I wasn't told to do so."

"Did you report that?"

"No."

"Why not?"

Brayden said nothing.

"Constable! Don't play the fool with me. What has been done to find her effects?"

Brayden suddenly realised he was on thin ice and now might not be the best time to try to brazen it out.

"I don't know, Inspector," he admitted miserably. Frustrated Tomlinson realised the investigation was in danger of going off the rails.

"What did they teach you at the Depot?" Brayden did not answer. Tomlinson frowned and continued with his questioning.

"Did you survey the scene before or after the body was taken away?"

"I looked around."

"And what did this look reveal to you?"

"There were many footprints that I assumed came from the students."

"Did you think to look at the footprints and compare them with what the students were wearing?"

"I didn't think it would be productive." Tomlinson sat for a moment *He's probably right about that. But that's about all. How did this guy ever get through the Training Program?*

"Ok! So, you looked over the area where the body had been found and then what?"

"I'm sorry, Inspector, I don't follow you."

"What did you do next?" Tomlinson hid his exasperation.

"Me? About the body. Nothing, there was nothing I could do there."

"Don't be obtuse with me, Constable. What can you report of the skeletal remains you found?"

"As Sergeant Alvarez told me to, I sent for an expert, Inspector," Brayden answered confidently.

"How did you go about that?"

"I asked around. I was told there was one at the University, so I went there. I thought one of them, Holroyd, wou d be a good choice, but the dean told me he wasn't qualified and recommended van Vervoort."

"Have you had a report from him?"

"No, but he gave that lecture."

"And you think that is all that is needed?" Brayden did not answer.

"What about those items he found at the site? Did you give him permission to take them?"

"No!" Brayden sensed he was in trouble and mumbled his response.

"Even though they were found at a crime scene?"

"They weren't near the woman's body, so I didn't think it was a crime scene." Brayden tried to excuse his failure to observe correct procedure.

"And you decided that all by yourself?" Tomlinson looked stonily at the by now very unsure constable. Tomlinson sighed then resumed on yet another tack.

"What about the search for child abusers?"

"I haven't got to that yet, Inspector." Brayden suddenly looked like a whipped dog.

"Then just what have you been doing?" Brayden remained silent. Tomlinson looked at him a little longer before saying.

"If you have nothing to add now, you can go. I'll call you when I'm ready."

The hapless Brayden left the room, but heard Tomlinson call for Alvarez.

Tomlinson looked at Alvarez with disapproval. "I think you might have exercised more supervision at the site. That young twit clearly failed in performing his duties. Remember that next time, Sergeant." Alvarez looked embarrassed. Tomlinson resumed.

"We may have an almighty clusterfuck on our hands. Take the kid off the case and get him focused on the search for abusers. Meanwhile, put him under supervision somewhere he can't do any more damage and do an assessment whether to keep him. I'll find you someone who can help you on the murder." He paused. "This won't play out well upstairs."

He was right.

***

Holroyd returned home to find that Pearl had left a message. Holroyd's suggestions had been followed and everyone was very excited and pleased. They had stopped for an English Tea at a small Café, and everyone agreed the tea was far inferior to Chinese teas and found the scones and fruitcake far too sweet. The pressed cucumber sandwiches on the other hand were delicious. Holroyd smiled. The next item on the agenda was a visit to the British Museum.

Holroyd looked at his watch, decided it was too late in London to phone and sent an appreciative message instead. He made himself a cup of tea and was about to sit down when there was a knock on the door and a Chinaman and another who might have been Korean waited outside.

"Professor Holroyd? Please excuse our unannounced visit, but may we come in?"

"I'm sorry, but who are you?"

"Permit me to introduce myself." Reaching into his pocket the Chinaman extracted a business card which he offered with both hands. Holroyd examined the Chinese and English writing that proclaimed the owner to be Mr. Li Feng, Consultant with a Hong Kong address and telephone number. No such introduction was made of Li's companion.

"Thank you, Mr. Li. But may I ask why you wish to talk to me?"

"We represent a client who has instructed that we meet with you to offer you an engagement to help resolve his interests."

Torn between wanting to find out more and retiring to bed, Holroyd gave in to his curiosity. "Well then, please come in."

Once inside and seated, Holroyd offered tea that was politely accepted. As they sipped their tea, Holroyd waited.

Li opened the conversation. "Our client wishes to engage you to help recover some items that are linked to the body that your colleague uncovered."

"Would you not be better to ask the man who made the find?"

"Our client insists we approach you."

Holroyd considered this statement.

"I don't see how I can help given someone else is handling the case."

"You misunderstand me. We have no interest in the body, but we are interested in recovering the items that were found there."

"I'm sorry. You said recover, or did you mean obtain?" Holroyd asked.

"Recover."

"That would mean that your client once had possession of the items," Holroyd observed. "And you mentioned items not just an item. I am aware of a crucifix, but are you telling me there is more?"

"Yes," Li answered unemotionally.

"But from what I have heard that body has lain there for centuries." Holroyd felt as if he had been punched in the gut. *Oh hell! So, van Vervoort was right after all? There's more to be found?* "Then how would your client be able to show let alone prove a legitimate claim?" Holroyd asked with curiosity.

Li broke the silence. "I can see you are puzzled."

"That understates my thoughts," Holroyd said dryly.

"Oh! How so?"

"The crucifix was found on tribal lands after lying there maybe centuries. From what you tell me your client thinks he has a claim to it. I just wonder if your client understands the difficulties he would have to overcome before such a claim would be supported."

"He understands very well, and that is why he instructed us to contact you," Li smiled.

"I'm flattered, of course. But my field of knowledge is ancient Chinese maritime voyages, not finding support for ownership claims."

"My client is fully aware of your field of knowledge." Li paused. "Your work on ancient Chinese voyages is well known and relevant in this matter. He is also aware of your success in resolving a recent territorial dispute[4]. I believe resolutions of territorial ownership claims are also outside your normal field of knowledge, but perhaps not under specific circumstances." He paused, "or am I mistaken?"

"No, you are right. But the solution to that dispute relied on records of ancient Chinese voyages. I don't see the relevance in this case." Holroyd was puzzled. "Are you suggesting that the man arrived here on some ancient Chinese voyage?"

"I am not suggesting any such thing," Li said.

"But if that is not what you are suggesting, then I don't see how I could possibly be of any help to you. I think there are other people who might help you better than I can to establish whatever claim your client may have."

"Professor, I said I am not suggesting. I am telling you."

"Pardon?" Holroyd was thunderstruck.

"I said I am telling you."

---

[4] *The Dragon's Threat*

"Yes, I heard that. You are telling me that the dead man came here on some ancient Chinese voyage."

"Not some ancient Chinese voyage."

"A particular one?" Holroyd asked.

"Yes."

"Which one?" Holroyd leant forward suddenly gripped by excitement.

"That can be revealed to you once we have an agreement," Li said.

"What are we waiting for?" Holroyd was now eager to accept the engagement.

"There are some troubling matters that need to be resolved first."

"May I know what these troubling matters are?" Holroyd asked, but thinking he already knew the answer.

"There is the matter of your colleague's claims," Li observed neutrally.

"I can understand how the claims might prove awkward although I believe them to be specious."

"Pardon? Specious? What does that mean?"

"Sounds good, but actually wrong," Holroyd explained.

"Ah! Yes." Li nodded. "But they are, as you might say, a potential loose end that my client would want tied up." Holroyd nodded.

"May I ask why this interest in the crucifix? I can't help but feel there is more behind your client's request than just this one rather small item," Holroyd said.

Li looked up sharply. "I don't think I referred to the crucifix."

He's right, I did. Holroyd realised.

"I could deduce from your answers there are more items to be found, or should I say recovered."

Li nodded "You could deduce that."

"So, van Vervoort is right when he says there is treasure to be found."

"Yes, you could deduce that, however, I am not at liberty to tell you more at this point."

Holroyd had hoped that a negative answer could help undermine van Vervoort's claims, but that hope died when Li answered.

"But I will need to know what I am looking for if I am to help you," Holroyd persisted.

"Once we have an agreement, you will be given whatever information you need." Holroyd had no comment.

"Furthermore, you may come across further claims, and we would expect you to inform us."

"Of course."

"Then may I inform my client that subject to the terms of the agreement, you would be willing to undertake the task?" Li asked expectantly.

"Thank you for considering me. I am interested, but I think I will wait until I see the details," Holroyd said.

"Of course."

"Mr. Li. I cannot help but think we have met before." Holroyd looked closely at Li.

"That is highly unlikely. This is my first visit to Canada, and I have never been to England."

"Then in China perhaps?" Holroyd persisted.

"That too would be unlikely. I believe you were in China during the Cultural Revolution, but I was not in China during those years. Furthermore, I have never been to Fujinhaizhou which was the scene of your now famous activities, so I doubt we have ever crossed paths."

"No, I don't think it would have been in China. I think it was very recently in Vancouver."

"There are many Chinese living in or just visiting this part of Canada so perhaps you saw someone who might look like me on your recent visit there."

"You are probably right. I do apologise."

"Please don't worry about it. Thank you so much for receiving us." And with that Li and his companion left.

Holroyd was suddenly struck by a thought. *If Li was one of the men talking to the curator when I first went there, then those items stolen at the museum are linked to van Vervoort's find and that means Li is looking for the treasure. I wonder if Li will prove to help or hinder my quest.*

22.

Hummersdorf left the office to return home where he relaxed with a drink by his side. He unfolded the newspaper that had been delivered to his door that morning but not had time to read until now. Meanwhile, Manning was out in the kitchen washing the supper dishes. *Nice to read an actual Broadsheet instead of having to watch or listen to a superficial opinion of happenings in the world.*

The headlines, predictably, were focused on a report of van Vervoort's lecture and his statement of more treasure to be found. Further down the column was a description of Holroyd's outburst, but qualified by Hummersdorf's dismissal of Holroyd's credibility. *That's what's needed to keep that upstart in his place* and Hummersdorf felt a glow of satisfaction.

Strange! Nothing about the bitch up on the reservation. That should have made the front page. Never mind, it's not my concern anymore.

Putting the newspaper aside he turned on the TV only to tune in to some boring sitcom. Switching channels, he caught the end of the hockey game in which the Montreal Canadians were massacring the Toronto Maple Leafs. *That's hardly news!* Before he could change to another channel, the phone rang.

"Hi, Joe!"

A feeling of unease crept over Hummersdorf as he recognised the voice. "What are you doing, calling me?"

"Oh? So, now I can't even call my closest relative? That's hardly friendly."

"So, what do you want?"

"What do I always want from you? A little affection would be nice, but since you ask, I need money."

"How much this time?"

"A couple of thousand will do."

"That's outrageous."

"I don't think so, given what's at stake. Anyway, if you have doubts, ask your old man and I'm certain he will be only too ready to help."

"Who is it?" Manning called from the kitchen.

"Just one of the students."

"Nice one, Joe! Not quite true, but it should keep that pansy partner of yours satisfied." The laughter in the voice carried down the wire. Before Hummersdorf could answer, Manning came into the room. Hummersdorf assumed an authoritative tone on the phone.

"I don't take calls from students at home. Please call my secretary in the morning and set up an appointment. Good evening," he said and hung up. He sat for a moment and then started to tremble and sweat.

"What was that all about?" Manning asked but then stopped. "What happened? You look as if you've seen a ghost." Hummersdorf sat silent but tears started down his cheeks.

"C'mon Joe! What has happened?"

"I'm being blackmailed," he finally confessed. Manning sat down and put his arm around the weeping man.

"Who by and why?"

"There's someone who knows my past life and threatens to go public if I don't give him money." He gave another sob. "If I don't pay up and he does go public, I'd be finished."

"But you've told me of all your past misdeeds. Or is there something you haven't told me?" Hummersdorf nodded and whispered "Yes."

"Ok, out with it and stop crying!"

"I can't," Hummersdorf said and with that he got up and went into the bedroom shutting the door firmly behind him, leaving Manning sitting alone, puzzled, and worried.

23.

Holroyd poured himself a stiff drink. *What do I do now?* Morosely he sat thinking over recent events and wondered what else could possibly go wrong. With that thought he went to bed and a restless sleep. The call woke Holroyd in the early hours.

"Quan Li has been arrested." Pearl was in tears and clearly distraught.

"Who?"

"Quan Li, my nephew."

"What on earth for? What happened?"

"We went to the British Museum and were looking at the Chinese exhibits. Quan Li said that many of the objects had been stolen by the British Imperialists."

"That's probably quite true."

"But then some English man commented about being polite when visiting another country."

"But surely you were speaking Chinese."

"Yes, but this Englishman could speak it, too."

"Quan Li told the man not to listen to other people's conversations."

"The man got very angry and other people gathered around to find out what was happening. Then the Englishman spoke English and explained what had happened."

"Go on."

"Other people started making comments about Chinese tourists coming here and trying to cause trouble, and Quan Li got very angry. He started by saying the English never accepted responsibility for all their murdering and looting. They had never learned to behave in a civilized manner. Someone started to shove, and my mother was pushed onto an exhibit which fell and broke into many pieces."

"Oh my!"

"The police came, my mother was crying, and Quan Li was blamed for everything." Pearl broke into tears.

"What happened then?"

"The police took Quan Li to prison. I don't know what to do."

"I'll come home right now." He hung up. He searched for the next available flight home. He was lucky to get a direct flight leaving that afternoon and dialed Hummersdorf's number even though he knew he would probably wake the dean. As he waited for Hummersdorf to answer, he realised his quests had been put on hold and he wondered for how long.

After explaining the situation, his request for a week's leave of absence was granted. As he hung up the phone, Holroyd could not fail to notice the dean's satisfaction. Packing nothing but an overnight bag he made his flight.

On leaving the aircraft at Heathrow, Holroyd with all the other passengers proceeded to immigration and customs. As he approached the exit, he was intercepted by a Customs Officer, led into a room, and asked to sit while waiting to be called. He noted several others most of whom sat surrounded by suitcases and bags. He was finally called over to the inspection desk and asked to open his bag for inspection.

"May I know why I was selected for inspection?" He asked while zipping his bag closed.

"Usually, we select arriving passengers at random unless we have reason to do otherwise. In this case we are looking at all passengers arriving from Vancouver."

"May I ask why?"

"There have been increased attempts at smuggling in drugs from there. Something about gang warfare."

"Oh yes, I heard about that."

"Hey, you, stop!" there was shout from another part of the room and Holroyd stepped back to see what caused the disturbance. Two men, one carrying a metal container were running as fast as they could towards him chased by a couple of customs officers.

One of the men crashed into him causing him to fall. He fell on something, perhaps the customs table or perhaps the metal container the man was carrying, and he lost consciousness.

***

"Mr. Holroyd? Is it?" The man in a white coat looked at his clipboard before looking at Holroyd and asking with a distinct Indian accent. "How are you feeling?"

"Wh . . . wh . . ." Holroyd mumbled, confused by what he saw. *What's this? Who is that? Where am I? Who is this Holroyd he keeps talking to?* The man repeated his question, but got no better answer. Turning away from the patient, the man spoke to a nurse.

"Keep Mr. Holroyd under observation. Make sure he doesn't get out of bed for now. Let him rest but call me immediately if there any signs of nausea or pain. For the time being give him only fluids and we'll see how he responds over the next 24 hours."

***

"Mr. Holroyd?" the Indian man in the white coat looked at his clipboard before looking at Holroyd. "How are you feeling today?"

"Where am I? What happened to me? Who are you?"

"Ah! Much better I see. I am Doctor Nathakilsvami. I am your doctor, and you are in the Princess Margaret Hospital, Windsor after your fall."

"My fall?"

"Yes. It appears you fell and banged your head at the Airport. You are suffering from a concussion, and we are keeping you under observation until we can be certain there is no serious injury."

"I don't remember any fall."

"Temporary amnesia is not unusual in cases like this. All being normal you should be back in fine form in a day or two."

"Oh!" Holroyd thought about what he had been told.

"We managed to contact your wife and she is on her way here." *My wife? I'm married?*

Nathakilsvami nodded to a nurse outside Holroyd's vision, and he was given a couple of tablets and a glass of water. He fell asleep immediately.

Holroyd woke feely groggy.

"Pearl?" he looked at the woman sitting by his bedside.

"You're awake!" She stood up, bent over him, and gave him a hefty embrace accompanied by tears and kisses.

"Excellent." Nathakilsvami's voice floated from somewhere outside Holroyd's vision. "How are you feeling now, Mr. Holroyd?"

"Much better thank you, Doctor."

"I'm going to give you an examination, and if there are no problems, I think we can let you go home. But please, no strenuous activity for the next few days."

"I have to get back to Canada."

"I would strongly advise against that. At least for another week."

On arriving in his flat, Holroyd surveyed with dismay the changes in his arrangements. Very little remained of the comfortable surroundings he had left just a while ago, but he was given no time to comment. Pearl tearfully threw herself into his arms while her mother trailed behind complaining in a loud voice. It took a few minutes for peace to be re-established after which Pearl repeated her version of events ending with the news that Quan Li was in custody and due to appear in magistrate's court the following afternoon.

Holroyd was tired but called on an old school chum for legal representation.

The next day accompanied by the women folk; he attended the court. The magistrate was severe but spared Quan Li further custody pending trial.

Standing outside the Court looking to flag a taxi, Holroyd heard an unmistakable voice.

"Peter, Old boy! What are you doing here? Thought you were out in the wilds of Canada."

"Oh! Hello, Merry!" Holroyd turned to see who had hailed him. "Well, as you can see, I'm here."

"Ah! Yes, and so is the lovely Pearl! What brings you to this dismal place?"

"A spot of bother our young guest managed to get into."

"Ah! The fracas at the British Museum. Awkward that, what?"

"Oh! I'm sure we'll sort it out."

"Excellent. Look, while you're here can we have a talk?" Merry seemed anxious, but Holroyd looked at him with surprise.

"I'm sorry, but I really don't have the energy." And he explained he was still recovering from the fall.

"Pity. You see, it has to do with some gold that has surfaced in unusual places, and I think you're involved."

"What?" Holroyd was taken aback.

"Something to do with a treasure trove I'm told you found on an Indian Reservation."

"I found no such thing."

"I'm told you found the location where the trove had been buried," Merry insisted.

"That's not true either."

"But someone wants to engage you to get it."

"How on earth . . .?" Holroyd was completely taken by surprise.

"I think you might want to know a few things before you accept the engagement."

"I haven't even got to thinking that far, and anyway I have this little matter to settle first."

"I might be able put in a word or two in the right places to give you a helping hand there. Let's say dinner at the Athenaeum. I seem to remember you enjoyed our last dinner there." *Oh yes, a lot of fun that was!*

"Oh! That's very kind of you, but …"

"See you at seven." And with that Merry took his leave.

Holroyd had a lot of explaining to do on the way home. Pearl knew some of the story, but Quan Li was thrilled at the adventures of a family member. Pearl's mother grumbled about the dangers Holroyd had attracted and how he had placed Pearl in such a situation.

***

Once arrived at the Athenaeum, the doorman fetched Merry and immediately they went in to dine.

"So, what's all this about? And before you go any further don't even speculate about the possibility that once I've finished my present assignment. I'll do another job for you. This one isn't quite the balmy cruise you promised and the one before that was exciting enough."

"Steady on there, Peter! That's not fair! But rest assured this is not about asking you to do anything for us. This is to fill you in on some matters you should know before you sign on any dotted lines."

"Oh?"

"Don't look so innocent. Finding a three-hundred-year-old corpse while on a student foray can be awkward. And in this case, I'd have to say doubly so."

"How so?"

"Finding the body so near to some buried treasure is one reason, especially if they can tie it to your search for an ancient Chinese vessel, finding it on Reservation lands is another, and the fact that nearby they found the body of an indigenous woman following up on residential school abuses would probably clinch it."

"Residential school abuses? How do they come into this?" Holroyd repeated with his fork stopped halfway to his mouth.

"Oh! The death of the woman has a possible impact on the university's plans for expansion, I rather think your dean might be a tad miffed. But let's get down to the things you need to know." Merry took a swallow of wine.

"As I told you, we are concerned that some of the assets being moved out of Hong Kong may have been illegally gained. We have since learned that Hong Kong and Beijing have several individuals in their sights and may include your prospective employer as a prime target."

"Who is that?"

Merry ignored the question and went on with his narrative.

"If your employer is indeed a person of interest, he's got some interesting ties in the Golden Triangle. If you sign, you might be trawled up with the rest of the catch."

"Golden Triangle? What or where is that?"

"It's the area where the borders of Thailand, Laos, and Myanmar meet at the confluence of the Ruak and Mekong rivers." He went on to explain that Myanmar is one of the main producers of opium and the control of its production and export is partly exercised by remnants of the defeated Kuomintang troops. Law enforcement agencies know that ties between those troops and Hong Kong have been maintained, but don't have a clear picture.

"But I have no knowledge of any of that," Holroyd protested.

"That might not be accepted as a valid defense, should your potential employer be hauled in."

"I don't see how that would work out."

"You never know what Beijing might do. Trouble is, if you are enmeshed, there's not a thing we could do."

"That's very encouraging." And with that Holroyd returned home.

"Hello Uncle!" Quan Li welcomed him as he closed the door.

"Hello, young man! Shouldn't you be in bed as this hour?"

Quan grinned. "Auntie doesn't know I'm up."

"Well off you go before she finds out."

"But I was hoping we could talk a little."

"It's very late. Let's keep it till the morning when we're fresh."

"But I was asked to make sure we had a talk."

"Asked by who?"

"My mother's uncle's third daughter. She is a very important person, and I don't want to disappoint her."

"Important? How so?"

"She is in a high government position in Beijing, and she knows of your work when you were last there. She is very impressed by you."

"I see. So why does she want us to talk?"

"I was telling her of my visit and of your meeting with that British Lord and that you would be having dinner with him tonight."

"Did you tell her I happened to meet that British Lord outside the Magistrate's Court?"

"I think I forgot to mention that."

"Probably very wise of you."

"She would love to hear of your next activities with him." Holroyd could hear the excitement and even awe in Quan's voice.

"Well, we mustn't disappoint her then, must we?" Holroyd tried to sound enthusiastic. "But you, young man, are off to bed. Go on."

Quan Li trundled off to bed and Holroyd went to see what messages he had missed. One was from the dean. Checking his watch, and noting the time difference, he called Hummersdorf.

"Ah, Doctor Holroyd! I hope you have recovered from your accident."

"Thank you, Dean. Let's say I'm up and about and should be returning shortly."

"That is what I called you about. The Board has decided that adding this accident to all the other matters that concern you, your invitation is rescinded." Holroyd felt as if he had been poleaxed.

"What?" he said weakly.

"I'm sure you can understand our problem. We really couldn't hold your course until you return at a yet unspecified date and only then if you have been given your medical discharge. I presume you have not yet received that?"

"Not yet. It's supposed to happen next week."

"That's what we thought. Anyway, we decided to assign your class to another qualified professor."

"And who would that be?" Holroyd asked with foreboding but expecting the answer he got.

"Why, Doctor van Vervoort. Who else?" Holroyd had no energy left to reply.

24.

"Professor Holroyd! I am Quan Li's cousin, Wen Mei Li." The call came in the morning.

"Good morning, Wen Mei Li. This is an unexpected pleasure. How may I help you?"

"I was wondering if you might be free for a coffee and a chat."

"But I thought you are in Beijing, and I am in London," Holroyd observed mildly.

"So am I. Did Quan Li not tell you?"

"No, he failed to mention that to me."

"Beijing is where my office is, but I am in London now. So would you be free for a meeting?" Wen Mei Li said.

"I'm not sure because I have family matters to attend to after which I have to return to Canada."

"Ah! Yes. But has not your return been delayed because of your accident? And I hear your engagement at the university is on hold. So, I was thinking perhaps you would be free this morning. Would ten thirty suit you? There is a small café around the corner from you. Let's meet there." *This is quick! Why the urgency? If it's a social chat, I'll have kept my women folk happy, but if it's official I'd better find out sooner than later.*

"Oh. Don't be shy. I will happily provide the coffee or tea," Wen spoke again. Holroyd could hear amusement in her voice.

"How can I refuse an offer like that?" He let his laughter escape. "I'll be there."

Holroyd saw Wen sitting at a small table outside the café. She was wearing a dark blue business suit, and white blouse that came to her throat and what people would call sensible shoes. Her hair was jet black, cut to a fringe in front, and at the back hung just below the neck. All in all, the epitome of a Chinese bureaucrat.

"Doctor Holroyd! So pleased you could come." He sat down as she waved at the waiter who acknowledged the call, but continued to serve other customers. "I bring greetings from Li Wen Yao, who hopes you are well."

"That is most kind of him. Please pass on my best wishes." *Li Wen Yao? He is with the State Security Bureau, so who is she?*

"Thank you I will do so. He recommended that I get in touch with you as he was most impressed with the services you rendered China when you worked together."

Worked together? That's not quite how I would have described it.

"You must be wondering ..." She was interrupted by the waiter and ordered tea and coffee with two croissants. "I trust that is satisfactory, Professor?"

"Oh yes, thank you."

"As I was about to say, you must be wondering why I asked for this meeting."

"Errr, yes I am."

"As I was in London and I knew Quan Li was visiting here with your wife and her mother, I intended to meet up with my family. I get so few occasions when I can do so."

Oh! Good! A social reason.

"But I thought I should clear it with you first."

That's unusual, why not set it up with Pearl? They are after all relatives albeit distant ones.

"But then Quan Li mentioned you met with Mr. Hantington."

"Nice of him to do so." Holroyd tried to remain noncommittal.

"He is very excited that you are such a famous and well-connected man who is in the family."

Holroyd smiled at Wen Mei Li's compliment. *Where is she going with this?*

"Oh! He speaks very highly of you." Holroyd offered hoping it sounded like genuine praise and not a noncommittal civility.

"That is polite of him." She took a sip of tea, but from the expression on her face, was not very pleased with the brew. She put the cup down and took a bite out of her pastry.

"But enough pleasantries. There is a further reason for our meeting."

Oh! Oh! Here it comes.

"I work for Li Wen Yao, who after his brilliant work in Fujinhaizhou is now the Deputy Director." She paused to let

Holroyd consider what this meant. "As you will remember his area of expertise is in White Collar Crime and we have become aware that once again you are in contact with someone in whom we have an interest."

"I am not aware of any such person." Holroyd was taken by surprise.

"But you have been offered an engagement by him," Wen Mei Li observed drily.

"I'm not aware of who that person might be." He gave a short summary of the approach that had been made. "The name of the person behind the offer was not given to me."

"So, a Chinese man offers you an engagement, but you have no idea who is the client? I find that rather curious."

"Yes, I agree with you! However, no final offer has been made for me to consider and so I have let the matter rest until whoever it is gets back to me," Holroyd observed.

"But you do know the outline of what they want you to do," Wen Mei Li insisted.

"Yes, they want me to recover some lost items."

"Recover some items?" Wen seemed surprised. "Did they tell you what these items were?"

"Not precisely, no." There was a pause.

"That seems unusual."

But before she could go on, Holroyd asked "What caused you to get in touch with me?"

"Your contact with your prospective employer."

"And why would that cause you to contact me?"

"Because this person is involved with drug trafficking and is trying to evade the government's regulations on wealth by moving capital out of China. Canada is one place where he might be heading."

"I have no idea about such matters. My field of interest is . . ."

"We know exactly what you maintain is your field of interest," Mei Li interrupted, "However, my colleague pointed out that your interests have previously extended beyond that field and so we wondered whether that is so once again."

"What do you mean?" Holroyd began to feel uneasy.

"Even though the People of China acknowledged your contribution in recovering many Chinese treasures, we noted that you seemed to be close to the criminals involved in that matter."

Holroyd threw his hands in the air. "That was all cleared up."

"That case was all cleared up and you were considered to have been innocent of any crimes." She paused. "In that case."

"Are you accusing me of some sort of crime by helping this unknown person? That's preposterous!" Holroyd became uneasy and started to bluster.

"We shall see. However, I do advise you to be very careful before you accept any offers from that man. I would be very disappointed if we had to include you in our investigations." She paused before adding "As I am sure the family would be."

She got up, placed a twenty-pound note on the table and walked away. Holroyd was thunderstruck and looked up from the pound note to the woman, staring at her with his mouth open as she walked away without a backward glance.

Holroyd left the café and started home, but passing a newsvendor noticed the headline of one of the broadsheets: 'Standoff on the West Coast of Canada between Indians and treasure seekers.' He went in and bought a copy. Opening the paper, he saw that coverage was quite lengthy and was accompanied by a couple of photographs. He decided to return to the café and order another coffee while reading the coverage.

He read that treasure hunters from Canada and the US had descended on tribal lands that included a native burial site, after a university Professor, Paul van Vervoort, claimed that treasure estimated to be worth $64 million or more was buried there.

The Band had refused access to their lands and the hunters had become aggressive after being ordered off. One hunter, identified as an American, attacked a villager who was taken to hospital in a serious condition. Guns had been produced on both sides and the RCMP had to restore order, but the Army may also have to be called in.

'When interviewed, Professor van Vervoort strenuously defended his claims and denied any responsibilities for the situation that has developed. "The development of this deplorable situation lies squarely on the shoulders of Peter Holroyd who first authorised the students to enter First Nation lands without permission and desecrated the First Nation burial site. When I announced the discovery of the treasure and its history, he refused to accept my findings. The university has fully backed me up, and I can only hope that any suitable response will finally put an end to Holroyd's pretentions and career." 'Doctor Peter Holroyd could not be reached for comment.'

Holroyd was stunned. van Vervoort had laid the blame for the consequences on his shoulders, and he had a queasy feeling the university would agree. *How am I going to counter this? I don't think going public will do the trick. I'll have to go back to clear my name. But how on earth can I do that if I don't have a position to go back to?* Deep in thought, he folded the paper and went home.

***

Holroyd sat at his desk and considered the challenges he now faced. First, he had to get over his injury and then get back to Canada. Once there, he thought he could address both van Vervoort's outrageous accusations and his dismissal.

"We have to leave soon." Pearl appeared at the door. "Quan Li goes before the Judge today." Behind her, Holroyd could see his mother-in-law watching him and anxiously hovering over Quan Li who, if anything, looked defiant. Holroyd debated whether he was fit enough to attend court, but then weighed the consequences if he did not. Reluctantly he went.

Quan Li's case eventually came up. The magistrate looked sternly at the youth who tried to look as contrite as his pride would allow him.

"Mr. Li," legal counsel interrupted the magistrate.

"If it please your honour, my client should be addressed as Mr. Quan or Quan Li."

"What? Why?" The Magistrate frowned.

"The Chinese put their family name first, unlike our own practice."

"Hrrrmph. Very well."

The magistrate looked at a folder open on his desk. He looked up and summarized the charge. While he understood the desire to express feelings, he did not condone the way it was done. Accordingly, Quan Li was cautioned to keep the peace and fined five hundred pounds. Holroyd heard Pearl gasp and his mother-in-law stifle a whimper while Quan Li looked crestfallen, but said nothing.

As they left the court, Holroyd saw Wen Mei Li coming over to them.

After expressing hope Holroyd had fully recovered from his accident, Wen turned to the womenfolk and the conversation carried on in a spate of Chinese that Holroyd made no attempt to follow. Wen left.

"What was that all about?"

"She expressed disappointment at the punishment and then promised to come and visit us."

"Oh! Lovely!" Holroyd exclaimed hoping Pearl would miss the sarcasm.

"Yes! That will be nice," Pearl agreed. Holroyd had nothing further to add.

25.

Holroyd was at a loss. *I need help.* He picked up his phone and dialled.

"Peter, old boy! How's the head? Recovered, have we?" Merry answered the call.

"Not quite yet, thanks. Still a few aftereffects but I expect they'll disappear shortly."

"Good show! So, what can I do for you?" Holroyd explained the call from the dean.

"I say! That's awfully unsporting of them. But I see you've managed to cause quite a stir over there. I'd say you're not the flavour of the day."

"I need to go back to clear my name and was wondering if you knew someone who might get them to change their minds," Holroyd said hopefully.

"I see your point, but I'm not too sure about what I can do. I don't have many contacts in that part of the world, at least none that I can think of who might be helpful. Sorry, old chap, not much help there, I'm afraid."

"Merry, you owe me for the China job. At least, I think you might try." Holroyd sounded as if he was getting desperate. There was pause.

"Steady on there! That's a bit much!" Merry protested. He paused. "Alright, I'll make some calls, but I can't promise anything."

"Thank you, Merry. I'd be grateful." The call ended but Holroyd's mood didn't change much.

***

"Your Lordship, I was expecting your call." Wang answered the phone. "Our mutual acquaintance suggested an exchange between us would be helpful. How may I assist you?"

"I'm calling because a little bird told me you are rethinking your support for that Canadian West Coast university."

"It seems some birds have sensitive ears."

"Yes, strange, isn't it? But I was thinking you might want to consider the possible benefits of your donation."

"I am well aware of the benefits to research that my donation could bring. But there seem to be some problems in pursuing my desire."

"Oh, yes! The kerfuffle over the intrusion onto Band lands."

"Exactly."

"I wasn't thinking of those benefits I was thinking on a larger scale, benefits that would diminish the likelihood further problems."

"Oh! I was unaware there could be further problems."

"Perhaps you haven't been advised on renewed interests from Beijing and maybe from other sources."

"No! I was unaware there were any interests, renewed or otherwise, that could cause me more problems."

Wang prevaricated even as a trickle of cold sweat formed on his back. "However, I appreciate your Lordship's concern and will certainly investigate if there is any truth to what you may have heard."

"I do think that would be wise, as I am told some of the interested parties can be quite insistent and even dangerous."

"And how would my donation deflect such interests?"

"Sometimes a whispered word in the right ears leads to changed outlooks."

"And you think you might be in a position to whisper such words into the right ears?"

"I think we both understand each other."

"Indeed. But besides my donation, is there another matter that could influence your decision?"

"Now that you mention it, yes there is." Merry brought Wang up to date on Holroyd's dismissal.

"Holroyd, you say. Is he not the one that caused all the problems?"

"I doubt it. But let me just say that your help in getting the university to reverse its decision would be most helpful and appreciated."

"Then, your Lordship, how could I possibly refuse to help."

"That's awfully decent of you. But don't let me disturb you any further. I have some calls to make."

Wang put down the phone and stared out of his office

window at the city and beyond. In the distance he could see ships at anchor and the islands that guarded the entrance to Hong Kong's harbour.

The phone rang again, and Wang lifted the receiver.

"We have tried on several occasions to search at the location, but were foiled each time. The first time there was an intruder."

"I see. Will he cause trouble?"

"Unlikely, unless she returns from her grave."

"She? Who was this woman?"

"We could not enquire."

"Did you assist her to enter her eternal sleep?"

"No."

"I see. So, why did you not complete your search?"

"We were concerned that others might come looking for the woman and we left to make sure we were not observed."

"Continue."

"We tried again, but there was a watchman, and we couldn't proceed."

"A watchman? Why are they suddenly so interested?" There was no reply.

"The watchman?"

"Neutralized. I don't think he saw us."

"Neutralized or terminated?"

"Neutralized. I did not want to attract another investigation. However, we came across two items and recovered them."

"Excellent, so it was not lost." The satisfaction was evident.

"And there are developments. One that is encouraging is a university professor found the crucifix. The other one is one that could prove worrisome. There are whispers that an item has surfaced where it should not."

"I see. Follow it up." The caller understood he had received his orders in no uncertain manner. As Wang hung up, there was a knock on his door and his secretary entered carrying a parcel.

"This just came by delivery for you."

"Well, what is it?"

"I haven't opened it."

"Why not?" He allowed a note of irritation to creep into his voice.

"It's marked personal to be opened by addressee only."

"Since when have you decided that you don't open my mails?"

"The delivery man stressed it was to be opened by you, and you alone."

"I was not aware that delivery services included instructions on opening parcels."

"Oh! This wasn't a normal delivery service. It was a private individual," His secretary pointed out.

"Who is the sender?"

"There's no information." Wang was just about to make a remark when the phone rang and looking at the number, he ordered the secretary to leave the parcel on his desk and get out. Once the door was closed, he picked up the phone.

"We have heard reports that not all is going as we had agreed," the caller at the other end started. "We would be disturbed if our smooth arrangements had been reordered in a manner of which we might be ignorant."

Wang swallowed before answering. "You may rest assured that nothing untoward has happened and you may pass that on to our associates in Ho Chi Min City."

"I am most pleased to hear that. Your cooperation is noted and always valued. Our friends have asked me to pass on a token of their high regard for you, which I believe you have already received."

"That is most considerate of them. I have received it and am most appreciative."

"Excellent. I am sure our friends would not be happy if the value of their gift were not to be fully recognised. I shall pass on your assurances." And the line went dead.

Wang put the receiver down and looked at the parcel. Finally, grabbing a pair of scissors he cut the string and ripped off the wrapping paper. Inside was a box wrapped in red silk. Carefully, he unwrapped the silk and opened the box.

Inside was an exquisite model of an ornate Chinese

coffin. He sat back staring at the model. He felt a cold shiver go down his spine. *That message is clear enough. Do what they want or suffer the consequences. Who or what had aroused their suspicions?* He thought over what he had just learned and concluded the future was not promising. A speedy liquidation of his assets and an early departure would be prudent.

He turned back to his computer and brought up a file that only he could access. Reading the file, he started making notes before calling his broker.

Finished with the call, he sat back and thought, *it's time to recover what's mine and this time no one will stop me. I think that professor, Holroyd, needs a little encouragement.* He picked up the phone and gave instructions.

26.

Holroyd heard the doorbell ring and got up to see who it might be. Before he could do so, Pearl answered the door and was greeting Wen Mei Li. Clearly this visit was a family re-union and remembering his last meeting with her, Holroyd decided it would be wiser to duck back into his study. He could hear an animated spate of Chinese coming from the next room and thought *They're having fun.* His thoughts were interrupted when the door opened, and three grim faced females entered the room.

"Doctor Holroyd, we meet again!" "Peter! What have you done?" *"Zhe shi bu dui."* All three spoke simultaneously. Holroyd faced the onslaught with the sinking feeling he was outnumbered.

"One at a time, please." Holroyd grasped for time. Pearl launched the attack.

"You did not tell me you have been fired."

"That's not exactly true."

"Then explain what is exactly true." Holroyd reported what the dean had said.

"And how is that different from being fired?"

"Being fired means I won't be able to go back. I'm on a temporary absence."

"That is splitting your hair!" and before he could reply she started to cry. "You are keeping secrets from me." and before Holroyd could frame an answer, she changed tack "You don't love me at all," she sobbed.

187

"That's not true." He stood up to hold her in h s arms, but she pulled back.

"Then why is Wen Mei Li telling us you are working with a criminal who is wanted by the Chinese police?" She resumed the attack from a different direction.

"That's also not true." Holroyd shot Wen as venomous a look as he was capable.

"More splitting of your hair?" Pearl's sarcasm was palpable. "And now you accuse Wen Mei Li of lying? How dare you. She is family and a senior police officer."

Holroyd was taken aback. Before he could say arything, she continued "After all I did for you. I saved you from one criminal and now you are working with another one. I thought you were an honest man, but now I am not sure. I think you lied to me, and you don't love me at all." Pearl was working up a full head of steam and Holroyd could see no immediate escape.

"Look at my face and see how ugly I have become because you don't love me. Now, no one will think I am beautiful anymore." She started to cry again.

"That's not true at all, you are the most beautiful..." He could not complete the sentence before Pearl launched another attack.

"You don't mean that; you are just like all those white men telling lies to hide your deceits. Mother warned me against marrying a foreigner."

Her mother said something in Chinese that Holroyd did not understand. Seeing he was puzzled, Wen Mei Li jumped in smugly.

"Her mother points out you never give Pearl any gifts," she paused before driving the knife in deeper. "As any husband who loves his wife should." Wen Mei Li was enjoying his discomfort. Holroyd realised this was going to cost him plenty and he hoped his bank balance could meet the demand. He turned to Pearl.

"Darling . . ."

"Don't you Darling me." She pulled back and ran out of the room still crying. Her mother trailed after her hugging her and making soothing noises.

"I warned you." Wen looked at him with a hint of triumph. Holroyd glared at her and was about to speak.

"Please, Doctor Holroyd, I suggest you consider living in less interesting times." And with that she turned, and he heard her leave.

Holroyd was shaken to the core and slumped into his chair. Quan Li entered.

"I think you should go to *gugu*. She is troubled." Holroyd stared at the boy. *Not half as troubled as I am.*

There was no peace to be had. Pearl continued to cry and to berate him. Holroyd was becoming worried. *This is going on longer than I expected.* He sat alone in his living room when the door opened, and Pearl announced, "I am going to the hospital."

"What on earth for?" Holroyd jumped up alarmed. *Don't tell me she's going to have a breakdown!*

"Because I want to see my doctor!"

"But why?"

"Never mind, it doesn't matter, and you don't care anyway."

"That's not true. Let me come with you." He went over to her.

"No!" She slammed the door in his face and left the house before he could catch up. Looking out of the window, he saw she was accompanied by her mother and Quan Li. *What's wrong with Pearl?*

***

The intercom rang and Hummersdorf focused on a report answered it absently.

"You're wanted on the phone."

"I thought I told you I wasn't to be disturbed."

"Yes, but he told me to put you through."

"Who is it?" Hummersdorf asked.

"He wouldn't give me his name, but said it was urgent."

"Oh! Very well! Put him through."

"Yes?'

"Have you had any further thoughts about your students?" Hummersdorf started to sweat.

"Who are you?"

"As I told you at our last meeting that is unimportant. But there is a further matter that concerns us. We have heard that you have fired a professor in whom we are most interested."

"What?"

"Please ensure his safe return before we become irritated." And the line went dead. Hummersdorf sat back trembling. *This is getting out of control.* The intercom buzzed and his secretary announced:

"The president is on the line for you, Dean."

"Put him through."

"Joe, sorry to bother you, but I wondered if you could give me an update on where we stand with Holroyd."

"We don't stand anywhere. He's gone."

"Gone?"

"He asked for leave to return home for a family emergency. Of course, I granted that, and he immediately went home."

"Did he say he would return?" asked the president.

"Not immediately because while over there, he suffered an injury from which he hasn't been discharged as far as I know."

"Fine, but did he say he would not return?"

"Well no. I decided that if he wasn't able to give a definite date for his return, we couldn't wait for ever and so I cancelled the invitation."

"Did you clear this with anyone?" The president asked, but Hummersdorf heard an undertone of concern.

"I didn't think it was necessary. Granting leave for family emergencies or sick leave is within my power for administrative matters."

"Granted, but rescinding an invitation is hardly an administrative matter. And let's not forget you promised the Board you would inform them of any action you proposed to take."

"Which the Board promised to support."

"Can't support something we don't know about," The president observed drily.

"Are you going to support me?" Hummersdorf asked suddenly feeling vulnerable.

"I'm not sure because Holroyd might have a case against us for wrongful dismissal."

"He'd have a hard time proving that in court."

"Well, I can't comment on that. We'd have to see how that would play out."

"Thanks! That's very encouraging and makes me feel a whole lot better. Anyway, it's done. But can I count on the Board's support?" Hummersdorf persisted.

"We won't do anything until we know the details but, in this case, probably not."

"What? Are you saying you'll override me?"

"I'm hoping it won't come to that." Hummersdorf suddenly recognised where this was heading. "You want me to back down and bring him back?"

"I think everyone would be happier that way."

"If you think I'm going to bend over and take this, you're dead wrong. I won't reverse my decision." Hummersdorf was becoming loud and aggressive.

"Now calm down, Joe! Just bring Holroyd back, will you?"

"I'll resign first." Galvanised, Hummersdorf brazenly promised.

"That, Joe, is an option, but I suggest it shouldn't be necessary." Hummersdorf swallowed the retort he was about to make. He became very cautious and tried to find out what had caused the president to call him.

"What brought this on?" he asked.

"I got a call from the chancellor. Let's just say it's in the interests of the university that Holroyd comes back or resigns of his own volition."

"I doubt he'd do that" Hummersdorf shot back.

"Then the choice is clear. Bring him back, Joe. The sooner the better for all of us." The line went dead.

Hummersdorf collapsed in his chair grabbed a tissue and wiped the sweat off his brow. He called in his secretary.

"Send Holroyd an email asking him to set a date for his return," he growled.

"Oh!" She stood there with her mouth hanging open.

"Well? What are you waiting for?"

The Secretary shot him a look. "Didn't we just terminate him?"

"Yes, and now we are un-terminating him."

"Un-terminating? Is that a word?"

"Just do it."

"In your name?"

"No, in yours," he snarled at her.

"But … "

"Get on with it, woman. Just get on with it and see to it I'm not disturbed." He was almost yelling at her.

"Yes, Dean Hummersdorf," she said and hastily closed the door behind her as she went to do his bidding. *Has he lost his wits? This will not end well. Not well at all.*

She typed the email, considered whether to clear it with Hummersdorf before sending it, but in the end pressed the 'send' button and hurriedly left for the day.

Alone in his office, Hummersdorf poured himself a drink and then another.

***

Holroyd's unease continued as he waited impatiently for Pearl's return. While waiting he opened his emails and read Hummersdorf's latest message.

"This can't be right," he muttered to himself "It's not even signed by Hummersdorf. It must have been sent in error not knowing the invitation has been withdrawn." He deleted the message and went on to other correspondence. The phone rang, but he ignored it as the door opened and Pearl entered accompanied by the others.

Holroyd was relieved to see they were smiling. *Thank God! She got a clean bill of health. That's one less thing to worry about.* Before he could utter a single word, Pearl announced.

"Peter! I am with child."

Holroyd stared at his women folk standing in the door-way. He sat there with his mouth open as he felt a sudden exhilaration. *I'm going to be a father again*! "What? You never told me."

"I didn't want to tell you until I was sure."

Holroyd was overwhelmed by joy, everything else was forgotten. He jumped out of his chair and ran to his wife holding her tightly and covering her with kisses. Dimly, he heard his mother-in-law raising her voice as she said something in Chinese. Pearl nestled in his embrace was smiling happily.

"Peter! Mother says to treat me and our child gently!"

"I am!"

"I know, but mother is worried you will crush us."

195

"Tell her to go and prepare some tea and you ccme and sit."

"The child is not due for several months but until then you have to start treating me like a valuable piece of delicate jade."

"You are valuable and delicate, but you are not a piece of valuable jade. You are far beyond anything like that." He kissed her again and again as her mother brought in tea and biscuits. Pearl was smiling happily as her mother launched into voluble Chinese.

"What's she on about?"

"Oh! She's planning for all the things we will have to do."

"Like what?"

"Getting a baby room ready. Buying clothes and toys for when he arrives."

"He?"

"Yes." She laughed with joy.

"Isn't it rather soon to know?"

"Oh, no! Mother rang her fortune teller who said the signs are all there for a boy." She laughed. "I am so happy."

Holroyd was too, until he started to think again of what lay ahead. *A baby room! More rearrangement of the flat? And I guess returning to Canada is off limits.* His thoughts were interrupted by a spate of Chinese between the women folk.

"Quan Li will be leaving to go home. He can pass the good news to the rest of the family," Pearl translated.

"And your mother?"

"She will stay here, of course. She will help me with our son."

"And what will I do?"

"You will do what every father should do. You will look after all of us."

"At least that means Quan Li will be safe," he mused.

"Safe? Why should he not be safe?" Pearl sat up suddenly concerned. Holroyd was about to answer when the phone rang again. Holroyd tried to ignore it, but the caller did not hang up. Finally, Pearl said in an annoyed tone, "Peter, please answer that phone and tell them to go away." Holroyd lifted the receiver.

"Professor Holroyd? Mrs. Finch here. Dean Hummersdorf's secretary. The dean wants to know if you received his email and propose to answer."

"Oh! That was from Hummersdorf was it? It wasn't signed so I took it someone didn't know the dean had fired me and sent it in error."

"Oh, no sir! It was sent on the dean's explicit orders."

"Then since the dean fired me, he might do me the courtesy of telling me personally instead of delegating the task to you." He paused but she made no comment.

"Tell the dean, if would be so kind, Mrs. Finch that I will expect his call and I will be happy to give him my answer."

"Thank you, Professor! I'll pass your message on to him."

"Thank you, Mrs. Finch. Have a good day," and he hung up. He did not have long to wait.

"Professor Holroyd? Dean Hummersdorf is on the line for you." Holroyd heard a click.

"Doctor Holroyd? Joe Hummersdorf here."

"Good afternoon, Dean. To what do I owe the pleasure of this call?"

"Oh, come off it, Peter! Let's not be so formal and above all let's not play games." Holroyd bridled as he registered the use of his Christian name.

"I wasn't aware that we were playing games. In fact, I wasn't aware we had anything to talk about."

"My secretary tells me you received my email asking you set a date for your return."

"I certainly did receive such an email, but it was unsigned. Given our previous conversation I assumed it must have been sent in error, or perhaps as a joke in bad taste."

"I was appalled when I discovered it had been sent like that." Hummersdorf paused as if to take a deep breath and continued to press for a date of return by offering to include Pearl and associated costs.

Holroyd was astonished. "That's extraordinarily generous and attractive, but I won't accept until my wife agrees." He ended the call without waiting for as response.

"What was that about? Why did you not tell the caller to go away?" Pearl asked in a querulous tone.

"That was the university. They want me to come back."
As expected, Pearl was not overjoyed.

"But didn't they just fire you?"

"Yes!"

"I hope you told them it would be very inconvenient."

"Well, sort of."

"What is this 'sort of'?" Pearl sat up. "You have been
fired, you have been accused of working with a criminal, and
now you have a child on the way. Why not tell them you're
not coming back? At least not coming back now."

"Well, you see...." He got no further.

"No! I do not see. You want to leave me here all alone
to bring our child into the world so you can go back and do ....
Do what?" She burst into tears. "You don't love me! You
never did."

"Dearest! That's not true! I love you and I always will."

"Then stay here with me and tell your university to
leave you alone."

"They've invited you to come along."

"Go to Canada? *Ni youdian shenjingbing ma*?" She cor-
rected herself. "Have you gone crazy? You want me to bring
our child into the world in the middle of a frozen wilderness?
I won't go!"

"But if I do stay here, none of you will be safe to go
back to visit in China."

"What? Why would we not be safe?"

"Wen Mei Li warned me that the family in China might become a target if they decide I was working with some suspected criminal."

"You mean Wang Lin Fei."

"Who?"

"She told me you are thinking of working with Wang Lin Fei."

"I didn't know his name. Why did Wen Mei Li tell you the name?"

"Oh! There are few secrets between family members. That way, we know what to keep hidden from others who have no need to know."

"And I'm not family?"

"Yes, you are, but you are not Chinese." Holroyd had not expected that and mulled this over in his mind before realising there was no adequate response.

"Anyway, I haven't accepted anything because I haven't received a definite offer," he grumbled hoping that was the end of the conversation. It proved to be a vain hope as Pearl persisted.

"They wouldn't do anything if you don't work with him."

"Don't be too sure." He then explained how two Canadians had been held in jail for over three years because Canada had arrested a Chinese business executive. They were released to the day the executive was released.

"Don't you see? Two men held in retaliation for a charge that was later shelved."

"But that's not the same at all! You are not that important."

Thanks, love, true but a little more recognition would have been nice.

"Maybe not. But it is a risk." Once again, she burst into tears. He went over to her and hugged her tightly until she calmed down.

"I'm not going to leave you, dearest."

"Then what can we do?" she said with a plaintive sniff. Holroyd noted the 'we' and breathed a silent sigh of relief.

"Tell them to go away."

"I rather think that if there is any contact at all, Wen Mei Li may not believe me if I tell her I told them to go away. You know how policemen think."

"So, we need to think how to stop them from contacting you again."

Pearl silent for a few moments.

"What do you know about this Wang?" she asked, and Holroyd explained what he had been told.

"That's what we found out about Xun Fan Ting before we knew exactly who he was[5]. Maybe this Wang is like him."

---

[5] The Dragon's Threat

"How can we find out?" Pearl did not reply immediately, but Holroyd saw that she had now shifted her focus and was becoming involved.

She gave a conspiratorial smile. "I may have a way to find out more."

27.

Pearl sat down and opened a file folder.

"Wang is a very old family name that started at the time of the end of the Shang Dynasty and the beginning of the early Zhou Dynasty. That was about three thousand years ago. The name means King." She looked at her file.

"Over the following years, they lost their noble status, but used the name to show their once high status. Today, there are over 90 million people in China with the family name Wang, about one million in Taiwan, and some 60,000 in Hong Kong."

"Are all these people related in some way?" Asked Holroyd.

"Not necessarily, but many are. Probably relationships would be stronger in the South of China like Hong Kong and Taiwan."

"Where did you find all this out?"

"It's based on national censuses and freely available."

"Well done!"

"You forget I was the Deputy Librarian in Fujinhaizhou." She smiled demurely but her eyes betrayed her delight at his reaction.

"Anyway," she continued. "I suddenly remembered why the name Wang was familiar. It reminded me of my graduate work."

"How so?"

"I studied the Qing Dynasty methods of torture and punishment."

"What?" Holroyd was surprised. "I would not have thought that would be something you'd be interested in."

"I was curious to see how those methods compared to what happened during the Cultural Revolution."

Holroyd became curious. "And what did you discover?"

"Many of the acts of the revolutionaries were similar to what was practiced under the Qing but did not go so far as the Qing did."

"How, so? Oh wait! We can get back to that another time. Let's stay with Wang for the moment."

Pearl nodded. "I next went to the British Museum and to the Bodling Library …"

"You mean Bodleian."

"Oh yes." She nodded. "They allowed me to look at some old books and records."

"But access is strictly controlled. How did you get in?"

"I told them I was a graduate student doing research for you." She grinned.

"You little minx." Holroyd laughed. "Any success?"

"Yes. At the Bodling I found a collection donated by a man named. . ." She looked at her file. "Edmund Backhouse."

"Oh! That scoundrel. He was a charlatan, did you know?"

"Charlatan? Is that some sort of clown?"

"No! But in his case, probably yes. However, he did donate some valuable stuff to the Bodleian. The British historian Hugh Trevor-Roper wrote a book about him. I may have it in my library, and you should read it someday. But go on, what did you find?"

"There are some official records of rebellions that took place after the Qing destroyed the Ming."

"Oh! Around the 1650's or so."

"Yes, I think that is right."

"Go on." Holroyd became enthralled.

"One report was of an execution of a man named Wang. But the record was incomplete because it did not include why he was executed. I asked a classmate of mine who works in the National Library in Beijing to see if she could find more." She paused tantalisingly.

"Go on." Holroyd let his impatience show.

"She sent me a reply." She read from her file. "When the Qing conquered the Ming, resistance continued, particularly in the Western and Southern areas of China. One man, Zheng Chenggong escaped to Taiwan and established a kingdom there."

"Yes, he was known as Koxinga in the West," Holroyd observed.

"Yes. Please don't interrupt." She looked at him as a grade schoolteacher might look at an unruly student before continuing. "In one battle several rebels were caught and tortured to learn the whereabouts of leaders' locations, weapons, treasures and so on. After torture they were executed. The method of execution was often quite severe. One man, Wang Qu Ling, was given a lot of torture because they thought he had buried lots of gold somewhere near Guangzhou.”

“What was so special about this man?”

“He was one of Zheng Chenggong’s closest counselors.”

“Ok, so what happened to him?”

“He was executed by Ling Chi.”

“Who was Ling Chi?”

“Ling Chi is not a person, you funny man. It means death by a thousand cuts. The executioner would cut little pieces off the victim until he died. They often started by cutting off the nipples as that was very painful but did not immediately kill the victim.”

“Oh! That’s barbarous!”

“It was thought to be less painful than burning alive. Wang Qu Ling was originally sentenced to be burned alive, but the emperor decided to be merciful.”

“Merciful? Death by a thousand cuts was more merciful than being burned alive?”

“The emperor thought so.”

“But that’s terrible.”

“Oh, but you shouldn’t be so shocked. Your Queen Mary was quite happy to burn many of her subjects alive. I think people still call her Bloody Mary.” Holroyd had no answer and quickly changed the subject.

"That's really interesting, but how does that help us?"

"Wang Lin Fei is a direct descendant of Wang Qu Ling," Pearl announced proudly.

"How could you possibly prove that?"

"Family histories or genealogy charts in China are very precise because we keep in touch with our ancestors."

"You mean you would not want to keep in touch with the wrong ancestor in case you miss something?" Holroyd remarked teasingly.

"More because we don't want our ancestors to disapprove and punish us for something that another relative did." Pearl was quite serious.

"Good work! So perhaps Wang Qu Ling did take the treasure and thought it safer if it were sent away from China." Holroyd stopped, and then exclaimed "I think you have hit the nail on the head!"

"What do you mean? I was not hitting any nails. I was telling you of my research," Pearl sounded plaintive.

"No dear. It means you have rightly identified what all this is about."

"I am pleased you think so. But why do you say that?"

"Because when Wang's men approached me, they told me I was asked to help recover a treasure." Pearl looked at him questioningly. "I asked what they meant by recover because it means getting back something you have lost. They as good as told me it was treasure that van Vervoort bragged about finding." He stopped "That means the treasure in Canada might be

Wang Qu Ling's treasure. But if that's true, how are we going to prove it?"

"You'll have to go back and find out, won't you?"

28.

Hardly had Holroyd unpacked his bags when the phone rang.

"Professor Holroyd?" the unfamiliar voice asked. "My name is Alan Eddy. I am the legal counsel to the village. I wonder if we could meet."

"Mr. Eddy, for reasons I am sure you know, I am not sure that's a good idea."

"Oh! I am not suggesting we meet in my official capacity. I was hoping to discuss the find by your colleague."

"I don't think I could add to what you may have heard from him. Anyway, that's not something we should discuss right now." Holroyd was torn between wanting to discuss exactly that and the propriety of meeting with a representative of the village at loggerheads with his employer.

"I assure you, nothing that passes between us will go further without your express permission."

"Then what do you want to talk about?" Holroyd asked curiously.

"Could there be an alternative explanation for the find?"

Holroyd paused before answering. "I think that's possible."

"Would you be prepared to fill me in on such a possibility?"

"Mr. Eddy, are you aware of my theories of ancient voyages?"

"Oh yes. One of your students, who is a member of our Band, told me about them. Specifically, she mentioned the possibility that ancient Chinese ships may have stopped off here."

"As you know then, it's only a possibility until there is proof."

"Could the find be such a proof?" Holroyd paused. *Is Eddy calling me on a fishing expedition, or does he know something that he wants confirmed?*

"Why would you think it might be?"

"Let's say, I have some information that I would like to verify." *What?* Holroyd was both surprised and curious.

"You have aroused my curiosity. With the clear understanding that for the moment our exchanges remain off the record until I agree to release them, I think a meeting might be acceptable."

"Lawyer-client confidences," Eddy promised.

Holroyd agreed. "Then come over when you're ready."

"On my way."

Once Eddy had arrived and after some small talk Eddy opened the discussion.

"What I'm curious about is the truth of van Vervoort's claim that the crucifix is part of some pirate treasure that got buried on our lands." Eddy opened the discussion.

"I am not at all convinced he has it right... at least not entirely right."

"I might have a clue that could give some support to his claim." And Eddy went on to tell Holroyd of the shaman's visit to Old John.

"So, Old John implied that a treasure had been buried in or near your village some time before a war of the Nine Tribes. What war was that?" Holroyd asked becoming very attentive, but hiding his excitement.

"A series of territorial battles that took place along the mainland coast starting about the late seventeenth century, but there were similar battles here on the Island. Our village got destroyed around that time." Eddy explained how neighbours to the north sacked the village burning the houses and stealing whatever was of value. Luckily, many folks were able to get away and came back once the English started settling here and enforcing peace.

"So, one possible scenario might be that when your village was razed, the conquerors might have known of the treasure and dug everything up and carted it all away," Holroyd suggested.

"Possibly."

"What happened to the conquerors?" asked Holroyd.

"They got obliterated later."

"By whom?"

"A combination of another tribe and English traders."

"Do you have proof of all that?"

"Of the attacks, yes. Of the treasure, nothing more than Old John's testimony. Unfortunately, Old John has since passed away."

"So, that testimony was incomplete and he's dead now. I don't think that would be very convincing."

"It would be if it's oral tradition and if there was a more complete story," Eddy suggested.

"Such as?" Holroyd looked at Eddy.

Eddy paused and then went to suggest that support for how the crucifix arrived would be more convincing.

"You don't believe what van Vervoort said?" Holroyd asked.

"I'm not sure, because I've never heard of any foreigners, let alone pirates burying a huge treasure on our lands."

"Someone must have done so if Old John was correct," Holroyd pointed out. "I suggest we need further research into that tradition to see if there is anything that might corroborate Old John."

Eddy nodded and left.

Hardly had Eddy gone when the phone rang.

"Welcome back, Doctor Holroyd. I trust you have recovered from your travels?"

"Thank you, yes."

"My employer is most eager that you let him know where you stand with the conditions he requires before he can offer you an engagement."

"Oh! Mr. Li. I'm sorry, but I have not made any progress yet. As you may know, my stay in London was quite eventful."

"Yes indeed. I trust you have fully recovered from your unfortunate accident."

"Yes indeed, thank you."

"And I trust the rest of your stay was enjoyable?"

"Oh yes, thank you for asking." Holroyd waited wondering where Li was heading.

"My employer has asked for a report and would not be happy if there was nothing to tell him."

"I rather think that might be a problem for you."

"Oh! I assure you; I would not be alone."

"Are you threatening me?" Holroyd's tone conveyed outrage mixed with a qualm of fear.

"Not at all. I am just letting you know my employer's wishes." Holroyd was tempted to tell Li to go to hell, but he was intrigued.

Li continued. "I'm sure you appreciate the situation, Doctor Holroyd, and will get back to me quite soon."

The line went dead.

Holroyd sat back realising he was going to have to disengage from Wang. "No, Mr. Wang! I regret I cannot accept your engagement, thank you very much. I hope you will fully understand that family and professional matters have left no time to be of assistance," he muttered to himself. "I doubt Mr.

Wang will be gracious enough to accept a refusal, and that's hardly comforting."

29.

Holroyd picked up the Dong Xi Yang Kao but couldn't concentrate because the light from the desk lamp was too bad. He tried to move it, only to find the cord was not long enough to move it far enough. Frustrated, he moved the chair to be nearer the light and saw the envelope that had been included in the original package he had received, but had forgotten. He ripped it open and found two pages that the sender thought might be of interest. Holroyd looked at the first one closely and reached for a magnifying glass.

Written in Ming dynasty calligraphy, the text was quite lengthy, but he thought he recognized '寶船' as Koxinga, and '國姓爺, 東寧王國' as the Kingdom of Tungning (The name of Taiwan under Koxinga).

On the second page he saw a woodcut print of a broad-side *Baoshan*[6] under full sail. At the bottom of the print was a Chinese Chop the equivalent of a signature or seal. He mused. *It's obviously not linked to the book because the book was written some 50 years before Koxinga came onto the scene. Such voyages were quite common, so this must be a record of a voyage for a special reason. But if this has something to do with Koxinga, why is this a Baoshan?*

He was puzzled because under the Ming Emperor Hongzhi China's Ocean-going fleet had been destroyed, and supposedly by 1525, none of the big ships were left. *Koxinga only established his Taiwanese empire in 1661 so it's unlikely*

---

[6] *Chinese treasure ship of the Ming Dynasty*

that he had access to a Baoshan. Perhaps this was a metaphorical treasure ship carrying a huge treasure, but with no consideration of the actual ship or ships used.

Holroyd focused on the crew who were clearly identifiable as sailors by their clothing and topknot hairstyles. On the quarterdeck, a couple of men whose headdress and robes identified them as officials stood looking out at Holroyd. He looked at the print more closely and focused on the base of the fourth mast.

A figure stood there with a tonsured head but no cap, dressed in a belted robe with what looked like a cross or crucifix hanging from the belt.

"That must be a western friar. What's he doing on a Baoshan? And is that crucifix on his belt similar or even the same as the one van Vervoort found? But would a mere friar carry such an ornate crucifix? So, if the crucifix is the one van Vervoort found maybe that's a prelate!" He stopped. *If this is a record of the ship carrying Koxinga's gold with a cleric on board and it arrived here at the West Coast my theory would be validated. What I need to do is to find evidence that a ship left Asia with a friar or prelate on board. If so, maybe it sailed from the Philippines which were then governed by Catholic Spain.*

Holroyd made a few notes before putting the paper down and returning to the Dong Xi Yang Kao. But the question bothered him like an irritating fly. He put the book aside and made himself a cocoa nightcap. Sipping the sweet brew, he thought further about the piece of paper and decided a translation would be the best first step. Looking at his watch he decided he could call a colleague in Taiwan and ask for a translation. She promised to help. An answer was in his email box the next morning.

'I'm paraphrasing the contents but will send you a proper translation later.' He read 'It's a report of a vessel carrying taels of gold and other valuables setting out from Taiwan to Manila to save the treasure from the advancing Qing armies. It doesn't state the exact amount, but given the capacity of those vessels I'd guess it might have been more than a couple of tons. On board is a European, named Rizzi (I think), who is to ensure safe delivery of the cargo to Manila. It's sent under the seal of the Lord of the Seas or some such high-sounding title. Curiously, I've been looking at the history of Manila, but I don't recall any mention of a ship like this arriving around that time. Perhaps it was lost at sea. Further, there's no mention of any Rizzi, but there was a Dominican friar in Manila named Riccio who had extensive contacts with people in China including Koxinga. Got put into prison for some reason but was released later. Perhaps it's the same person. I'll try to update you soon.'

So, it's possible that Koxinga's treasure was sent to Manila for safety in a Baoshan because Koxinga trusted this Rizzi. "Is this Rizzi the same as Riccio? If so, what was his role?"

If the Chinese had little or no knowledge of what lay to the east of the Philippines, is it likely that the ship with all that treasure would have travelled into the unknown? More likely, if the ship did arrive in Manila, the treasure would either have been unloaded and stored in Manila or would have been shipped for passage to Acapulco.

"But who would have authorised it be sent on and to whom? Did this Riccio have the authority to do so or was it sent surreptitiously?" He wondered aloud. *Assuming the treasure was transhipped to be sent to Acapulco, perhaps it was blown off course[7] and arrived here.* Satisfied with that as a possible explanation, he thought he had better have a look at the situation in the Philippines at the time the treasure ship might have arrived there.

*****

Holroyd after searching the internet learned that in 1662, the Spanish governor in Manila received an embassy sent by Koxinga demanding that Manila submit to his rule and that the Spaniards pay him tribute and taxes. Koxinga appointed Riccio as his official emissary and at some point, was chosen to receive Koxinga's treasure. *That corroborates what's written on the paper I received.*

When Riccio returned to report to Koxinga, he discovered that Koxinga had died.

Holroyd thought it unlikely Riccio would have kept the treasure for himself but would probably have been ordered to have it shipped to Spain via Latin America. It was more than likely that the head of the Dominicans in Manila would have demanded a government official or a member of Riccic's order to accompany the shipment.

Holroyd stood, stretched, and went to brew a cup of coffee and make a sandwich. As he did so, he thought again about the skeleton. *If the skeleton was that of a Dominican friar maybe there is a record somewhere of the man's*

---

[7] *One such case was found have happened when the Santo Cristo de Burwas lost in 1693.https://www.nytimes.com/2022/07/12/us/beeswax-shipwreck-oregon.html?action=click&module=RelatedLinks&pgtype=Article*

disappearance. I suppose it might be possible. I think a call to the Catholic Archdiocese is in order.

30.

Alverez stood at the door "The autopsy on Elisa is in. It confirms she was strangled, and the murderer used a wire."

"What about her personal effects? Have we found them?" Tomlinson asked.

"Not yet."

"What about where she was staying?"

"The Band policeman went over to where she was staying but there was nothing. No mention of a cell phone or a laptop. He did say her car was missing. So maybe the laptop and the cell phone could be in the car."

"And no one questioned that?"

"The villagers thought she had just moved on," Alvarez answered. Tomlinson nodded, and then mused aloud.

"I'm still puzzled why Holroyd sent those students into that area. His story about looking for past Chinese ships there doesn't fit."

"How so?"

"It's never surfaced before. He's claims to be basing his ideas on a book that experts have dismissed as fantasy. Yet, despite the dismissals, Holroyd, a reasonably respected academic from what I've been told, is pursuing the idea. So, what does he know that others don't? On the other hand, if he had some idea that there was treasure there, sending his students in to look for possible signs of a previous visit by someone would make sense."

"But Elisa was murdered before the students went in," objected Alvarez. "I don't see a link between the students' visit and Elisa."

"Could Holroyd have gone there to search by himself, got interrupted by Elisa, and murdered her?"

"But there's no suggestion Holroyd ever went there. And why would Elisa go there? There's nothing to suggest she knew Holroyd so why go to meet him? I'd say there's no link."

"Don't assume there's no link. If Holroyd knew or believed there was treasure there, he might just have gone there to look for it. Keep Holroyd under observation. I think there must be a link even if we haven't found it yet."

31

Holroyd met again with Eddy. "I might be able to suggest a plausible scenario for the arrival of the treasure." Holroyd explained the history of Koxinga's gold.

"A bit tenuous, isn't it?" Eddy sounded doubtful.

"Not necessarily because I have possible evidence that the ship had on board a cleric, possibly a friar." Holroyd answered and showed the paper that had been included in the package he had received from England.

"A cleric? That might explain the skeleton with the crucifix!" exclaimed Eddy.

"Possibly." Holroyd seemed uncertain.

"You sound doubtful."

"The treasure was destined to go to a Dominican friar, Rizzi or Riccio but, if so, how would a friar have such a crucifix?"

"Why?" asked Eddy.

"It's too ornate." And he explained the Dominican Order's views on personal possessions.

"Let's speculate for a moment and assume your version of events is correct. Where did the treasure arrive?" Eddy asked, obviously interested.

"I may even have a suggestion for that." Holroyd explained what he had seen in the private collection. "If those pieces are part of the treasure, it would prove that it arrived here. If that's correct, then the skeleton could be linked to it."

"Like van Vervoort claimed?"

"Yes, I think that part is correct." He stopped. "I think we need to find out whose skeleton that is, and where he came from." He stopped again. "If we accept van Vervoort is correct, that treasure is or more likely was buried on your lands, then perhaps the people who attacked your village found it. In turn, the looters lost it when English traders arrived and grabbed it. Then, they or their descendants might have disposed some or all of it over the years."

"That might be impossible to prove." Eddy sounded doubtful.

"I'm not too sure about that."

"How so?" Eddy looked up expectantly.

"Suppose for a moment it was an English trader who somehow got whatever was buried there. And let's suppose for the moment the treasure was gold. What would he have done with it?" Holroyd paused.

"Go on." Eddy was carefully following Holroyd's thoughts.

"It would be taken someplace where it could easily be reached when needed. At first, he might sell some, or all of it to buy land and build a house here."

"Accepting that as one scenario, how would we find out?" Eddy asked.

"From what you told me, the raid that could have re-covered the treasure took place in the middle of the Nineteenth Century. Thus, a newly rich trader might have built his house shortly after that time. Let's say two to ten years after the raid."

"I'm following you this far."

"Wouldn't there be records of who bought and built on property for that time?" Holroyd asked.

"I'm not sure about that. However, Victoria, the capital of British Columbia, was established in 1866 around the time of the Gold Rush. I think we can assume for the moment that records were kept from then on."

"The Gold Rush would provide a perfect cover to explain how someone suddenly had a lot of gold," Holroyd exclaimed.

"That would take some digging. First to find who was rich and bought property and then discovering how they became rich. We might discover that everyone claimed to have found gold," Eddy mused.

"True, but let's not forget that gold out of the ground would have to be sold to an assayer or at least someone who could pass it on for refining. I would think such an assayer or middleman would have to be licensed to do so and keep records. If that is all true, then there would also be records of any refined gold tendered for sale, or perhaps bank records if the gold was stored in one."

"We can't possibly take on such a search. We haven't the authority or the manpower," Eddy protested.

"You might not have to."

"How do you mean?" Eddy asked.

"If the hoard was large enough, it would be unreasonable to sell or store it all at the same time. In fact, it could be that the possessor and his heirs put gold out for sale at different times over the years. They might even be doing that today."

"How would we know?"

"One clue would be if some of that gold appeared on the market today. Now, when I say market, I don't mean the legitimate market because those markets get rather nosy when gold appears, and no one can explain how," Holroyd said.

"Has that happened to your knowledge?"

"Perhaps." And he confided what he had learned from the Mounties.

"There's one question that occurs to me. If the gold arrived here late in the 17th Century but the benefits of owning it only started to accrue in the middle of the 19th Century, what happened to it over the 150 to 200-year interval?" Eddy asked.

"Good point. Assuming this was a huge amount, it would have had to be hidden or at least stored somewhere large. I'm guessing the people storing it would not have used it immediately or at least not used it to the extent that others would have noticed," Holroyd supposed.

"Finding a storage large enough to hide a huge amount of gold and keep it hidden would take a lot of effort. I mean, it would have been a community effort to say the least." Eddy paused. "I don't recall any mention of such a project among my people or any neighbouring people."

"Would a community be able to keep such a secret for such a long time?"

"Perhaps not, but possibly if the original people involved died such as say in an inter- tribal conflict, and the others never knew about it."

"Then how would anyone know enough to recover it later?" Holroyd asked.

"No idea!" Eddy admitted. "What's next?"

"I think you've opened a new approach to what happened at the site. I'm going to talk with some people to see what they think. We can get together again when that's done."

Eddy left and Holroyd was left to his thoughts. *There are just too many loose ends! I think my next move is to follow up with that call to the Archdiocese and find out if a cleric disappeared while travelling to the West Coast.* He picked up the phone and waited to be put through to the Archdiocese's records department.

When he was connected, he explained that he was looking for any records that might give details of the death or disappearance of a cleric, possibly a Dominican Friar, or Vancouver Island sometime around 1660 or slightly later. He was somewhat brusquely informed that their records did not go nearly that far back. Persisting in his quest, Holroyd then asked where he might find such records if any existed and was referred to the Vatican Archives for which a telephone number was grudgingly given.

A call to that number introduced Holroyd to the labyrinthine intricacies of Christendom's most ancient bureaucracy. His search was not made any the easier by the linguistic inabilities of many of the contacts to which he was sequentially referred. Finally, he reached a Canadian priest in the Vatican Library who listened carefully to the request.

"I can't think of any such records off hand. But at the same time, I wouldn't rule out the possibility. There was a big thrust to evangelise East Asia around that time and many of the missionaries were sent out to the Philippines from Mexico and I would assume some returned by the same route."

"Would any of the ships that might have brought a missionary back to Mexico also have been carrying cargo such as say, treasure, for a religious order?"

"Of course. The Church would try to benefit from the trade between the Philippines and Mexico and use whatever ships were deemed reliable and economic. I doubt that having a separate fleet would have been justifiable. So, if you can give me any details that would help narrow the search, I can go and see what's in the archives."

"That would be most helpful. I'll be happy to send you what I know."

The reply when it came was more than Holroyd had hoped for. He read:

'There are reports from a Dominican, Fray Felipe Pardo, later Archbishop of Manila detailing with, among other matters, the arrival and departure of ships from Manila and members of the Order as passengers and the cargoes that belonged to the Order.

One such ship, the Nuestra Señora de Valladolid, departed Manila in 1665, heading for Mexico carrying 'gifts received from the Prince Zheng Chenggong (Koxinga) to be transported to Spain via Mexico.

Among the passengers is a Fray Alfonso di Seville O.P. who is returning to Spain after many years of devoted service.

Curiously, I found no description of the gifts being transported. Also, and again curiously, there is no mention of the ship's arrival in Mexico, but I am still looking.'

'Even more strange, there is a letter in the file, sent by the Congregation for the Propagation of the Faith addressed to la Duquesa di Montefero in Spain conveying the Holy Father's sorrow and informing her of the loss of His Excellency, the Bishop of San Felipe de los Bosques Tropicales, who was lost at sea returning from Manila on a mission from the Holy See. The date of the loss seems to coincide with the voyage of the Nuestra Señora de Valladolid, but I can't vouch that he was on the ship.'

So, it is possible that the skeleton was that of this bishop and to give van Vervoort his due, that might explain the crucifix. But what of the sword? Did Bishops in those days carry or fight with swords? Until I know who those remains belong to, I'm not much further ahead. Whoever died here, it means a ship, possibly the Nuestra Señora stopped here. Why? What then happened to the ship?

Holroyd found the next report when he again logged into his emails.

'There's a report from a priest in a now disappeared village in Northern California of the arrival of a man who claimed to be off a shipwreck that happened off or at least near Cape Flattery. The document has deteriorated for various reasons, and I can't read all of it, but I think the name of the ship could well have been the Nuestra Señora de Valladolid. The report is quite detailed about what happened to the ship.'

'The voyage from Manila was difficult due to heavy weather, and several people on board died and were buried at sea. The ship got blown off course, and food and water supplies ran short. The captain decided to head for where he thought there might be land so that he could replenish supplies, but lost control when a sudden freak storm drove the ship towards shore. Men were sent aloft to reef in sails when a gust of wind and a fluke wave caused the ship to heel over while simultaneously hitting some underwater object because of which several men fell from the yards either onto the deck or into the water.'

'This man got ashore, but as far as he knew no one else did. The man thought the ship got dismasted and might have been holed beneath the water line, but he couldn't be sure. The ship was still afloat and got pulled back out to sea by the undertow. The last he saw was that it was blown northwards, probably towards the Straits of Juan de Fuca.'

Holroyd stopped reading to visualise the scene. *Although there is no mention of the ship stopping here, it might have drifted here after being dismasted.*

The email ended with the opinion that because there is no mention of a landing, Fray Alfonso could have survived or have been among those who died on board. The report was signed with a 'Hope that helps.'

"So much for proving my theory that the Chinese got here first." Holroyd sighed. "Looks like van Vervoort wins that point even if he doesn't know why or how. So, let's see what might have happened the wreck."

Holroyd brought up charts of the area around Cape Flattery including those that showed prevailing winds and currents. After some calculations he concluded that under the influence of winds and tides, the wreck could have ended on the southern coast of Vancouver Island east of Port Renfrew and west of Sooke Basin maybe around Jordan River. *If so, it is probable that some of the crew survived and salvaged the treasure,*

"The captain would have known that he faced a lengthy journey back to Acapulco down a coast for which he had no charts." He mused aloud, "He might have concluded he would have to stand out to sea to avoid getting wrecked on shore again and calculated that without repairs suitable for an ocean voyage he risked losing his ship, his crew, and the cargo if he encountered another storm."

Failing adequate repairs, his best bet would have been to land the cargo for later retrieval providing he could find a spot that was deserted, accessible to land a huge treasure trove, and allow for some form of concealment. A sandy beach and a seaside cave might be such a spot. Having found one that satisfied his requirements he would have recorded the location in the ship's log or on a separate piece of paper, perhaps even on leather.

Holroyd went back to his computer to search for caves near Jordan River and found the Mystic Beach Cave located about seven kilometers away. The cave is described as approximately 15 to 20-metres deep with one entrance facing toward the Strait of Juan de Fuca, and another entrance facing toward Mystic Beach. *Tall enough to stand up at the entrances and in the middle and it can only safely be entered at low tide. That could have fitted as a place to hide the trove.*

He noted that there had been archeological finds at Jordan River that established there had been a First Nation village there, and visualised what the captain of the Nuestra Señora would have done. Once landed, the survivors would have searched for supplies.

If the village existed at the time the Spaniards landed, the Spaniards might have contacted the settlement, although given the Spaniards' attitude towards indigenous people any encounter may not have been friendly.

If an encounter had resulted in the deaths of any Spaniard, it's possible the villagers collected and kept souvenirs from the dead rather like the Inuit who kept souvenirs from the ill-fated Franklin expedition to the Northwest Passage. However, the villagers may not have known the significance of the souvenirs or trophies and so not learned about the treasure trove which then remained hidden for the next two hundred years.

The discovery by a trader or another visitor of a souvenir that a villager possessed might have provoked enough curiosity to start enquiries and then to explore along the coast. If so, both the cave and its contents might have been discovered. Recovery in secret might have been possible, and any sudden appearance of riches could be explained as a lucky goldrush find. *That's a plausible scenario, but how to prove it will be more difficult.*

"I can hardly see anyone supporting an expedition now to investigate the caves at Mystic Beach in the hope of finding evidence that the trove had been hidden there," he mused aloud. "There ought to be another way." He paused before a sudden thought entered his mind. *O'Mallory gave me an approximate time frame when his ancestor got those two items that were stolen from the museum. The time frame could fit the scenario of the trove being recovered from caves near Jordan River. If so, how did O'Mallory acquire it? I think I should visit him and have a long chat.*

Holroyd called O'Mallory, but when no one answered he left a voice message asking for a meeting.

32.

Holroyd replaced the phone after calling O'Mallory when the doorbell rang. On opening the door, he recognised Wang's representative Li Feng accompanied by two others neither of whom would have been seen in a corporate boardroom. Before he could say anything, he was pushed aside, and the three men entered.

"Please sit down, Professor," Li indicated a chair. Curious about the visit and the brusque way he was being treated, Holroyd controlled a tremor of fear.

"Mr. Li. This is outrageous. There can be no explanation for this behaviour. I would have been happy to welcome you had you first called to arrange a meeting. However, you did not, and I am not at all pleased that you barged in like this."

"Yes, that is probably true. However, we can no longer observe the niceties of normal meetings. My employer is not pleased at all with your lack of action and, as he is pressed for time, he has instructed us to manage the request he had of you."

"I certainly won't undertake anything for him if this is how he conducts his affairs."

"He has come to the same conclusion, so he has decided that we are to pursue the matter, but for that we require your information."

"I'm sorry to disappoint you, but I have no information to give you."

"I find it so hard to believe you that I won't."

"That, of course, is your privilege."

"We are not the only ones who so believe. I am sure you are aware that the police think you have more to tell them about what can be found at the site where the woman was found."

"Well, then the police are as wrong as you are," Holroyd retorted.

"Really? Then perhaps you might explain to me what you were searching for at the museum in Vancouver?"

"I wasn't searching for anything. I went to see the exhibits there as I was told it is a magnificent collection of West Coast art."

"And that is the sole reason you went there?"

"Yes."

"And did you see only West Coast art?"

"Yes."

"Did you not also see two gold pieces that I would assume you would not have classified as West Coast art?"

"Not that I can recollect."

"Oh, but I am quite certain you can remember. You asked the curator there about them."

Holroyd was surprised. *So, I was right! Li was one of the men I saw talking to the curator when I was visiting the museum!*

"Oh, those two pieces. Yes, now that you remind me, I did ask the curator. He was unable to tell me anything about them."

"And you did not follow up?"

"Why should I have? The items in question were stolen the next day and besides, the museum is a display of an individual's collection that includes not only West Coast art. Collectors sometimes acquire and display objects that may not reflect a specific relevance. I assumed that to be the case here."

"That assumption leads me to assume that you have not fully applied yourself to meet my client's wishes. Would you not agree?"

"You would not be entirely wrong. As you probably know I was away on family business and sick leave. I certainly did not concern myself with anything else during that time."

"But you have been back since then and we know you have met with the village's legal counsel. I would not believe you if you told me you had spent that time discussing the weather or the price of milk."

"You are right we did not discuss those subjects."

"Then what did you discuss?"

"I don't think that is of any concern to you. After all, I have not been engaged by your client."

"Professor, you have no idea what is and what is not of concern to me. And as for an engagement, my client has decided to dismiss that detail. So, what did you discuss?"

Holroyd remained silent.

"My client demands your cooperation; I would recommend that you meet his demands."

"Unfortunately, as I said, I don't have any information that would merit compliance."

"Are you sure?"

Holroyd kept silent. Li looked at one of the men and nodded, whereupon Holroyd received a stinging blow to the head followed by another.

"Well, Professor? Do I need to go further?"

"Oh! Go to hell!" Holroyd retorted.

"I may well do so, but if you continue to be obstinate, I assure you, you will be there to welcome me. Do you seriously want to take the risk?"

"You wouldn't dare."

"I would not be so confident," Li advised.

"If I'm dead, you won't get any information out of me."

"Aha! That suggests you do have some information for me. So, let's avoid any more unpleasantness and you tell me what you know so that I won't have to ask my men to exert themselves."

Holroyd thought for a moment. "You're wrong about one thing."

"And what is that?"

"It's very unlikely that anything came here on a Chinese ship."

"Oh?" Li was surprised. "We do know the ship carried an unspecified but large amount of cargo under the control of the Dominican Friars in Manila. We believe the crucifix was part of that cargo or at least came from the same source. But now you tell me it was not a Chinese ship. So, what was it?"

"I believe it was a Spanish trader that regularly sailed between Manila and Acapulco and was carrying treasure from Zhen Cheng Gong or Koxinga as he was known in the West." Holroyd admitted.

"Excellent!" Li beamed with satisfaction.

"Let's say all that is correct, then how does your client fit into the developments?"

"Koxinga entrusted the whereabouts of the treasure to Wang Qu Ling who passed it on to his sons before being caught and executed by the Qing. Mr. Wang is the direct descendant of Wang Qu Ling who, as you may know was Koxinga's trusted Lieutenant." *Well done, Pearl, my love, you had it exactly right.*

"So, what happened to the ship?" Li asked.

"I can't tell you precisely, but I think she probably sank." *I can only hope he doesn't know about the Vatican report.*

"And just how do you come to that conclusion?" Li asked.

"Simple logic. A ship leaves point A to go to point B but never arrives and there are no reports as to what happened to it. Since we're talking of a sea voyage, either the ship went to another point, or it sank. Spanish or indigenous settlements dotted the coast between here and Acapulco and while the ship may have ended up at one of them, it is improbable that it did so unnoticed." He paused to let Li consider this logic. After a moment's silence, Holroyd continued, "The only way it could have vanished, therefore, is by sinking far enough out to sea that there would be no noticeable evidence."

"Yes, I can see your point. So, you would have us believe the ship and its cargo sank without trace somewhere out to sea."

"After stopping here to get water which is where one of the crew or a passenger was killed. I believe that to be the most likely scenario," Holroyd added.

"And of course, even if one could locate the wreck, recovery of the cargo would entail a significant salvage operation," Li remarked agreeably.

"Oh yes!"

"Doctor Holroyd do not insult me with fairy tales. Fascinating and even plausible as your explanation may be, there is one minor detail that relegates it to the land of fantasy," Li resumed a threatening tone.

"Oh?"

"As you noticed, there were the two items in the collection that were not indigenous art. I doubt they had the capacity to swim ashore from a sunken wreck. In addition, a *yuanbao* has been offered for sale on the black market, and we both can guess where that came from. Not, I assure you, from the depths of the Pacific Ocean."

Holroyd sat silent. *So, I was right*! Li looked at him impassively.

"You see, Professor, you do know quite a bit. I believe you know more than you have admitted. Or perhaps you do not know more, but I am sure your mind has considered several possibilities. I think it would be in our mutual interests for you to share those possibilities."

Before Holroyd could answer, Li's cell phone rang. He listened before acknowledging whatever he was told and stood up.

"We are leaving, but don't worry, we will be back in contact again. In the meantime, I trust you will conclude that cooperation would be in both of our best interests." He motioned to his henchmen and together they left shutting the door behind them leaving Holroyd furious at the treatment he had received but trembling and afraid of what might lie ahead.

33.

Holroyd was still unsettled after the encounter with Li, and to distract himself from the memory, he opened his electronic copy of the academic journal to which he subscribed and often contributed. Glancing over the list of contents, he noticed an article published by van Vervoort. It was a detailed report of the discovery including an excellent photograph of the crucifix and van Vervoort's conclusions as to its provenance. *That was quick. Usually the publication of a peer-reviewed article takes at least a couple of months.*

He started reading but became increasingly irritated as he continued. The first part of the article repeated what Holroyd had heard at van Vervoort's lecture. However, at the end of the article, Holroyd read 'This discovery lays to rest the spurious if not specious suggestion by an English so called academic that the Chinese were the first to visit the West Coast of Canada.'

Holroyd could not believe what he was reading. In addition to the misgivings, he had raised before the reference to an English academic clearly was written with himself in mind. Even though his name was not given, other academics would know to whom van Vervoort was referring. In essence, the article was both wrong and possibly libellous. Holroyd sat there alternating between stunned disbelief and fury. Finally, he called the editor of the journal with whom he had good relations.

"Harry! Peter Holroyd here. I hope I haven't caught you at an inconvenient time."

239

"Peter! Not at all! I was expecting this call. I guess you've read van Vervoort's article."

"I have!"

"What do you think of it?"

Holroyd tried to control his feelings. "It's tripe and probably libellous."

"I can see how you might think it's libellous, but our legal team tell me that whereas it's close, it doesn't meet the threshold to render us vulnerable."

"That's a matter for debate, but I do think you might have passed the article through me before publication."

"Hold on, there. We tried to get in touch. The University told us that you had been let go and had returned to the UK. Your university in England had no knowledge of your whereabouts. As we had a deadline, I made the decision to go ahead without waiting for you."

"Clearly you didn't try hard enough. We'll talk more on this later, but in the meantime, you have a problem with the main thrust of the article." Holroyd gave an overview of his findings so far. Harry listened and then said:

"That's all very interesting Peter, but the difference between what van Vervoort has written and what you are telling me is that the ship was not on a voyage of exploration and evangelism to the North but a trader from Asia that probably got blown off course?"

"Yes." Holroyd stopped. "But the real story is it's Koxinga's gold."

"What's that?" Holroyd gave the details. There was silence before "Bit outside your field, isn't it?" Harry sounded a little more interested.

"Yes, and no. Sometimes something of interest pops up that demands further exploration." Harry considered this point.

"What I'm hearing you say is that that a clerical passenger travelled on a ship that may have been carrying treasure, but lost its way and ended up on Vancouver Island. Other than the reason for the ship's voyage and the suggestion there was no pirate activity, I don't quite see how van Vervoort's claim is false." He paused. "At the best, your version quibbles with details that really do not upset van Vervoort's main point."

"Oh! Come off it, Harry! You're ignoring that fact that van Vervoort's claims have caused that standoff at the reservation. I suggest you might find yourself embarrassed if you do not at least throw doubts on what he's claiming." Holroyd protested.

"Hang on, there, Peter. We publish articles but we don't take responsibility if readers draw their own conclusions."

"Even if the article is tripe?"

"I haven't heard you convince me it is tripe," Harry objected.

"It is if any treasure was found and recovered years ago."

"And was it?" Harry sounded more dubious.

"I have reason to believe so."

"Are you prepared to publish that?"

"Not yet."

"Sorry but without an article to that effect, there's not much I can do."

"Oh, have it your way, then," Holroyd gave resigned sigh. "I'll consider whether I'll write it up for you, but at the same time I'd rather you gave van Vervoort an out because if he sticks to his story, its likely to be embarrassing for him."

"But as I understand it, there's no love lost between you two."

"True, but not to the extent that I want to see him disgraced or even dismissed. That is, not if he is prepared to substantially edit or withdraw the article."

"I doubt he would do that."

"So do I, but I'd prefer you give him the chance."

"All right. I'll see what we can do. But I'll hold you to submitting your article." With that the call ended.

***

Holroyd listened to the recorded message on his inbox. "Not the best conversation I've had with van Vervoort. Shorn of all the expletives, mostly aimed at you, he refuses to change one word of his article much less withdraw it and invites you to do your darndest."

"As you wish." Exasperated by van Vervoort's attitude, Holroyd decided he would do just that.

***

The hum of conversation stilled as Holroyd entered the lecture hall and placed his briefcase on the desk. He surveyed the class and was pleased to see the hall was filled almost to capacity. *I guess my spat with van Vervoort has raised the interest levels in what I'm about to say.*

"Welcome back, Professor." Came from somewhere in the middle of the crowd. There was some clapping and a few "Hear, hears."

"I'm happy to be back and continue with our lectures." But before he could launch into his presentation, he was interrupted when a voice asked,

"Excuse me Professor, but while you were away, Professor van Vervoort told us to dismiss your theories on the grounds they were pure speculation for which there was no proof."

"Yes, I am aware of Professor van Vervoort's views."

"Are you right, or is he?"

Holroyd paused, and then looked up at the audience.

"I hadn't intended to discuss this morning the differences between Professor van Vervoort's claims and mine. But I can understand there may be sufficient interest in the matter for me to postpone what I was going to say and instead open discussion to outline the basis for those differences."

"Is he wrong, Professor?" one student insisted. Holroyd paused.

"I think he is enjoying a curate's egg for breakfast."

"What's that?" Several students asked.

"For those of you who do not know what that is, let me ask if any of you ever encountered a bad egg?" Several students shook their heads.

"That's not too surprising in this day of food inspections. When an egg goes bad, both the egg white and the yolk go off. When it is cracked there is an unpleasant sulphurous smell." He paused to let the students consider this.

"Now, the story goes that a humble and obsequious curate was invited to breakfast with the bishop but when he cracks his boiled egg, the bishop exclaims, 'Oh dear me. You have a bad egg.' But the curate not wanting to embarrass the bishop's hospitality replies 'Oh, no, My Lord. I assure you parts of it are excellent." While some students gave appreciative grins, others looked puzzled.

"If something is described as a Curate's egg, it means that the whole thing is bad even if there is a claim that parts of it are good."

"So, are you saying that parts of van Vervoort's presentation are good but overall, it's bad?" Before he could answer that, another voice called out:

"Are you accusing Professor van Vervoort of incompetence or fraud?"

"I'm not prepared to answer or comment on that. I am however, drawing to your attention how in this case Professor van Vervoort has made claims that cannot now be supported."

"I'm not sure that I see a distinction," muttered one student and others indicated they agreed. At that point, the bell rang to signify the end of the lecture and the students filed out.

Predictably, the reports of the lecture spread and once again Holroyd was summoned to the dean's office.

***

Hummersdorf's face was blotched red and white, and he looked as if he had just sucked a lemon.

"What on earth is wrong with you?" He opened with a full barrage barely containing his fury. "You reward my generosity inviting you back, by trying to undermine a respected colleague. Now you have stirred up a wasp's nest among the students. Why do you keep clinging to your unsupportable theories even in the face of undisputed facts? Are you jealous because he made a significant discovery? And to add icing to the cake, the police think you are involved in that wretched woman's death."

"Jealous of van Vervoort? That's an asinine question." Holroyd cast discretion aside and went in full bore. "I don't dispute that he found the crucifix and the pieces of cloth, but he omitted some other relevant finds so that his case is a mix of fact and fantasy, though I have no idea as to the relative proportions. Furthermore, if I have stirred up a wasp's nest among the students, that pales in comparison to the standoff at the reservation that he let loose and where, I remind you, people have been injured. As to the suggestion that I have anything to do with the woman's death, I can only say the police are very much mistaken. I suggest you should not give that idea credibility at all." He took a deep breath and continued.

"I think, Dean, you might want to disengage yourself from van Vervoort, and step back from any ideas I might be involved in the murder." He paused before adding "If, that is, you have any intention of remaining dean." Hummersdorf looked as if he had been badly stung.

"How dare you make that statement? Do you think everyone, but you is wrong? Who do you think you are? If you think that you have any right to behave as you are behaving, I will have no alternative but to…" He stopped, suddenly mindful that Holroyd's position was not his to question alone.

Holroyd continued angrily. "Since I have come here, you and van Vervoort have done everything to stop my search for proof that a Chinese vessel first came here. You have cast aspersions on my credibility at every turn, to the point I have to ask myself are you that close minded or is there another reason that drives you to do that? If this continues, I'll have no alternative but to register a complaint."

Hummersdorf sat down and looked as if he was about to breakdown. "I haven't felt so humiliated since a group of kids caught me in the park with that …." He stopped as he realised he was about to reveal a secret that he wanted no one to know about. He slumped back in his chair. "Can't you just keep your confounded opinions to yourself?" he asked in a somewhat calmer but plaintive tone.

"Opinions? Is that what you think they are?" Holroyd did not yet calm down. "Do I have to remind you that there is a difference between unfounded opinions and supportable conclusions? If so, perhaps I'm not the one who should keep his mouth closed."

"This … this is outrageous!" Hummersdorf looked as if he had been kicked in the groin. Outraged, he made to rise but collapsed in his chair and looked as if he would start to cry. Holroyd stared at the man and in a sudden feeling of compassion looked around for a chair and sat down facing Hummersdorf who was by now visibly trembling.

"Dean, I think we should take a moment to calm down before we go much further." Hummersdorf nodded and reached into a drawer from which he pulled a bottle of whiskey and a glass and poured himself a stiff measure.

"Might I be allowed to join you?" Hummersdorf looked up in surprise but then took out another glass and poured Holroyd a drink. The two men took a swallow and looked at each other in silence.

"I'd rather we worked together during these rather difficult times. Somewhere, you and I got off on the wrong foot so can we stop and regroup? Perhaps together we can find a way to solve some of our differences to our mutual benefit," Holroyd suggested.

"I'm not sure we can."

"We might start by clearly identifying those differences."

"No need for that. I think you know them as well as I do." Hummersdorf seemed to be ready to reassume his adversarial behaviour.

Holroyd looked at him. "I know what we have talked about, but I don't know what's behind those discussions." Hummersdorf looked at him in silence.

"For instance, I know that I caused you some problems when a student complained that I had treated First Nations unfairly," Holroyd said. "And further problems when I let the students go to the burial site. I will admit that I acted without full realisation of the sensitivities involved."

"Yes, and look at the trouble that caused."

"But surely, we could have avoided or at least mitigated those consequences had we stopped to think rationally."

"Are you accusing me of behaving irrationally?"

"No, I would not suggest that at all, but I would suggest that you have been poorly advised." Hummersdorf did not respond.

"The differences between me and van Vervoort revolve around differences in interpreting facts. Academic differences are a part of a university's existence and surely only require a university's involvement if such differences threaten the university's credibility or funding. I think that does apply in this case and should result in a careful examination of both his and my views. I for one, am quite prepared to submit to such an examination." There was a silence.

"Have you read van Vervoort's article?" Holroyd then asked quietly.

"I have not yet had an opportunity to do so," Hummersdorf admitted and shifted uncomfortably in his chair.

"May I suggest you do so at your earliest convenience. Meanwhile, you might want to adopt a neutral position until you have done so. That would help avoid any embarrassment for the university should any questions arise as to its soundness." Holroyd did not need to point out that by so doing Hummersdorf's own position might not be questioned.

"And what about the police inquiries?"

“I am sure they will soon realise they are barking up the wrong tree.” *I can only hope!*

“I see.” Hummersdorf finished his drink and stood up. “Perhaps you have a point.” He stopped, sat silent, and then, “Thank you for your openness and your offer to cooperate. Let me consider what you have said, and we will discuss further.”

34.

"O'Mallory here! I got your message and I think a meeting would be worthwhile. Would you be free to come over to my house at, say, eleven?" Holroyd listened to the voicemail, and after making sure there were no other engagements, decided he would go and summon an Uber.

Arriving at the address, he rang the doorbell and was surprised when no one answered. He tried again and pushed against the door which, again to his surprise, opened. He entered and called out, but again no one answered. He then noticed papers strewn on the floor and alarmed, he went in further only to hear a sound coming from a room on his right.

"Hello! Anyone there?" He called entering the room. It was in chaos with books, papers, and furnishings scattered over most of the floor. One pile of books lay in a heap at the base of a section of bookshelves that was complete y bare. Some of the books, which by their bindings must have been quite old, looked as if they had been ripped apart.

Lying on the floor was an elderly man obviously in trouble. The face was showing signs of abuse and blood was pulsating from a cut on his throat. A knife with blood on it lay nearby on the floor. Holroyd went over to him and looked for something to try and stop the bleeding, but nothing was immediately at hand. Fumbling with the buttons, he ripped off his own shirt and held it against the throat. The old man responded by weakly reaching for Holroyd's hand.

"Save the dispatch!" the man croaked. "Save the dispatch." And with that the man gave a sigh and sank back.

250

Still keeping the shirt in place with one hand, Holroyd found his cell phone with the other and dialed for help. The police and an ambulance arrived but from the paramedics' reactions, they had come too late.

Holroyd was taken to another room and told to wait until his statement could be taken. He thought over the old man's last words about saving a dispatch. *To what dispatch was he referring? There were so many papers strewn about that room I wouldn't know which one to save or, for that matter, why.* Still wondering, he looked around the room in which he had been asked to wait.

The room was furnished for dining in rich surroundings. Wealth was displayed by masterpiece paintings on the walls, rich hangings on the windows, and on shelves by porcelain vases and gold or gilded figurines, the prices of which Holroyd dared not to guess. The whole setting reminded him of the collector's treasure vault he had seen in China, and he got up to examine some of the pieces. One item caught his attention.

A small black stone statuette of Hermes wearing nothing but a gold hat with wings reminded him of a similar piece by the renaissance sculptor Donatello. Simply put, it was magnificent. But then Holroyd noticed it had been placed on top of a box-like base that seemed out of harmony with the beauty of the statuette. Gingerly, Holroyd lifted the Hermes and put it down beside the box.

He reached for the box and examined it closely. It was clearly old, was made of wood and had some intricate carving all over it. Holroyd looked closer to see what patterns had been put there. He saw some armorial shields and an abundance of flowers, all of which reminded him of a 17th Century Spanish tapestry he had once admired.

One flower, resembling a daisy, caught his attention for its intricate details and he touched it only to hear a click and feel it move. Curious, he swiveled the box and saw that one side had come away to allow access into the interior. Looking inside he saw a small, opened stoneware jar and what looked like a letter written on sheets of leather. Carefully, he removed everything but before he could examine further, he heard someone coming and quickly put the objects in his pocket before closing and returning the box to its former position. He was putting the statuette back on the box as the door opened and Inspector Watson entered.

"Doctor Holroyd! Sorry to have kept you waiting sir. Please take a seat and let me get your statement down." The inspector looked at Holroyd and then surveyed the room.

"Doesn't look as if anything has been touched in here. But we'll be examining just to be sure." He paused. "Those things look valuable. That statue, for instance, ought to fetch a good price." He pointed at the Hermes before sitting down and taking out his notebook.

"You said you contacted Mr. O'Mallory to arrange a meeting. Was there a specific reason for requesting that meeting?" Watson looked at Holroyd.

"I had some further questions about some items in his possession."

"Some items, you say," Watson repeated. "Now, to what items are you referring?"

Holroyd repeated his curiosity about the stolen items and watched as Watson finished writing down his statements.

Watson looked up from his notebook and asked, "As you will remember, sir, you were interviewed by Inspector Hollingsworth about those two items. Now I find you at the scene of Mr. O'Mallory's death. Unless your presence at both these events is coincidental, I'm asking why you were interested in those two gold pieces."

"I wanted to know more about where they came from."

"Do you have a particular interest in them?"

"They seemed so out of place and in such poor condition to have been included in the exhibits." Holroyd decided this was not the time to give his reasons in full.

"No other reasons?" Holroyd detected a tone that suggested doubt and suspicion.

"None at all, Inspector."

"I see." The inspector paused and looked at Holroyd.

After a few more questions he was told he could go home, but not to leave the city and to come down to the station to make a formal statement.

***

Realising that relatives need to be informed, Watson checked O'Mallory's next of kin. There were two children, one of whom was a stockbroker in Vancouver and decided to go over there.

In Vancouver, Watson was taken to the offices of O'Mallory's son in the upper stories of a high-rise office building with views of the harbour and the mountains. After introductions, and the expressions of condolences, Simon O'Mallory asked how he could be of help.

"I'm investigating the death of your father," Watson started. "Do you have any idea who might want to harm your father and why?"

"Not at all. I'm shocked by the whole matter. Father was a man who did a lot of good for many people."

"Our thinking is that the attacker wanted something of value he or she knew or maybe only thought your father might possess."

"Such as?"

"Money, jewelry, an antique, or art piece, stock certificates. Items perhaps you, or someone in the family might know about."

O'Mallory nodded in agreement.

"All of us have been well provided for by our father, so why would any of us want to attack him?"

"When you say 'us,' I presume you mean yourself and your sister."

"There's also my half-brother Joe Hummersdorf."

"Hummersdorf? What's his connection?" Watson expressed surprise.

"Born out of wedlock."

Watson sat silent before commenting "Another reason might be that some sort of revenge motivated the attack. Of course, there is also the possibility that the attacker has nothing to do with the family."

"I'd say that is the most likely. Now, Inspector, I have a meeting scheduled, so if there is nothing else, I have to leave."

"Just one more question, sir. Does the name Holroyd mean anything to you?"

"No. Why should it?"

"He's the man who was in your father's house and reported the murder."

"Perhaps that's the man you should be investigating then." O'Mallory rose and gathered some papers from his desk in preparation for his meeting.

Watson nodded and started to leave, noting he might want to meet again if further questions needed answering.

35

Once home, Holroyd took out the jar and the leather document. Looking at the jar he remembered in the 17th Century perishables were often stored in such containers, and thought the document had probably been stored inside.

Next, he began to examine the document only to find there were two items. One item was a note written in English. He read: 'Exchanged with (what was probably a name), for two pounds of tobacco and three yards of woolen cloth, a stoppered ceramic jar containing leather pages that look like a written report.' What might have been an illegible date and signature was at the bottom. *This looks like a bill of exchange.*

Next, he looked at the second item. The handwritten entries were scripted in Spanish or Latin only some words of which he recognised. He read names and dates followed by the word 'muerto' and reference to 'cuevas' followed by what seemed to be bearings.

He realised that this was probably the notebook of some Spanish sailor, but nothing seemed to indicate who that sailor might have been. *Could this refer to the loss of the Nuestra Señora?* Intrigued, he debated whom to call to help with a translation and finally settled on a young Spanish assistant professor at the university. After a short conversation, she agreed to look at it. He photographed the pages and sent the pictures over to her.

***

"Holroyd here." Holroyd picked up the phone.

"Good evening, Professor! It's Maria Sanchez. I hope I'm not disturbing, but I'm calling about the photographs you asked me to look at."

"Oh, yes!" His heart gave a jump. "No, you're not disturbing me at all. What have you found?"

"They're really interesting. They are photographs of what appears to be from a diary of a Spaniard who was living somewhere near the sea and near a pueblo dos Indios. He, or maybe even she, records the happenings at that time. I think possibly the writer was the leader there."

"I very much doubt it was a she, but go on."

"I could not read the whole of the first pages because they look as if they have been in the water and so illegible. I was able to determine that the document was addressed to some high personage because I did recover the words 'Your Excellency' and something about a small boat sent to the south to get help. There is also mention of someone who was the Commander of the Manila Garrison."

"Is there a name?"

"Not that I could read other than he must have been a person of importance because it refers to a 'Don' but that's all."

"Pity. But please go on."

"What I could determine was that the document contains details of what happened to a ship and its cargo. The writer specifically requests that the families of individuals mentioned in the letter be informed of the misfortune that befell the ship and that personal items that have been kept with the cargo be returned to them. Anyway, he tells of the difficulties finding foods, building shelters, and even building fort fications. He also records the hopes and prayers for a rescue. There seems to have been trouble because he records fights among the Spaniards including some who get killed. He also records deaths from hunger, wounds or injuries, and illnesses. And there were fights between the Spaniards and los Ind os." She paused. "I'm thinking this may be the records of some ship's survivors."

"Perhaps there is mention where they put the cargo."

"Not that I could see. But there may be something if I go over the whole document in detail."

"That won't be necessary just now." *It must be from the Nostra Señora. But how did O'Mallory get this record, and how did it survive when O'Mallory told me the family records had been destroyed in a fire?*

"Is there anything else you noted?"

"Yes. There are also some figures that seem to be ascensions because I see symbols that I think represent planets or stars, but I can't be sure."

"I think ascensions are quite likely." He paused. "Are there any dates?"

"Not that I can see. Would that be important?"

"Yes, because if we have dates, we can apply the ascensions and so locate where all this took place."

"I see. I will look further."

"Excellent! Thank you so much for your help."

"Do you want me to do a complete translation? That may take some time."

"That's very kind of you to even think of it. But no, not yet. I must do some more research at my end to decide whether the effort is worthwhile." *Accepting this document to be the last record of the Nuestra Señora, I think the skeleton up at the reservation could be that of this Garrison Commander. A Garrison Commander might have a sword and the crucifix.*

He went back and photographed the first document and decided to forward it to Alan Eddy to see if Eddy could help decipher the name with whom the exchange had been made.

"It's a name from one of our people." Came back from Eddy. "He was one of our chiefs about the mid 1800's." *So, this chief trades for the container probably not knowing what was inside. How did he get the container in the first place?*

"What else can you tell me about him?"

"I'll get back to you on that."

Holroyd went back to the list of what he thought were likely ascensions. If he could identify the astronomical bodies to which they referred he could identify the latitude, but not the longitude, because accurate time pieces would not be built for another 100 years. But then it occurred to him the latitude might be sufficient if, as he thought, the observations were taken on land. A line of latitude that intersected with a shore-line would give a precise location of where the observations were taken.

He remembered his navigation lesson from the days when he had been at sea and calculated a latitude of 48 to 49 degrees, North. Opening a world map, Holroyd drew a horizontal line across the Pacific Ocean at that latitude and noted that the line intersected with the Canadian Coastline at approximately Barkley Sound. *That's quite a way up the coast from Jordan River, but if the hulk drifted up that far that could be the location of where the treasure ended up.*

Holroyd opened his computer to learn about Barkley Sound. First Nations occupied most of the west coast of Vancouver Island including the Sound, for some four thousand years, living a semi-nomadic existence between the protected islands and bays of the Sound.

Archeological sites including stonewalled fish traps, shell middens and the remains of long houses in terraced abandoned village sites attest to their existence long before Europeans arrived. Large caves exist on several of the islands in the Sound.

Europeans arrived towards the end of the 18th Century and trading started soon after, with fur sealers eventually setting up a permanent post that subsequently grew to become Ucluelet. Fishing was excellent and some gold was discovered but not enough for profitable exploitation.

Holroyd shut down his computer. *That looks like where the treasure probably landed if indeed it was, but I need to find corroborative evidence that it was landed, hidden, and found. My guess would be one of O'Mallory's ancestors found it, but which one and how to prove it?*

36.

Manning and Holroyd settled on the patio with drinks and Manning asked how Holroyd was settling in.

"It's not been quite what I expected, but I think I'm coping."

"Yes, from what I hear it hasn't been a very smooth ride."

"I should say not."

"I gather the police suspect you of involvement in Elisa's murder."

"Well, they're really wrong about that."

"It's not a nice thing to have hanging over you," Manning commented. "I hope they get it right soon." He sat for a moment thinking and then "How are you getting on with your quest?"

"The skeleton and the crucifix are evidence of a visit earlier than originally believed by a foreign ship that was probably European. The cloth with the crucifix suggests the ship dates from the time that corresponds to this treasure people are all excited about."

"So, Paul was right when he claimed the skeleton does not show a Chinese ship visited here."

"I'll give him that, but only to the extent there was no Chinese visit at that time. It does not prove that no Chinese ship visited here before that time."

"You don't give in easily, do you?" Manning laughed.

"I confess I'm puzzled by the degree of van Vervoort's animosity towards me," Holroyd mused. "I mean, I've experienced animosity, but never to this degree and with such vehemence. What's his background?"

"He and Joe graduated from here as undergraduates after which I've been told Paul went north somewhere. He disappeared for a while before reappearing with his doctor's degree in anthropology with a minor in archeology. Apparently, he was in contact with the team that investigated the ancient stories of the indigenous Heiltsuk Nation people that during the last Ice Age sheltered somewhere along the coastline in Canada. According to the Hakai Institute the team proved these stories were true by discovering a 14,000-year-old settlement on Triquet Island. The discovery included the remans of charcoal, tools, fishhooks, spears used to hunt marine mammals, and even a hand drill used for lighting fires. Paul published a paper on the find but he failed to give credit to the other members of the team."

"You mean he claimed he was the team leader?"

"Not in so many words, but people felt he implied it."

"That's outrageous! I'm surprised he wasn't disciplined in some way."

"He was protected."

"Oh? How so?"

"Joe and Paul graduated together from here and became quite close. In those days, sexual orientation was still an issue and Joe was caught quite literally with his pants down. Paul was somehow able to hush the matter up before anything was said officially. Joe owes Paul, and helped Paul to get appointed here. I think that's all there is to say."

"Oh! I see." *van Vervoort must really have helped in hushing up Hummersdorf's earlier indiscretion.*

Manning went to refill the drinks and bring out some munchies. Once settled again he remarked:

"Joe was telling me about your meeting with him. I think you made the right offer. Joe can be very stubborn, but he's open to reason. The trouble is that he's caught between a rock and a hard place."

"How so?"

"On the one side there are the differences between you and Paul. It's not Joe's field of expertise so he has no real basis by which to judge who may be right. I gather you are open to have your ideas reviewed but Paul is not. Given Paul's history, if Joe doesn't support Paul, Paul will create a fuss and Joe desperately wants to avoid that sort of confrontation. Paul is faculty and you are a visitor, which means that Joe has to live with Paul after you've gone."

"I fully agree with you. That's why I suggested he should adopt a more neutral position."

"I tend to agree," remarked Manning.

They sat silent for a few minutes until Manning's cell phoned chimed.

"Excuse me for a moment." Holroyd heard him say "No, can't help you." He disconnected the phone. "Sorry about that. Joe's son, Rod. Sounds agitated."

"How does that work, if you don't mind me asking?"

"You mean between Joe and Rod?" Holroyd nodded.

"When Joe came out, his wife was furious. Made such a fuss that Joe's father basically cut her off from everything. She was not happy and from all accounts can be vicious. She sued to get custody of Rod after which relations with Joe and the old man remained frosty. As Joe tells it, Rod got on well with his grandfather. Still, he didn't get to have much contact because Joe's ex tries to keep them apart." He paused. "Really nice kid. Very bright, good at sports, and I think ambitious. He could go far."

Holroyd sat silent and then asked, "Does he hold a grudge for what happened?"

"I don't really know, but if he does I haven't been able to notice it, but as for the ex, that's a totally different matter." Holroyd sat mulling over what he had just learned.

"How about with his father?"

"Again, I don't really know. I've felt there is something not quite right, but I don't think it's something I should press."

"Family issues can be troublesome," Holroyd agreed.

Manning went to refill the glasses.

"I hear you discovered O'Mallory's murder." Manning started after he returned.

"Yes."

"I'm told he asked you to go see him. Any idea why?"

"Not really, other than perhaps he wanted to discuss two gold pieces that I thought didn't fit the collection of native arts and he had asked me to find out more about them."

"What about them?"

Holroyd explained his curiosity and then added the fact they had been stolen.

"That's strange!"

"I'm thinking those pieces may be part of the treasure everyone is talking about. That being so, I believe O'Mallory was murdered by someone who thought the old man knew where the treasure was hidden," Holroyd explained. "When I arrived at O'Mallory's house the place looked as if it had been ransacked, but many valuable items were left behind. That suggests to me the thieves were looking for something in particular."

"Do you think they found whatever it was?"

"I have no way of knowing that."

"O'Mallory didn't leave a clue?"

"Again, I have no way of knowing that." Holroyd decided to keep secret O'Mallory's last words and the discovery of the diary.

Manning sat thinking before acknowledging, "That does sound plausible. Proving it might be more difficult." They sat in silence until Holroyd remarked "He told me the stolen items were a sort of family heirlooms."

"I wouldn't have thought it wise to put family heirlooms on public display but who knows what went through the old man's mind?" Manning mused.

"I agree," and after a moment Holroyd asked, "What happens to the collection now?"

"I don't know if he bequeathed it somewhere, but if not, it'll go to his heirs."

"Do you know who they are?"

"Not all of them, but Joe is among them." Holroyd was surprised.

"How?"

"The old man was quite prolific," Manning grinned. "I think he had a couple of children by his marriage though I have no idea where they are now. But he also had at least a couple of kids outside marriage and Joe is one of them."

"Who was the other?"

"I have no idea. Joe might know but he's only mentioned it a couple of times without going too much into detail. We'll probably find out when the will is probated. The lure of money brings all sorts of people out of the woodwork," Manning grinned.

"Does Canada have any bastardy laws?"

"I don't know about Canada or the other provinces, but in British Columbia illegitimate children inherit the same as legitimate ones. I think that law was passed in 1927 or so."

"I'd have to say that's much more enlightened than in Britain. A similar law wasn't passed there until 1987." Holroyd paused. "So, the dean stands to inherit what I suppose could be quite a fortune."

"Yes. Might not be that great a windfall. The old man was very generous, and we have been able to live quite well, as you can see."

The sound of the doorbell and knocking interrupted further talk as Manning went to see who was there. He returned with Rod. The young man was clearly agitated and stopped when he saw Holroyd.

"Oh! I'm sorry. I didn't know you had a visitor." Rod looked confused.

"I was just about to leave." Holroyd started to get up. "I think this is not something I need to be here for. Thanks, for the drinks and chat, Ron. I'll leave you two to talk."

"No! Please stay." Holroyd was surprised but settled down again.

"Well, Rod, what brings you here?" asked Manning.

"Mother."

Holroyd started again to get up.

"Please stay, Doctor Holroyd," Rod said. "I just want to find out what's happening, and I think it involves you." Both Holroyd and Manning were surprised.

"She accused you of stealing something that she says is rightfully hers," Rod continued.

"She what?" Holroyd was shocked.

"She said something about you knowing where Grand-dad's treasure is hidden."

"She's definitely wrong about that," Holroyd muttered.

"But you might have an idea, Peter," Manning inter-jected.

"Having an idea and knowing are two very different things," Holroyd shot back. There was silence.

"Perhaps you should stay for the moment." Manning turned to Holroyd. "Let's hear what Rod has to say." Holroyd settled down again but felt distinctly uncomfortable at the probability of becoming involved.

"Well, Rod?" asked Manning.

"Mother has gone ape." He paused and gave a weak smile. "Sorry, Doctor Holroyd, I meant to say my mother is behaving very strangely and I'm worried."

"I think you had better start at the beginning, Rod. Doctor Holroyd knows enough about your family to follow whatever explanation you might have for that remark."

"Mother was ranting about Granddad before he was found murdered. That wasn't so strange because the old man and she haven't been on good terms for years. But after the murder was discovered, she went off the deep end. She's been going through her stuff, ripping up papers, crying, and even screaming. She keeps calling Granddad a fucking bastard who got what he deserved. She won't talk to me and even told me to get out of the house."

"Did you report that to the police?"

"No. I don't want to get involved or her either."

"I think you have to," Manning commented.

"Look. I really don't think I should be involved. Ron, if you don't mind, I'll leave now." Holroyd got out of his chair and prepared to leave.

"Let me see you to the door," Manning agreed and got up. Just as he was about to exit the house, Holroyd turned to Manning. "You know, I think this is something the police might want to know. Could it be that the mother went there to search for something?" Manning looked at him.

"I hope not. But I think you're right. Leave it with me."

37.

Holroyd opened his computer to find an email from Eddy reporting what he had discovered about the old chief who had been dismissed for selling the war trophies.

'I checked around to see what I could find. There isn't much, but from what I did learn is that about 300 years ago foreigners arrived in a small boat and were driven off when we attacked them. Several of the foreigners were killed and we recovered trophies including weapons, clothing, and some other items as spoils of war. One of the totem poles in the cove was put up in honour of the chief at the time. I think the skeleton probably was one of those killed, but I don't quite follow how the body, or the crucifix was left there. I would have thought it would have been discovered and buried long before now.'

That fits! Holroyd sat back. *The Nuestra was abandoned in Barkley Sound and a small boat was sent south to get help. It lands here to replenish supplies and the crew gets attacked. One of the trophies could well have been the jar. If so, the trader who bought it from the old chief was an O'Mallory ancestor.* He paused, *I think I need to confirm that to complete my task for Merry, but it doesn't help me in my quest.*

***

"There's something we missed." Alvarez entered with a report sheet. "On the night of Elisa's disappearance, one of our cruisers came across a car stopped on the road near where the body was found."

"Go on."

"We ran the license plates and it's registered to Joseph Hummersdorf."

"You mean Hummersdorf went up there?" Tomlinson sat up.

"Looks like it."

"What on earth for?"

"No idea. And another thing. The driver was texting when the cruiser went to ask what was up. So, I called Dupré over at the telecom company to see if he could tell us anything about who was texting. There were three calls registered in that area on that night. One was a local phone, another was an out-of-province number, and one was an unlisted number. The local phone call went out at about 8.15 in the evening, the out-of-province call at 8.18 and the last call from the unlisted number at 9.29. That one was a voice call to an unlisted number in Asia." Alvarez paused with a small grin before continuing "You're going to love what Dupré told me," He paused again. "The local phone is registered to Hummersdorf."

"You're kidding me!" Tomlinson was surprised "Ok! Go question him."

"Got it." Alvarez paused, "so Holroyd didn't drive or use the phone."

"Probably not. But let's not exclude him just yet."

***

"Mr. Hummersdorf," Alvarez began.

"That's Professor or Dean Hummersdorf."

"My apologies, Professor." Alvarez gave Hummersdorf a long stare before looking down at his notebook. "We want to ask you some questions about the night that Elisa went missing."

"I'm sorry. Who?" Hummersdorf sucdenly became nervous and shifted in his chair.

"I think you know of Elisa, so let's not pretend otherwise."

"I know she has been murdered," Hummersdorf grudgingly acknowledged.

"Where were you on the night of the first of October?"

"At home, I would think. Let me check my diary." He reached into a desk drawer and brought out a leather-bound diary. Opening it he scanned the entries until "Yes, here we are. I was at home." He passed the opened book to Alvarez for inspection.

"Yes, sir. I can see that. Was anyone with you?"

"My partner, Ron Manning."

"You were at home all night?"

"Yes."

"Both of you?"

"Yes."

"Neither of you went out for anything?" Alvarez insisted.

"No."

“So, what did you do?”

“I don’t follow you, what do you mean?”

“Just go over how you spent your evening together after you got home.”

Hummersdorf sat thinking, “Let’s see. I got home after Ron. We had supper and then watched TV.”

“About what time would that have been, sir?”

“I’d say 6 or 6.30 in the evening.”

“What did you watch?”

“Jeopardy, the news, a documentary on whales. Then we went to bed and fell asleep.”

“At the same time?”

“No. I went first, and I don’t know what time Ron went to bed.”

“About what time did you go to bed?”

“I’d say maybe 10.30 or a few minutes later.”

“And about how much later would Mr. Manning have joined you?”

“As I said, I don’t know exactly. My guess he would have turned in maybe half an hour after me.”

“I see.” Alvarez consulted his notebook. “You have a 4x4 do you not?”

“Yes.”

“Did you use it that night?”

"I just told you I did not go out that night."

"Yes, you did say that! But what of Mr. Manning?"

"He didn't go out either."

"You're sure of that?"

Hummersdorf nodded.

"Then did you lend your car to anyone?"

"Goodness, no! I don't lend things."

"Does anyone besides yourself have keys to the car?"

"Ron does."

"Did he lend them to anyone?"

"I very much doubt it."

"But if neither of you went out that night, would you have an explanation as to why your car was stopped on the highway near where Elisa's body was later found?"

"What? Who says so?"

"One of our constables asked why a car was stopped by the side of the road without its flashers on. After running the license plates, we found it was registered to you."

"And who was driving?"

"That, sir, is what we are here to determine."

"Well, whoever it was, it wasn't me, or Ron."

"I see. Then perhaps you could think of who it might have been."

"I have no idea." Alvarez waited, but Hummersdorf said nothing.

"Do you have a cell phone, sir?" Alvarez changed to another line of questioning.

"Of course."

"May I see it, please?" Hummersdorf reached into his pocket and handed it over.

"Could you unlock it, please?" Hummersdorf did so and handed it back. Alvarez inspected it before looking up.

"Do you have any others?"

"Yes, I have another one at home. I use that for my personal stuff."

"Do you happen to remember the number, sir?" Hummersdorf recited it and Alvarez consulted his notebook.

"Yes, that fits. Now any other cell phones?"

"No."

"Are you sure, sir?"

"Of course, I'm sure. Where is this line of questioning going, may I ask?"

"Three phone calls were made on the night of Elisa's disappearance between around 8 pm and 9.30 and all in the vicinity of where the body was found." He paused. "One of those calls came from a phone registered under your name and that was not from this cell phone. Therefore, it must have come from the phone that you say you use for your personal calls."

"But that's impossible. I keep that phone at home and as I told you, I was nowhere near that area that night." Hummersdorf was beginning to sweat as he realised where this was going. Alverez looked at him in silence.

"I see, sir," he said after a few moments. "I would appreciate your stopping by the station at your earliest convenience to sign a statement. Oh! And bring your cell phones ... both of them." And with that the interview was over.

***

Alvarez stood at the door and looked in. "They found Elisa's car about 15 klicks away from the village, half submerged in a roadside pond with two boys dead inside. I called the local boys up there and her laptop was recovered. It's on its way here."

"Was her phone recovered also?" Tomlinson asked.

"It's not listed on the report."

"So, Hummersdorf or someone driving Hummersdorf's car goes up there. We have Hummersdorf's phone being used at the scene. We don't know if, and if so, why Hummersdorf went there. On the other hand, Holroyd could have had a reason to go up there, but we don't know if, how, or when he went there." He paused.

"Too many unknowns. He paused. "Unless there's a third person."

"A third person may have had nothing to do with the murder. May have been passing the wrong place at the wrong time," Alvarez suggested, and Tomlinson nodded.

"True, but that is hardly a place that people just wander into. I'd say there would have to be a reason for going there and so far, we don't have a cast iron reason, only suspicions."

"There is one way that might help narrow the possibilities. What time did Hummersdorf or whoever was driving the car get home?"

"Go on."

"If we examine the timelines from the time the first text went out and allow for a reasonable time to meet and drive home, Hummersdorf should have arrived home between 10.00 or 10.30 at the latest. If, on the other hand he stayed to bury the body he could not have arrived much before 11.00. I wonder if any of the neighbours saw him arrive? Do a door-to-door inquiry around Hummersdorf's place."

"Most people are getting ready to go to bed at those times."

"Not necessarily everyone, some people are insomniacs. But we won't know until we've done a door to door."

***

After the door to door, only one positive report came in. Mrs. Stubbington, 78, widowed, and living next door to Hummersdorf had been up to let in Muffles (her rather large tabby cat). She told the inquiring officer she had noticed someone getting out of Hummersdorf's 4x4 at about 11.15. She was certain about the time because she had just watched her TV station signing off a few minutes earlier. She was certain it was Hummersdorf getting out of the car but admitted she had not seen the face.

"Then how could she be certain it was Hummersdorf?" asked Tomlinson.

"Because she saw his grey hoodie even though he was on the other side of the car."

"I think it's time we had a look at Hummersdorf's car. Get a team over there and see what's inside and do a thorough search for fingerprints."

Just then came a knock on the door and a constable stuck his head in. "The IT boys just wanted you to know they managed to flash up the murdered woman's computer, but recovery of her files will take longer because they are double encrypted. They pinged her phone and did get a location." and he passed in a piece of paper. Alvarez took and glanced at it.

"This is at or near Hummersdorf's place."

"Narrow it down and if it's his address get a warrant and go search his place."

An hour later the phone rang. "We found the phone between the seats in Hummersdorf's 4x4."

"Ok bring it in and have forensics check for prints to make sure. If we're lucky it'll have the killer's prints on it too."

"Should we bring Hummersdorf in?"

"Not yet. Let's first see what the phone can tell us."

38.

Holroyd had just returned from Manning's home when the doorbell rang. Irritated he answered to see Wen Mei Li standing there.

"Good evening, Peter. I hope this visit is not too inconvenient, but I wanted to have a chat." Holroyd was surprised.

"I had no idea you were in Canada, much less here."

"I had further business in Toronto after I completed my business in London. I decided I would benefit from a slight change in my travel arrangements to stop and visit you to congratulate you on becoming a father."

"That's very kind of you but surely not the only reason for your arrival here."

"No. I also want to talk to you about Wang Lin Fei."

"I have had no further contacts with him."

"That's not quite true, is it? But may I come in? I don't think this is the sort of discussion we should have standing on the doorstep." Holroyd reluctantly stood aside and let her in. Torn between Chinese etiquette that demands a visitor be offered tea and the desire for her to leave, Holroyd decided to follow Chinese norms.

They sat facing each other talking about family matters as if this was a purely social visit. Finally, Holroyd's impatience broke through.

"You said you wanted to talk about Wang Lin Fei. So how may I be of service?"

279

"Peter! I am surprised at you! What could be more important than family matters?" Holroyd suddenly realised that the relationship had changed since their last meeting. Wen Mei Li wasn't threatening him now, she was seeking his cooperation and that raised the question what she thought he had that she needed.

"Yes! Wang Lin Fei is now definitely wanted in China, and I am hoping you will be able to assist me."

"How?"

"He has disappeared, and I think you have had recent contact with him or his men."

"Yes, they wanted information that they thought I had, but I didn't."

"What sort of information?"

"Before I answer, may I know why he is wanted in China?"

"We know he contacts and has dealings with people who control the drugs from the Golden Triangle although we don't know all the details yet. He will certainly be charged with drug trafficking."

"So, nothing to do with the ancient artifacts he wants me to recover?'

"No! What makes you think so?" Holroyd detailed his meetings with Li.

"I did not think it was of sufficient importance to start an investigation yet, but perhaps it's time we should examine it." She paused. "Excuse me, may I use the washroom?"

"Of course." And Holroyd opened the door to the small washroom off the sitting room. Scarcely had Wen locked the door behind her when the doorbell rang again. *This is beginning to be like Piccadilly Circus at rush hour.* Holroyd opened the door to see Li Feng and two Chinamen he did not know.

Li pushed his way in followed by his companions. One of the Chinamen closed the door and took off his hat and coat and faced Holroyd.

"Doctor Holroyd, we finally meet. Li Feng has told me so much about you. I am Wang Lin Fei." Holroyd began to panic.

Wen Mei Li needs to be warned before she comes out of the washroom!

"Mr. Wang! Mr. Li did not warn me that you would drop in." He spoke with an unnaturally loud voice. Both Wang and Li looked at him with surprise. "I'm sorry! Something is irritating my throat but let me just get something to drink." and he turned to go to the kitchen.

"I see you already have a *chazhuo* set up for two. Perhaps some more tea would help?"

Holroyd looked at the table with dismay. Wang or Li would want to know why the table was set for two and if either reached to pour some tea, he would realise from the temperature of the brew that someone had recently stopped by or perhaps might still be there. Quickly, Holroyd reached for a cup and poured more tea before anyone else could do so, but Li started looking around the apartment as if to find a hidden visitor.

"So, how may I be of service?" Holroyd watched as Li approached the bathroom and tried the handle. Finding the door locked, Li turned to Holroyd just as Wen Mei Li unlocked the door and came out.

"Oh! Hello." Wen Mei Li stopped and surveyed the room. "Peter, you didn't tell me you were expecting visitors. Won't you introduce them?"

"I am Li Feng." Li introduced himself before Holroyd could answer. "Now, who are you?"

"Oh! Let me give you my name card." And Wen Mei Li reached for her handbag but before she could open it, the henchman lunged forward, grabbed it, and handed it to Li. Li opened it and emptied the contents onto the ground to reveal a service revolver and bright red warrant card holder emblazoned with gold lettering. Li opened the card, read, and handed it to Wang.

"Now, what should I make of this?" Wang looked first at Wen Mei Li and then at Holroyd and back again. "This card tells me Wen Mei Li is a member of China's State Security Bureau from which I have to conclude that she is not here just for a social visit. As we all know Wen Mei Li and Professor Holroyd have met several times. I am puzzled by this visit to Doctor Holroyd. Just what is the connection here?"

"I hardly think that is any of your business." Holroyd, though distinctly uneasy, assumed a defiant tone.

"What you may or may not think is of no concern to me. But the presence here in your apartment of a State Security Officer with whom you have met several times suggests to me that you have not been entirely open with us, Doctor Holroyd. And that is very much a concern of mine." He paused. "Could it be that you have been collaborating with the Chinese police?"

"That is ridiculous. Why would I do that?" Holroyd tried to imply that Wang was being fanciful, but before Wang could reply, Wen Mei Li intervened.

"Doctor Holroyd was most helpful in resolving a matter in China and I came here to talk about that."

"I doubt that. As we all know, the matter was resolved, so what is there to talk about? No! Why are you here, Wen Mei Li?" Before Wen Mei Li could reply, Li whispered something to Wang who nodded.

"Mr. Li reminds me that we are here for a specific reason and while surprised at the presence of Wen Mei Li, we should focus on our primary task."

"Which is?" Wen Mei Li's tone expressed curiosity.

"We have some questions for Doctor Holroyd which he will be only too happy to answer."

"I very much doubt that." Holroyd maintained his brave front.

"Doubt you may now, but I am confident you will be sure by the time we are finished."

"Are you threatening Doctor Holroyd in my presence?" asked Wen Mei Li.

"Why not? You are in Canada now, Wen Mei Li, which means that as a Chinese police official you have no official standing and can be ignored for now." Wang turned back to Holroyd. "I am disappointed with the lack of progress of your efforts."

"How can you say that?" Holroyd feigned curiosity.

"You failed to report your findings at the museum."

"I had no idea they were part of the treasure," Holroyd countered.

"How would he know what was or was not part of the treasure?" asked Wen Mei Li. She paused before asking, "and just what is your interest in the treasure?"

"Oh! Did Holroyd not tell you? I am the direct descendent of the original owner. My ancestor kept very good records, so I know exactly what was included."

"Your ancestor?" asked Wen Mei Li.

"Oh! Yes. But that is not the issue now. The issue is where is the treasure? Given the existence of the items at the museum, we know that despite your imaginative suggestion, the ship did not sink." He paused. "What I think you can provide, Doctor Holroyd, is where the ship ended up."

"It could have arrived anywhere on the West Coast," Holroyd retorted.

"Indeed, it could, but we also know that O'Mallory obtained the two items that were on display at his museum, so it's clear the treasure was found and a link to O'Mallory exists. Furthermore, you obviously believed that O'Mallory would have a clue, otherwise why visit him?"

"I had no such belief. He asked me to come over and when I arrived, he was dead." Holroyd decided to omit any other details.

"I find that difficult to believe."

"Difficult to believe or not, it's fact," Holroyd pointed out.

"Are you sure you have nothing else to add?" asked Wang.

"Yes!"

"I see."

"How much would that treasure be worth today?" asked Mei Li.

"Probably two or three billion pounds." Holroyd gasped at this huge amount, but before he could say anything, Wang turned to Li.

"If Holroyd has nothing to add we can dispense with him, and the woman is an irritation I think should also be removed." Li nodded and turned to the henchman to give instructions at which moment the doorbell rang.

"Police. Open up." No one moved.

The doorbell rang again and was followed by a pounding on the door. Wen Mei Li moved quickly before anyone could interfere and opened the door. A plainclothes officer and two uniformed men stood at the door.

"I am Inspector Watson and would like to meet with Professor Holroyd."

"Thank goodness you've arrived. Come in, come in. Arrest those men," Wen commanded pointing at the Chinamen.

Watson looked at her and surveyed the room before asking "Arrest those men? Now why would I want to do that and who are you to give me such an order?"

"I am Wen Mei Li of the China State Security Bureau, and those men are wanted for their criminal activities."

"I assume criminal activities in China, madam?"

"Of course! Where else would I have an interest? And I am not a madam." One of the uniformed officers snickered.

"Well miss, without a crime in Canada or a formal extradition request from China, neither you or I have any reason or authority to arrest them."

Suddenly Wang interrupted Watson. "Officer, this woman was carrying an illegal firearm with which she threatened me and my associates. She should be arrested," and he handed the pistol over to Watson.

"Well, Miss? Can you explain this?"

"Of course! It is part of my equipment as a State Security Officer," Wen explained.

"Well, Miss, that may be so in China, but not here. We will discuss this at the station."

"You don't have the authority!"

"I do. And I have authority to question Doctor Holroyd."

"About what?"

"The murder of Mr. O'Mallory."

"I gave you a statement at the time. So why this demand?" Holroyd asked plaintively.

"Yes, you did, sir. But there are further questions. Doctor Holroyd, please come with me to the police station."

Holroyd noticed that Wang had suddenly become very attentive and understood. Wang had suddenly changed his mind, and now intended to intensify his search with Holroyd as the focus. *I've somehow got to stop him getting to me again.*

"Come along, sir," Watson ordered. Holroyd moved forward.

"Do you need us to come with you?" Wang asked.

"No, sir. But before you go, please leave us with the details where we can get in touch with you if necessary."

Wang nodded and handed a business card to one of the uniformed officers.

"You're letting them get away. You must stop them," Wen Mei Li protested with barely concealed anger.

"As I said, Miss, I need the authority to do anything about them. But if I might suggest you contact your people and have them send us an official request to arrest them, I'm sure we will be only too happy to consider it. Please come along now and explain why you are carrying a firearm illegally."

Holroyd leant over and whispered to her.

"I can explain when we are done with the police."

Wen looked at him obviously surprised and then said "Yes, I think that is what I must do."

39.

Holroyd was taken to an interview room in the police station. As he sat waiting for the interview to start, he remembered a previous interview room in a provincial police station in China. There, the arrested person was treated as a criminal and the walls of the interview room showed brown stains that might have been blood. Here the initial presumption cf guilt seemed to be absent. This room was clean, well lit, even airy and the walls were painted a light green.

"Well, Doctor Holroyd. You have been a busy man since your arrival in Canada. Not what I would have expected from a man of your stature." Inspector Watson and a constable entered the room.

"Thank you, but perhaps you could tell me why I am here?"

"We'd like you to help clarify some unexplained facts about the death of Mr. O'Mallory."

"I gave a full statement about that."

"Yes, you did. But since then, we have discovered your fingerprints in many places where, given your earlier statement, they should not be found. So naturally, we want to know why there is that discrepancy and what other discrepancies we might come across."

"You mean my fingerprints were found in the room where I was asked to wait?" Holroyd feigned innocence "I would have thought that's perfectly logical."

"Yes, sir. But you seem to have been busy touching so many items there that I begin to think you were looking for something. Perhaps you found it, so I'd like you to tell me what you found."

"I wasn't looking for anything and so found nothing."

"Yes sir, which does sound reasonable were it not for that secret drawer in the box on which a statue of a young man wearing only a hat with wings was standing. Looks like something was removed from the drawer and I think you could tell me what it was."

"Oh that! Yes, I was admiring the statue and happened to touch some carving on the box that released the hidden drawer. Inside there were only flakes of something looked like brown dried leaves." Holroyd tried to dismiss the incident.

"Exactly! Only the flakes weren't dried leaves, they were of leather... 300-year-old leather to be precise."

"You don't say! That's amazing!" Holroyd tried to sound surprised.

"And you know nothing of that?"

"Absolutely not!" Holroyd answered forcibly.

"Then perhaps you would be good enough to explain why you asked one of your colleagues to translate what appear to be pages from a 300-year-old diary or notebook?" Watson looked at Holroyd.

"I asked her to translate because my Spanish is nonexistent."

"Yes, sir. I understand that, but how did you get access to this notebook and where is it now?" He paused. "You see, I just find it too circumstantial that you are present when the O'Mallory collection get robbed, you are present when O'Mallory is murdered, and finally just after the murder you have access to a 300-year-old document that might have been kept in a secret drawer that you touched in the O'Mallory house."

"Let me correct you. Yes, I was present at the robbery, but no I was not present at the murder."

"But traces of O'Mallory's blood were found on your clothes."

"Yes, I tried to save him as he lay there bleeding."

"Yes sir, but what of this drawer?"

"As I explained I have no idea as to the contents. Finally, the document I asked Professor Sanchez to translate has nothing to do with O'Mallory, but concerns a project I am working on."

"Could you give us the details of this project?"

"I am looking for proof that my theory was right that the Chinese were the first foreigners to come here." Holroyd realized the answer sounded weak.

"I see." Watson looked at Holroyd in a manner that let Holroyd know his answer was unsatisfactory. "However, we're holding you on suspicion of the murder of Mr. O'Mallory."

"What? That's outrageous. Why would I want to do that?"

"Perhaps, not intentionally, but you roughed him up because you thought he had something you wanted, and he wouldn't give it to you. Unfortunately, you were too rough."

"That's completely wrong."

"Ok let's look at the time frame," Watson continued, "You get the call and go over there. You don't have a car so you either walked, cycled, or used public transport. Once arrived, you say you discovered the old man dying and call us. We know the times when O'Mallory called you and when you called us. The time between those calls is long enough for you murder Mr. O'Mallory and search if you came by public transport. We will question drivers who might have seen you getting on and off."

Holroyd said nothing.

"There's only your word that O'Mallory had been attacked when you called us. There was time between the call and the arrival of the patrol car for the attack to have taken place after the call."

"Oh, do stop! If that were even plausible, what if O'Mallory had been alive and able to accuse me even if the accusation was later in hospital?" Holroyd let his exasperation overcome his worries. Watson made no comment but continued.

"As to motive we have one possibility...you wanted whatever was in that drawer."

"That's the most asinine scenario I have heard," Holroyd said hoping his worry did not show.

"Is it? You are under investigation for the theft from the O'Mallory exhibition and about your involvement in the murder up at the reservation. You seem to be a common element in events that we had thought were unrelated. We will have to rethink our positions on that. Meanwhile, we will detain you here while we continue our investigations."

"Am I under arrest?"

"Not yet."

***

Watson went over to the Crown Attorney's office to discuss what the police had discovered. The Crown Attorney listened attentively.

"From what I'm hearing, you might have a possible motive in that Holroyd wanted to get some evidence to support his theory. I can't quite see that would be enough to commit a murder. And again, it would be illogical to murder O'Mallory if Holroyd thought O'Mallory knew about the treasure and its location. Add to that, you don't have Holroyd's prints on the murder weapon. I remain unconvinced the case would stand up in court."

Holroyd was released, but in the minds of the police he remained the prime suspect.

40.

Alvarez entered Tomlinson's office. "I was looking again over the report from the constable who stopped Hummersdorf's car. He followed someone driving a car that struck the cruiser at that time. I thought it possible that driver might have been involved in the murder in some way."

"I'm not sure the time frame fits. We know Elisa was texted just about the time the car struck the cruiser following which the constable gave chase. To me that suggests the driver left the scene before Elisa was killed. Did the constable catch him?" Tomlinson asked.

"No. The constable was stopped when a tree was blown over the road between the cars. Luckily, the license plate was recorded on the cruiser's dash cam."

"Go on."

"It was a rental car rented out to a Li Feng, Chinese national with a valid international driver's license." Alvarez paused.

"Chinese national? What do we know about him?"

"Immigration told me he is a consultant out of Hong Kong."

"How does he figure in all this?"

"I don't know, perhaps an innocent trip."

"Ok, I could buy that! But what would be of interest in that neck of the woods for a Chinese national?" Tomlinson wondered.

"Maybe he was there at the wrong time, but I agree that doesn't answer why." Alvarez paused. "One more thing. The local police just let me know they saw two Chinamen, and a Chinese woman at Holroyd's apartment." He gave a summary of what he had been told about what had happened there. He also reported that the police considered Holroyd to be the prime suspect in the O'Mallory case.

"What is this? A Chinaman was near Elisa's murder scene, and then some others were at Holroyd's apartment. Unless there's a convention of Chinese people going on here, I'd guess they were the same people." Tomlinson paused before going on "Then, Holroyd was present when O'Mallory's museum was robbed by some Asian and Holroyd is now the focus of O'Mallory's murder. Does anyone have any suggestion how these events might possibly be linked?"

"Not that I can think of. Perhaps the Chinamen can fill in some of the details."

"Right. Put out an alert for this Li Feng."

"On what grounds?"

"Possible suspect in a murder inquiry will do for a start."

"Is he a suspect?"

"Not yet, but he may be a witness to what happened on the reservation."

***

The RCMP at the Vancouver airport approached the departure gate for Cathay Pacific airlines flight to Hong Kong. People were standing in orderly queues according to their boarding priority, but the first-class passengers had their own

294

gate and were already boarding. The officers consulted with the desk agents and were informed that passenger Li had already boarded. Accordingly, they went down the ramp into the plane and were directed to Li's seat where he was sitting next to and engaged in conversation with a male passenger.

"Mr. Li?"

"Yes?" Li looked up with curiosity and then became wary as he recognised the uniforms.

"Come with us please. We'd like you to help us in an ongoing matter."

"But I'm about to fly back for an important business engagement."

"That will have to wait sir. We are detaining you in connection with a police inquiry."

"What inquiry?"

"The murder of an indigenous woman. Now come along, sir. We don't want to delay the other passengers."

"Officer, Mr. Li is engaged by me and cannot afford to miss this flight," the passenger sitting next to Li interrupted.

"I'm sorry sir. Please stay out of this." The officer looked at the passenger and turned back to Li. "Kindly do not resist. This way please." Li stood up slowly.

"You do not have the authority to take this man away," the passenger said forcefully and pulled Li back into his seat.

"Sir! You are interfering in this police matter. Kindly stay out of it."

"You do not have the authority! This is not a Canadian airline."

"But it is on Canadian soil. If you do not step aside, we will have to detain you as well."

"You would not dare!" he stood up as if to lunge at the officers.

The second officer moved forward. "Right! What is your name?"

"I am Wang Lin Fei. I am a Chinese citizen going about my legal business."

"Well, Mr. Fei I am detaining you for obstructing the police in the performance of their duties."

Just then the captain of the plane came down the aisle to find out what was happening. The police officers explained, and a member of the cabin staff corroborated what had happened.

"You realise Captain, you will not be given clearance to depart while these men are on board," one of the RCMP officers said.

Faced with this reminder, the captain turned to the Chinamen.

"As captain of this aircraft, I am ordering you to leave with the police officers."

By the time all passengers were boarded the police had escorted Li and Wang off the plane and held under investigative detention. The plane then departed on schedule.

Tomlinson called to advise he would come over to conduct an interview after which an arrest might follow.

***

Wang looked across the table at the police officers. He looked at ease as if he believed or knew he was in no danger. He scrutinised each officer carefully as if sizing up who might be the weakest link before launching his offensive.

"Why am I here? I am a Chinese citizen of Hong Kong, and you have no reason to detain me." He paused and again looked at each one in turn. "I have met Inspector Watson, but who are you?"

"I am Inspector Tomlinson of the RCMP, and we have detained you primarily because you obstructed a police officer in the execution of his duty. Let's start by asking why you decided to get involved."

"As I told the officers at the time, I did not believe they had the authority to detain us. Because we were on a Hong Kong carrier, I believed we were on Chinese territory and therefore your police had no authority to stop us leaving."

"But you were also highly protective of your companion, Mr. Li. Why was that?"

"I have engaged him as a consultant."

"A consultant to what?"

"I am interested in setting up business here, and he has been assisting me."

"And that is the only relationship between you?"

"Yes."

"Then perhaps you would explain what you were doing at Professor Holroyd's apartment?" Watson intervened.

"Professor Holroyd has information that would be useful in my business."

"And just what information did you think Professor Holroyd might have that would be useful?"

"I hardly think that could be of concern to you. It's a confidential business matter."

"Whether or not it's of concern to us is for us to decide."

"I assure you it not a criminal matter."

"But Mr. Wang, how can we rely on your assurance?" asked Tomlinson.

"Why would you not?"

"Because when I arrived, the woman Wen Mei Li asked me to arrest you," Watson broke in. "Why would she want that?"

"You will have to ask her. I suspect she has me confused with someone else. As I said I am only a businessman."

"And what is the nature of this business?"

"I am an investor, and I am considering investing here in Canada."

"Investing in what, sir?"

"I have not yet decided."

"I would like a list of the people with whom you have been in contact to set up business."

"I hardly think that is a matter for you to know. It's all legitimate."

"I'm sure it is, sir. However, I'd appreciate if you would give that list."

"I'll discuss it with my lawyers first."

"You are of course entitled to do so, sir."

"Do any of your business contacts include First Nation members?" Tomlinson shifted his line of questioning.

"No."

"Then why would Mr. Li Feng drive to a neighbouring reservation?"

"I cannot answer why Li Feng would go to a reservation."

"Perhaps he went there at your instruction?" Tomlinson persisted.

"Not any of my instructions. As I said, I cannot answer for all his activities."

"I see. Perhaps Mr. Li will be more helpful when we ask him."

"Perhaps. You will have to wait and see what he says. In the meantime, I will consult my lawyers."

***

Tomlinson and Alvarez sat down opposite Li Feng. He too, seemed at ease as if confident there was no case against him. Tomlinson opened the questioning.

"We want to know why you were driving to a reservation near here." Li Feng started in surprise as if he had not expected this opening of the questioning.

"What reservation? What is that?" Li assumed an air of ignorance.

"It is lands that belong to First Nations," Tomlinson explained.

"Oh! I have and have had no dealings with any First Nations. I am a Hong Kong consultant currently engaged by Wang Lin Fei. It follows that I have no reason to go to a reservation."

"That's not quite true, is it?"

"Are you saying I am lying?" Li decided to take the offensive.

"Let's just say the facts do not support your denial."

"What facts?" Li paused.

"The car rented by you was reported at the reservation and someone, probably yourself, phoned Asia from that location and at that time."

"You are mistaken."

"That may prove to be the case, sir, but if you did not go there, where were you?"

"In my hotel room watching a television program."

"Which hotel was that, sir?" Li gave the name and Alvarez went out to verify the claim. He returned and nodded at Tomlinson.

"The clerk at the reception desk confirms the registration but also said he saw Mr. Li leave at about 7.30 and not return until about 11.30 on the night in question."

"Well. Mr. Li?"

"He is obviously mistaken."

"I think not, sir."

"Which program were you watching?" Tomlinson resumed his line of questioning.

"I can't remember its name. It was boring anyway, and I dozed off halfway through."

"If you can't remember the name, what was it about?"

"I can't remember."

"I find that believable only if you never watched it."

"Why is this of such concern to you?"

"An indigenous woman was murdered at the time you were recorded as being there."

"Are you suggesting that I murdered this woman?" Li Feng asked nervously.

"We haven't got to that stage, sir. At least, not yet."

"Then what are you suggesting?" Li asked.

"That you were at the scene at the time when the murder took place. We think you witnessed it or maybe saw the victim before she died or came across the body after she died."

"But, as I said, I was not there," Li maintained.

"If you were not there, is it possible that an associate of yours was there?"

"I cannot answer for what any of my associates might have done that night."

"Give us the names of these associates so we can ask them where they were that night."

"Regrettably, who my associates are is a confidential business matter. I would want legal advice before I give you their names."

"You are, of course, entitled to get advice. But while you do, we know of one associate, Professor Holroyd with whom you met at his apartment. What is his role?" Watson observed.

"As I said, that is a commercial matter."

"Perhaps you lent him the car you rented, and he drove to the reservation. That is not commercially sensitive."

"As I said, I was in my hotel room, so I don't know about anyone driving my car."

"Well, sir, that does present a problem because if r one of your associates were at the scene, you must have been." Tomlinson paused. "Even though you maintain you were not." He paused again. "Would you care to reconsider where you were that night?"

"I have no reason to think I need to."

"I understand that, sir. However, we think differently and as long as we do, we will have to keep you here."

"That's outrageous," Li assumed an air of injured innocence.

"Perhaps it is, sir. But it is fact."

Li sat silently as if considering his options. Finally, he said "If I were to reconsider my position, how would that help you?"

"We are trying to establish who committed the murder, so any information about what happened at the scene could be helpful."

Li sat silent.

"It is possible that an associate passed that way," he said grudgingly, but then stopped. "If he did, it is possible he may have seen something."

"And was Professor Holroyd that associate?"

"No."

"Then who?"

Li did not answer.

"Let's not pussyfoot here. If you won't give us the name, we are still left with you as the driver. You're telling us your associate saw the murder! In your own words, then, what exactly did this associate see?"

"My associate told me he saw a man and a woman arguing about something. When the woman turned away, the man attacked her from behind and strangled her with a wire."

"And your associate did nothing?" Tomlinson asked.

"He was too far away. By the time he got to her, the attacker had gone, and she was dead."

"If he was so far away, how did he know she was strangled with a wire?" Tomlinson asked.

"That was discovered when he inspected the body to see if she was still alive."

"And did he then bury the body?"

"I assume he did."

"Why would he do that?"

"Obviously to avoid its discovery!" Li Feng implied he was surprised at the stupidity of the question.

"But what interest did he have in hiding the body?"

"You should ask him that."

"And where would we find this associate?" Li Feng remained silent.

"Please don't take us for fools and tell us he has left the country."

Li Feng shrugged his shoulders.

"Perhaps that is not the right question," Watson interjected. "I think the real question is why was his associate in that place."

Li Feng remained silent.

"I can't believe he had any interest in the woman which makes me think he had an interest in the place. Given what has been discovered there, I think he was there because he or someone believed a treasure was buried there or near there." Watson looked at Li.

Li leant forward. "As I said, I was not there so I cannot answer your question."

"That is fortunate because if the reason for being there is you or someone associated with you believed a treasure was buried there it ties you into the hunt for the treasure and thus possibly into the murder of Mr. O'Mallory."

"Who?"

"Mr. Li do not continue to pretend you are ignorant of O'Mallory. When you and Wang Lin Fei arrived at Holroyd's apartment you as much as admitted you knew about him."

"I don't recall ever mentioning the gentleman's name."

"Perhaps not, but your employer did."

"You will have to ask him then," Li said with a note of defiance.

"Well, doubtlessly you will find an explanation, if not now then later."

"Are you detaining me?"

"Oh! Yes! We can hold you for further investigation."

41.

Alvarez entered Tomlinson's office. "Forensics just sent over the results of their examination of Hummersdorf's car. They found a phone and it's Elisa's. They recovered her finger-prints on it and the messages between her and Hummersdorf. There's one from Hummersdorf setting up a meeting."

"Any other prints on the phone?"

"No."

"What about in the car?" Tomlinson asked.

"Most are from one person, probably Hummersdorf's and we'll follow up on that. But they also found a partial print inside the glove compartment. It's a match with prints we got from Elisa's residential school."

"That ties the abuser to Hummersdorf! What's the con-nection? That needs to be followed up." Tomlinson thought for a moment. "If that print was made the night when Elisa was killed, the residential school abuser is possibly the murderer. If that's correct, the question is if the murder was committed with Hummersdorf's knowledge." He went on. "Get back to Hummersdorf to verify his claim that only he drives that car. If anyone else used it find out who. Meanwhile, intensify the search for the abuser." He paused. "Given only Elisa's prints are on the phone, our suspect probably wore gloves when he left it in Hummersdorf's car." Tomlinson thought for a moment. "I can understand retrieving it from the body, but why keep it?"

"Maybe to frame Hummersdorf, or since Hummers-dorf's second phone is missing, perhaps he disposed of the wrong phone thinking it was hers." Alvarez suggested.

"So, who drove the car?" asked Tomlinson. "During the search of Hummersdorf's place, did we find any clothing that the driver could have worn that night?"

Alvarez checked the file. "They found rain gear including a set of gum boots in the car, but I don't see that they matched sizes or soil samples."

"Ok. Follow that up and see if there were any gloves that might have evidence they were used for the strangulation." Alvarez nodded.

"How tall is Hummersdorf?" asked Tomlinson.

"I'd say 5 feet 4 inches."

"And a 4x4 is about 5 feet 2 inches in height. So, at best, the old lady would have seen about two inches above the car. Maybe enough to identify the hoodie, but that's about all. I think we're at a dead end here. But maybe Elisa's files detailing her search for the abuser has some further information. How near are the IT boys to opening the files on her computer?"

"Haven't heard but I'll give them a call," Alvarez promised.

***

Li Feng tried to look confident as he faced the officers across the table. The fact that he was outnumbered two to one did not seem to disturb him.

"Why are you keeping me here? I have done nothing wrong, and I wish to return home," he demanded aggressively.

"You know, I think it would be in your best interests to cooperate with us," Tomlinson remarked.

"But why would I do that? I haven't committed any crimes here," Li protested.

"You failed to report a crime."

"What crime? The murder of the indigenous woman? I was not there and so can hardly report what I don't know about. Anyway, failure to report a crime even if I knew about it, is not an offense in Canada," Li Feng pointed out. "So, unless you wish to charge me with a crime, I would appreciate leaving so that I can return home."

Tomlinson looked at him impassively.

"I would not be too eager to return to China. I am informed they have a warm welcome arranged for you, even if you do not wish to discover that for yourself. And should we receive a request for extradition, we would of course have to consider it."

Li Feng suddenly shifted nervously. "You have no reason for that!" he protested. "I was engaged only to help recover Mr. Wang's property."

"Maybe so, but by the time you land there, be assured their reasons will be very valid."

"They have nothing on me," Li protested.

"Perhaps not, but I am told they will have established your links to known drug dealers, then by the time you arrive home, and any denials you may wish to make will sound rather hollow."

"But that's completely untrue," Li turned pale, and he stopped. "You have to help me."

"Then perhaps you will assist us in our investigations?" Watson asked.

"If I would even consider cooperating, what information do you think I have that would help you?"

"Perhaps none but let's just say we could take your cooperation into consideration."

"Consideration of what?"

"We'll let you know."

Li Feng sat silent. Then, "Very well. I will do my best. You understand, however, there are some things that must remain confidential between me and my client, but other than that, what do you want to know?"

"What was the nature of your engagement with Wang Lin Fei?"

"I was engaged to help recover some property belonging to the Wang Family."

"Explain that to us, please."

"I'm sorry but that would be a break of confidentiality. You will have to ask Mr. Wang."

"I see. Then let's turn to another question of interest. How did you, or your associate come to be at the site where the indigenous woman was found murdered?"

"Our presence at the murder scene was purely by chance."

"I find that hard to believe. Do you have anything to add to that?"

"No."

"Then let us go to the murder of O'Mallory."

"I really can't help you there at all. I admit we had intended to visit him, but we never got to that stage."

"Then how is it we found your fingerprints there?" Watson asked.

"That's impossible," Li protested.

"Facts don't lie," Watson observed. There was silence, but Li had become nervous. Watson nodded and gathered up his notes.

"Very well, Mr. Li. We will have to confirm some details and will detain you while we do that. We will let you know." The officers left the room.

"Did anyone check if Li's fingerprints were on the murder weapon?" Tomlinson asked.

"Yes, we did. His aren't and neither are Holroyd's."

"What about elsewhere in the room?"

"Holroyd's were found, but not Li's."

"So, what were you doing when you claimed Li's prints were there?"

"I was trying to rattle him," Watson admitted awkwardly.

"Now that won't sit well with the magistrate if it comes out in court," Tomlinson looked sternly at the inspector.

"I agree, it's not what I've been told is a career enhanc-
ing move," Watson admitted sheepishly.

42.

"Watson," the Inspector answered the call.

"Good morning, Inspector. I am Wen Mei Li. We met briefly at Professor Holroyd's apartment."

"Yes, I remember. What can I do for you?"

"I want to set an appointment for my report on why I carried a firearm. Also, I have asked my office to issue an Extradition request for the criminals Wang Lin Fei and Li Feng, but until the request is received, I thought that an informal meeting between us to exchange information might be useful."

"Please go on."

"I am aware, of course, of your ongoing investigations and am concerned that when the extradition request is delivered there could be confusion as to which takes precedence. Naturally, such confusion will be resolved in time, but I think we would both appreciate if the criminals do not escape in the meanwhile."

"Well, Miss Wen, I understand your concern, but I can reassure you that we will try to make sure that does not happen."

"Inspector, both you and I know that even with the best intentions such an assurance is at best an expression of hope. Let me suggest that we would take your agreement to a meeting as a sign of your cooperation in bringing international criminals to justice."

Watson did not reply immediately. "Miss Wen, thank you for bringing the matter to my attention. However, we are not the only jurisdiction involved. I will have to consult with my superiors and my opposite number in the RCMP."

"Of course."

When the meeting took place and introductions completed, each officer summarised the ongoing investigations. Tomlinson remarked on Holroyd's presence at the various events. "Seems Holroyd gets around more than I would expect from an academic."

"Has he always been around when there's a mess? Perhaps he's the one causing all this. He may be innocent when it comes to Elisa's murder but his role in the O'Mallory murder is less clear," Watson noted.

Tomlinson nodded and then added "We're stretched to our limits by the demands of our on-going investigations. My own view is that somehow all these events are linked but I have nothing but my view to support that."

"Have you considered the Chinese criminals could supply the missing pieces of the puzzle?" asked Wen Mei Li.

"We know they are involved somehow if only because of your meeting at Holroyd's apartment, but that's not really enough to go on."

"What you may not know, Mr. Tomlinson, is, that Wang Lin Fei approached Holroyd to undertake a search for the treasure everyone thinks is buried on the reservation. Wang informed us the property in question was Koxinga's treasure."

"Whose?"

"Koxinga." She explained the history behind the treasure.

"How would Wang have any claim to it?"

"He claims to be the descendant of the original possessor."

"Is he?"

"It's possible and we're checking into that."

"Does Holroyd have any interest in this gold?" asked Watson.

"Only in as much as it may support his theories on who visited this coast first. However, I think he has a good idea where it might have been hidden," observed Wen Mei Li.

"Just a moment please." Alvarez got up and left the room. When he returned, he handed a couple of photographs to Wen. "Would that treasure have included gold ingots, like this?" He asked.

"Most certainly."

"Ok that settles it. Someone found the treasure and put this one item up for sale. It looks like that professor, van Vervoort was right."

"I wouldn't be too sure. Other than van Vervoort's claim nothing suggests the treasure was hidden where van Vervoort found the crucifix. Holroyd certainly does not believe that."

"Could Holroyd have found something at O'Mallory's that identified the location?" asked Watson and explained about the hidden drawer.

"If Holroyd thought that O'Mallory knew where the treasure was hidden, it would give Holroyd adequate motive for the murder."

"Yes, it would," Wen Me Li interrupted. "But I know Holroyd and his background, and I don't think he would go that far. But Wang Lin Fei would."

"Why would he know anything useful?" Tomlinson asked.

"Because of what he revealed in Holroyd's apartment." And she gave a brief report on the encounter.

"Sounds promising, but how would we go about proving Wang's guilt?"

"You might not have to. Remember Wang and Li are wanted in China for crimes for which they most certainly will be executed. If they confessed to the O'Mallory murder they would be imprisoned here, but given the Canadian justice system, probably released after a few years. Given a choice, they might be persuaded to cooperate."

"What form would this cooperation have to take?"

"Besides confessing to the murder, I would want to know about their activities in the drug trade, and of course anything about their other business dealings," Wen Mei Li answered before continuing "I could say the extradition might be delayed while Beijing prepares the necessary paperwork. Such a delay might prove long enough for you to get an approval for an arrest because of your investigations. Any extradition would have to wend its way through the cumbersome Canadian legal system in competition with your accusations."

"Are you officially suggesting that?"

"Officially suggesting what? I am a member the China State Security here to pursue the extradition of these two criminals. I would not suggest anything else."

"And I don't think anyone here heard differently." Tomlinson looked around to see if there was any disagreement.

"It sounds to me as if we are saying other than finding O'Mallory, Holroyd has no involvement in the murders," Tomlinson ventured.

"I'm not convinced yet," replied Watson.

43

"The IT boys gave me an update on retrieving Elisa's files from her laptop. Seems she wrote her notes in what one of the guy's thinks is Dogrib. We have a problem because we don't have anyone here who can translate for us. However, there are some entries that look like they could be acronyms for names." Alvarez entered Tomlinson's office.

"Explain."

"There are a number of upper-case letters," Alvarez looked at the file. "For example, there's a couple of A's, an H, and a V. That H can't refer to Holroyd because he wasn't in the country, but it might refer to Hummersdorf and the V might just apply to van Vervoort."

"Those are big mights," Tomlinson observed and sat back.

"Hummersdorf and van Vervoort are pretty close, aren't they?" Alvarez asked.

"Seems like it," Tomlinson remarked. "So, it's just possible that van Vervoort could have access to Hummersdorf's car and used it without Hummersdorf or Manning knowing about it."

"Yes, and if I remember, van Vervoort is taller than Hummersdorf and could fit the old lady's description of who she saw returning that night."

"Given we don't yet know exactly what's in those files we had better wait before we start questioning van Vervoort. Meanwhile, let's see what else there is on file about the good professor." Alvarez nodded his understanding and quickly returned with an open file.

"There's nothing much on van Vervoort." He leafed through the file. "Currently holds a position here at the university and is living on campus with a young female about whom nothing is on file. He was married, but later divorced. Apparently, that was quite messy. His son, Mark aged 22, got hauled in on a drugs charge and several charges for being drunk and disorderly."

"Nothing to suggest that he was ever on a reservation in some capacity?"

"Who, the father or the son?"

"Either."

"No. Nothing on file about that."

"Then, perhaps the reference in Elisa's file doesn't refer to them."

"Possibly. But a reference to a 'V' is hardly common."

"Ok! So, van Vervoort senior is not in the clear yet. We keep him in sight. Also, check to see how many V's are registered in the area, and then see if any of those profiles might fit our professor."

44.

Holroyd answered the phone.

"Eddy here. You asked me to find out what I could about that old Chief."

"What did you find?" Holroyd asked with anticipation.

"It seems, that he sold some war trophies to an English trader and kept the proceeds of the sale for himself. The Band wasn't happy, and he got replaced."

"Is there a description of what was recovered?" Holroyd asked hopefully.

"No."

Holroyd thanked him.

"Can you tell me what this is about?" asked Eddy.

"I'm almost there, Alan. I promise you once I'm sure, I'll brief you fully." And with that the conversation ended. Holroyd sat back and thought. *So, the document was sold to an O'Mallory ancestor. I might as well start that article for Harry.* He sat thinking what exactly to write when the phone rang again.

"Peter, Harry here! It looks as if you were right." Holroyd had expected a call from the Editor of the Journal to remind him that a rebuttal article was expected, but as the article had not yet been written this admission came as a surprise.

"Oh? What made you give me that call?"

"I got a letter from the Spanish Embassy asking about van Vervoort's article."

"Don't tell me the Embassy agreed with van Vervoort's tripe."

"Not at all. Quite the contrary in fact."

"Do tell!" Holroyd sat back wondering what he was about to hear.

"You will remember the article had a photograph of the crucifix. Well, it turns out that crucifix has been identified as possibly one that was given by a 16th Century Pope to the de Perrefalta family."

"Who?"

"The de Perrefalta family. They were and still are grandees of Spain."

"Go on."

"If, as they suspect, the crucifix is the one that belongs to the family, they want it returned. They claim the family archives contain a drawing of a crucifix that looks very much like the one in van Vervoort's article. The report notes that the crucifix was handed down from generation to generation and was last given to Don Luis de Perrefalta, a *Capitan* in the Tercio de Albuquerque in the 17th Century. He then went on to become the Captain of the Spanish Garrison in Manila, but vanished while returning to Spain."

Holroyd experienced a rush of emotion.

"He didn't vanish. I think I know exactly where he is."

"Where?"

"In a box among the museum items stored at the university," Holroyd let his satisfaction escape down the line.

"Would you care to explain that?" Harry asked and Holroyd explained how a Captain of the Manila Garrison was mentioned in the document retrieved from O'Mallory. "Because the crucifix was found with the skeleton, I conclude the skeleton was that of Don Luis and I think a DNA comparison of the bones we found with the descendants might lead to a positive identification."

"Sounds good. I'm sure the family will be pleased and probably request the bones be returned to Spain for proper burial. I'll let the Embassy know."

"You might also ask van Vervoort what he's done with the crucifix and the gemstone. I'm sure the family would be happy to have them returned as well."

***

A heavily embossed letter with the de Perrefalta coat of arms was hand delivered to Holroyd thanking him for his services and inviting him to the formal interment of Don Luis' bones to be held in Spain. Holroyd put it aside pending discussions with Pearl. In the meanwhile, he watched the TV coverage as a charter jet landed, and a somberly clad delegation including a cardinal descended. They were received by a welcoming committee that included local, provincial, and even federal dignitaries. A few words were said by both sides before Spanish hidalgos carried the coffin covered by a banner ornately woven with the de Perrefalta family coat of arms to the plane. A Spanish guard of honour presented arms as it was ceremoniously loaded on board and the jet took off.

Pleased with what he had watched, Holroyd went back to his computer to complete his article. Satisfied that there were no changes to be made, he loaded the submission and sent it off. The response came back within hours.

"Peter, that's great! I'm taking a bit of a risk here, by not sending it out for formal review before putting it on our website. But I will add a caveat that it is for information and discussion pending peer review. It'll go out for review before formal publication in the next issue of the journal."

"That's rather unusual, isn't it?"

"Oh! Very much so!" Harry's laughter floated down the line. "But then the whole matter is unusual. I decided to follow this route because of the situation van Vervoort's claims have caused and so a rebuttal might help calm things. Who knows what could happen if his claims remain undisputed for long?"

"That's putting you and maybe the journal out on a limb. I mean, it's not just recording an academic dispute, but it could influence events directly."

"Oh! I quite agree. But then the usual publication process that can take months aims to influence thinking and thus events. I think his situation warrants reducing the time interval between submitting and publishing."

"Thanks, Harry. I just hope you won't be hauled over the coals for your decision."

"I hope so, too. But that's a risk I'm prepared to take with you." He hung up.

Holroyd disconnected the call, smiled, and even allowed himself to feel a bit smug.

Hummersdorf looked up from his desk and listened to the noise outside his door. Just as he was about to inquire, the door slammed open and a furious van Vervoort stormed in.

"Paul! What on earth is this about?"

"Have you seen what that fraud has published?"

"To which fraud are you referring to this time?" Hummersdorf feigned ignorance.

"Oh, don't be stupid, you know very well to whom I'm referring."

"You mean Holroyd's article? Yes, I have. It's very good."

"It's completely false and is obviously designed to smear my reputation," van Vervoort raised his voice in indication.

"Yes, I can see how you might think that." Hummersdorf remained outwardly calm but was fearful where van Vervoort might be going.

"Get him to withdraw it and then fire him."

"I don't think that's wise, Paul."

"What do you mean?" van Vervoort suddenly became cautious.

"There's too much corroborative evidence to claim the article is false. And if it's not false, then there's no cause to fire Holroyd."

"But he destroyed my reputation," van Vervoort assumed a plaintive tone.

"I rather think you managed to do that yourself. In fact, given what happened at the reservation after your lecture and article, it's been suggested you might want to consider leaving here."

"You're going to have to stop that."

"Not this time, Paul. This time you're on your own."

van Vervoort looked at Hummersdorf with an expression that switched from pretended hurt to cunning. "I don't think so, Joe. Remember, you owe me."

"That debt has been repaid many times over. I don't think any accusation you might make now will stand up in court. And if not, I'm resigned to face the consequences."

"Oh, you might well be right about that. But that's not to what I'm referring. I doubt this little nugget of information can so easily be swept under the rug," van Vervoort smirked convinced he still had the upper hand.

"I have no idea to what you're talking about."

"And I don't think you'll be happy when you find out."

"Oh! By the way, the police called asking if I knew where you could be reached. Apparently, you failed to report the items you found at the site. They would like you to tell them why."

van Vervoort glared at Hummersdorf before slamming the door as he went out.

45.

Tomlinson and Alvarez came down the steps of the magistrates' court, just behind Wang and his lawyer.

"Well, that didn't go as planned," Alvarez observed.

"You've got to give the old lawyer his due. He made his case." Tomlinson replied. "That firm has been around for over 80 years and wouldn't have lasted that long if they lost too many cases in court. Our case was weak. Other than suspicions and a few debatable facts, we really had nothing to justify an arrest."

As they went over to their cruiser, Tomlinson mused. "Too bad the Chinese haven't sent the extradition papers over yet. I hope they get themselves in gear before he gets out of the country. That other fellow, Li, could have been more helpful, but he's still dithering about how far he'll cooperate without a deal."

Alvarez opened the cruiser's door but stopped when there was a crash just up the street, followed by the roar of a car and a screech of tyres. A car careened down the street to disappear around a corner before anyone reacted.

"What idiot is driving that car?" Tomlinson asked angrily.

"Look!" Alvarez pointed in the direction of the lawyer's car. A door on the passenger side was hanging drunkenly down to the road and a body could be seen lying underneath it. Tomlinson turned to look as Alvarez ran over to the scene.

"Ambulance, at the Magistrate's Court! Now!" Tomlinson barked into his phone and walked quickly to the scene of the accident.

Wang was lying face down and from the crushed body either dead or unlikely to survive much longer.

The lawyer came round and stood there trembling. "This is terrible," he whispered with an ashen face.

"Sir, we have to call the Victoria Police and let them handle it. Perhaps you'd care to wait in the building until they arrive?" Tomlinson grasped the lawyer gently by the arm to face the courthouse. The lawyer went up the steps and disappeared into the building.

"That was deliberate. I think someone wanted Wang dead, either because of the treasure, or maybe because of his activities in China. Put out a call for the car; it should be noticeable with quite some visible damage," Tomlinson instructed. "I think Mr. Li will prove more cooperative after this."

Wang was pronounced DOA, and the car was found abandoned with stolen plates and without any fingerprints.

***

"Mr. Li." Tomlinson opened the meeting. "Your employer, Mr. Wang, was just killed in a hit and run incident. I think it was deliberate." He paused and then went on, "If that be the case, I have to ask why."

"That is terrible. But why ask me?"

"Because you were his consultant."

Li sat silent.

"You see, if it was deliberate it has to be because of his activities either here or in China, and that means you could be the next target," Tomlinson continued.

"I've done nothing that would give anyone a reason to attack me. I am, or rather was, engaged for a specific purpose that has no criminal objectives."

"Anyone that has you in their sights might not understand that."

"Then they would be mistaken."

"You might not be around to explain that to them." Li said nothing.

"Are you arresting me?" he finally asked.

"We'll let you know." And the interview was over.

Outside the interview room, Tomlinson turned to Alvarez.

"If the extradition papers don't arrive today, time will run out and we're going to have to let him go. I don't think we'd get an arrest warrant based on what we have right now."

"Oh! Speaking of that. Watson called before we started the interview. The hotel clerk now says that he is only sure it was a Chinaman who left the hotel that night. As Li was the only Chinese registered guest there, he had assumed it was Li, but he won't swear to it."

"So, we have nothing definite to support a warrant," He sighed. "Let him go for now but keep a watch on him."

When the extradition papers were delivered, Li was nowhere to be found.

46.

"Inspector, we found a box of personal stuff belonging to that teacher at Brentwood who was let go," Alvarez reported to Tomlinson. "Forensics tell me there were prints that matched some from that investigation at Elisa's school." Alvarez came into the office.

"At last, a bit of good news," Tomlinson sat back. "Who is it?"

"The names differ, so he used an alias here. But you're not going to believe the one he went by at Elisa's school." He paused. "Mallory."

"Say that again?" Tomlinson sat up as if he had been stung. Alvarez grinned and repeated, "Mallory."

"Could be coincidental, but somehow, I don't think so."

"Put out an alert for him. We need to find him, if only to hear what he has to say, though it might not be helpful," Tomlinson said. "Hummersdorf was born out of wedlock, but I wonder if there are any other illegitimate children. I'm calling Watson to see if he has heard anything. I think we need to make another visit to that son in Vancouver."

Inspector Watson suggested they should go over together to interview Simon.

47.

On arrival in Simon O'Mallory's office, Tomlinson and Watson were immediately ushered in.

"How can I help you this time?" Simon asked somewhat brusquely.

"I'm investigating the murder of an indigenous woman on the nearby reservation," Tomlinson answered.

"Oh? That's rather out of my field of activity, so how do you think can I help?" O'Mallory asked somewhat impatiently.

"Is there any link between your family and indigenous women?"

"I doubt that very much indeed. Other than my father who dealt with First Nations as part of his philanthropic works, none of us had any dealings with them. I doubt any dealings he had would lead to the murder of a woman on a reservation." Simon spoke dismissively.

"We came across the name Mallory in the investigation," Tomlinson said.

"Mallory, not O'Mallory? Then, I don't see what connection there could be."

"Even if the names don't match exactly, we think there may be a connection, sir."

"I see. May I know in what context?" Simon asked.

"Is there a member of the family that is, or has at one time been a teacher?" Tomlinson asked.

"There's Joe Hummersdorf. But you know about him."

"Yes, sir, we do. Is there anyone else in the family who would fit that description?"

"Yes, there is Lucas," Simon said reluctantly.

"Who is he?" asked Watson.

"Another illegitimate son of my father."

"Why did you not tell me that when I first visited you?" Watson frowned.

"I did not think it would be relevant."

"That was not for you to decide, sir! What can you tell us about him?"

"Lucas was taken away by his mother after she and my father quarrelled. My father never discussed the matter, and we didn't hear from her or from him."

"And you have not had any contact with him?"

"Not really."

"That doesn't quite answer my question."

O'Mallory sat silent before reaching into a drawer and placing a shoebox on the desk.

"He arrived at my office and asked me to help him with this." He pushed over to Watson who opened it and retrieved a cloth wrapped *yuanbao.*

"Hold on. Please don't touch that again without gloves, or at least a tissue. I will need to check that for fingerprints,"

Tomlinson quickly intervened. O'Mallory and Watson looked at him.

"We have an ongoing investigation into the sudden appearance of what looks like an identical ingot," he explained. "If this is identical, I believe we might be able to solve at least one murder and perhaps both. Would I be correct in assuming your half-brother wanted you to sell this item for him?"

"Yes. He said he was desperate for money."

"Did you ask him where he obtained it?"

"Yes, of course. He said my father gave it to him."

"And you accepted his explanation?"

"Oh, yes! I didn't follow what contacts he and my father had but it would not have been too unusual if they stayed in contact. If they did, I would expect Lucas to ask for help from time to time. I think my father would have given him one of these if asked. I don't know what reasons Lucas would have given to persuade the old man other than needing money. Nor do I know what Lucas would have done with it once he got it."

"Did you or your sister, or Hummersdorf receive ingots from time to time?"

"Oh! Yes!"

"Did you ever ask where your father got them from?"

"I did once when I saw an ingot like that in my father's study. He told me it was part of the family's fortune that he had inherited from my grandfather. I know he would put one on the market every so often."

"But you know the sale of bullion is hardly something you'd advertise on eBay."

"Of course, I know that. But it's not unusual in my line of work. I can assure you that such sales take place well within the law if licensed and trusted individuals conduct the transaction."

"And are you such an individual?"

"I'm not licensed for that, but I deal with people who are, and they accept my assurances when it comes to provenances."

"And do you act in that capacity with your family members?"

"Usually, yes."

"So, in this instance, you would provide such assurance," Tomlinson persisted.

"Normally, yes. But given my father's murder, I hesitated."

"And why would that be, sir?" asked Watson.

"I would think that's obvious, Inspector. Even I can wonder whether the murder and the almost simultaneous appearance of the ingot might be linked."

"But why did you not approach the police with your unease?"

"The disposition of ingots was not unusual in the family. The only difference was that this time was the first time Lucas asked me to put one up for sale."

"Surely, that would have alerted you enough for you to call the police?" Watson asked.

"Of course, and I fully intended to do so. However, I was immersed in a very important financial matter, so I never got around to doing so before you, Inspector, arrived."

"And you didn't think to mention it at the time?"

"It slipped my mind. As I said, I was focused on difficult financial negotiations. Anyway, you then asked me about the man who reported my father's death and I assumed from that there would be no need to involve Lucas."

"That was an unfortunate assumption, sir. A lot of police time could have been saved had you informed us of your half-brother's existence and his activities," Watson conveyed his disapproval and there was silence.

"Do you have an idea why he approached you this time?" Finally, Tomlinson asked.

"I can only assume he needed money more quickly than his other buyers would provide."

"Any idea who these other buyers might be?"

"No. And before you ask, I could hardly go around my contacts asking if my half-brother had offered ingots for sale. I assume he had his own contacts, but with whom I would not want to be associated."

"So, your half-brother arrived on the same day as your father was attacked?" Watson asked.

"Yes."

"That was quick."

"At the time, I didn't have a reason to question how he arrived, but he could have taken the seaplane," O'Mallory objected.

"Any idea where he might be?" Tomlinson asked.

"No, sorry."

"What about getting in touch with him?" Tomlinson persisted.

"No, but I think I might have a contact for his mother. I'll let you know."

"Thank you, sir. I suggest sooner would be much better than later. We'll be in touch." And with that the officers took their leave.

Outside the office, Tomlinson turned to Watson. "Check for fingerprints on the ingot and perhaps you might want to compare with those you found on the murder weapon. I'll send what we have over to you."

There was a complete match, and an arrest warrant was issued for Lucas O'Mallory. He was arrested and read his rights in a roadside diner while hitchhiking the Trans-Canada Highway East.

48.

"Lucas O'Mallory, we have arrested you on suspicion of the murder of your father," Watson began. "Is there anything you wish to say?"

"Go fuck yourselves," was the answer.

"That's not going to help you. However, you might want to explain why your prints were found on the murder weapon."

O'Mallory said nothing.

Watson looked down at his file, about to ask another question when Tomlinson entered and was introduced.

"What's he here for?" O'Mallory asked aggressively. "I've done nothing that would bring the Mounties into this."

"That's not quite true, is it?" asked Tomlinson mildly.

"What do you mean?"

"For starters, would you care to tell us how you came into the possession of the gold ingot you asked your half-brother to sell for you?"

"My father gave it to me."

"Willingly? Somehow, I doubt that."

"Prove it."

"That may take some time, but I think in the end we will," Tomlinson said sounding more confident than he really felt. "But let's change the subject."

"As you might expect, we found your prints on the ingot and on the weapon used to murder your father," O'Mallory shrugged.

"What you might not expect is that they matched some that were found at a Residential school at which abuses had been reported."

"So?"

"So, you taught at that Residential school."

"Nothing was ever proved, and I wasn't charged."

"True. But then you taught at a school near here and were accused of molesting students."

"Again, nothing proved, and I was not charged."

"True again. In both cases there was not enough evidence to make an arrest. But then." He paused dramatically. "Elisa turns up chasing an abuser at her school who is working here using an assumed name. She gets a message from someone claiming to have information, low, and behold! She ends up dead."

"So, what's that's got to do with me?"

"Perhaps nothing. But we found another fact we need to consider."

"What's that?"

"We found a partial fingerprint in the car. It matches yours."

"Do you really think, if I did commit either murder, I would leave prints somewhere? That's dumb! I'd have worn gloves."

"Oh! Yes! But you left a print."

"Bullshit!" O'Mallory became agitated.

"Then how come your prints are on the inside of the glove compartment?"

"Impossible, I wore gloves." The statement was greeted in total silence.

"You wore them?" Tomlinson asked softly. "Not you would have worn them?"

"Awwwww, fuck!" O'Mallory stopped, groaned, and slumped into his seat.

"Well?" asked Tomlinson.

"I want a lawyer."

***

The telephone rang. Tomlinson absent mindedly picked up the receiver "Yes."

"Inspector Tomlinson? Shaughnessy here. I've been engaged by Simon O'Mallory to represent Lucas O'Mallory. My client wants to bargain."

***

"Well, Lucas? Your lawyer tells us you want to bargain," Tomlinson opened the meeting.

"Yeah! I want a reduced charge and sentence."

"In return for what?"

"What do you want to know?"

"For a start, did you kill Elisa?"

"I'm advising my client not to answer that," Shaughnessy intervened.

"Then what is your client prepared to tell us?"

Shaughnessy turned to O'Mallory and nodded.

Lucas admitted that he had borrowed Hummersdorf's car, but without Hummersdorf's knowledge. He explained that he had entered Hummersdorf's home using a spare key hidden under a stone near the entrance, and had obtained the car keys by copying a set lying on a table inside the door.

"And did you arrange to see her?"

"Yes."

"Why?"

"I wanted to know what she had about me. I wanted to know if she thought I was the person she was looking for."

"Did you find out?"

"I'm advising my client not to answer that at this point as it could be taken as providing a motive for the murder." Shaughnessy leant forward. Tomlinson gave him a stony look, but went on with his questioning.

"Did you have wany wire with you?" Again, Shaughnessy leaned forward but Tomlinson forestalled Shaughnessy's intervention by quickly asking.

"How did you know she was looking for someone?" Tomlinson waited.

"I was told," O'Mallory admitted after a pause.

"Who told you?"

"Mark van Vervoort," O'Mallory answered in a sullen voice.

"Mark van Vervoort? Now, we know about him." Watson observed.

"And how did he know about that?" Tomlinson asked.

"He has some friends up there."

Tomlinson looked at O'Mallory in silence before asking.

"And are you the one she was looking for?"

Shaughnessy again intervened. "I'm advising my client not to answer that at this point, as it could be taken as providing a motive for the murder."

"I get the picture. But I must tell you there is a lot of evidence that points to your client's guilt and so far, I don't think he's been very helpful. I will tell you that he is now squarely in our sights as the murderer." Shaughnessy shrugged his shoulders.

"Let's go to the second murder," Tomlinson turned to Watson.

"Perhaps your client can be more open in that matter." Shaughnessy nodded.

"Well, Lucas. Did you kill your old man?"

"No."

"But your prints are on the murder weapon."

"I handled it, but I didn't use it."

"Are telling us you were there when someone else used it?"

"Yes."

"Who was that?" O'Mallory did not respond.

"C'mon, Lucas! You've just admitted you were there, and that you handled the murder weapon, so unless you have a name for the person who killed your father, you're on the hook for that murder as well." O'Mallory again said nothing.

"You'd better take us through the whole affair. Start from the beginning where you decided to go to your father's place. Why did you go there and with whom?" Tomlinson intervened.

"I wanted money. He refused and that's when he got killed with a knife. Just then I saw the gold on his desk. I grabbed it and was going to take the knife when I saw that English prof arriving. We ran out the back."

"There's that 'we' again," Watson observed. "Who were you with?"

O'Mallory didn't answer until Shaughnessy said "Lucas, I suggest you tell them now."

O'Mallory looked at his lawyer and sighed. "Mark van Vervoort." The police officers looked surprised. Watson asked "But his prints weren't found there. How come?"

"He wore surgical gloves we bought at the pharmacy down the road before we got to my old man's place."

"But you didn't wear any. Why not?"

"I didn't think I needed any. I wasn't going there to kill him or rob the place."

"Why was van Vervoort there in the first place?"

"I let him come along."

"Why?"

"Mark said that if I didn't, he would go to the cops and accuse me of Elisa's murder."

"Did he know something that would persuade us that he'd be telling the truth?"

"He saw me parking the car outside Joe's place after I came back from meeting Elisa."

"Why did he want to come along to your father's?"

"He said his father said there was treasure to be found, and Mark figured my father would know where."

"How did he figure that?"

"I never asked. Perhaps he thought the old man was rich because he knew where the treasure was."

"And did your father know that?"

"Oh yes. It was supposed to be a secret, but we all knew about it."

"Did you admit that to Mark?"

"Yes."

"Why would you do that?"

"I hated the old man. I hated how he treated my mother and me, how he treated his other kids. They had it easy, but we had to scramble for our living. He owed us."

"I see." Tomlinson paused.

"Did van Vervoort kill the old man?"

"Of course! Who else?"

"You?"

"My client denies that he did so," Shaughnessy quickly intervened.

Tomlinson sat back. "Is that everything?" When Lucas nodded, Tomlinson closed the meeting without making any promises until there had been discussions with the colleague forces and the Crown Attorney's Office.

***

Mark van Vervoort was arrested and brought in for questioning. He wore a dirty T shirt, torn denim jacket and jeans, and well-worn basketball shoes. He looked across the table at Watson and a constable and was if nothing, defiant.

"You've got nothing on me."

Watson looked at him and then looked down at a file on the table.

"I wouldn't be so sure about that," he looked up. "We have a witness who says you were at Mr. O'Mallory's house, and you murdered him."

"Prove it!"

"Are you denying it?"

"Sure, I am."

"So, you're saying you didn't go there? And you didn't search the place? And you didn't murder him?"

"Right," Mark agreed.

"So, we wouldn't have found your prints all over the place, and especially not on the murder weapon."

"No."

"Why not?"

"Because I wasn't there, and if I had been I would have worn gloves," van Vervoort leaned across the table.

"You mean gloves like the ones you bought at the pharmacy about a block away from the house."

"Nothing wrong with that."

"You're quite right about that, and of course they should stop any fingerprints from being found." He paused. "Trouble is, they aren't 100% reliable." van Vervoort suddenly became wary.

"What's that supposed to mean?"

"We can recover prints even if a person was wearing surgical gloves."

"I don't believe you."

"We'll soon see, won't we? Meantime, I'd like you to go with the constable here and change your clothes."

"What the fuck? Why would I do that?" van Vervoort began blustering.

"If you refuse, as you can do, then we will get a warrant. In the end those clothes will be examined, with or without your agreement."

"Get your warrant then," van Vervoort relapsed into a sullen silence and returned to his cell.

The warrant was obtained, and his clothes taken for forensic examination. Blood was found on his jeans and shoes and matched to O'Mallory's. He was charged with the O'Mallory murder.

49.

The Crown Attorney welcomed Tomlinson, Watson, and Armstrong into his office and opened the first of a several files folders.

"The charge against Mr. Lucas O'Mallory for the murder of his father." He read through the file. "This looks promising. You've established a motive, the opportunity, and prints on the murder weapon. Is there anything that could cast a doubt?"

"Only his version of what happened."

"Oh, yes!" he paused to read "He claims it was Mark van Vervoort who actually committed the murder." He stopped. "Unless van Vervoort confesses to the crime, I'd say there's a reasonable chance O'Mallory would be found guilty." He put the folder back onto his desk saying, "I'll discuss this with my colleagues, but even if we don't proceed with a murder charge, I'd say accessory to murder, and armed robbery would fly based on his admissions alone." He reached for another file.

"I think Mark van Vervoort can be charged with accessory to murder and armed robbery. Depending on what else you discover, a murder charge might also be possible."

"Now a possible charge against Lucas Mallory for Elisa's murder. Looking over what's here, I see he has admitted he went and met her and that you have evidence that supports his admission. However, I see he denies murdering her and the only possible witnesses that could shed further light on what happened are some unidentified Chinamen who have since died or disappeared. I don't think we'd get a conviction." He looked up.

"But we have motive and opportunity," protested Armstrong.

"We also matched Lucas' prints with a couple of old cases relative to sexual abuses and they matched," Tomlinson added.

"Were charges laid in those cases?" asked the Crown Attorney.

"No."

"Then I think the judge would rule them as inadmissible, and even suggest you had no right to keep them on file." Tomlinson shifted as if embarrassed.

"Furthermore, I think any judge is likely to deem most of what I see here as circumstantial in which case I'm doubtful whether a murder verdict would be certain. I'm sorry, but I can't recommend proceeding with a charge of murder with what you've shown me."

Tomlinson leaned forward. "We have some gloves that show Elisa's DNA on the outside, so that any DNA on the inside could be that of the murderer."

"That might be the piece that's missing, especially if you can show that only O'Mallory wore them."

"It's possible they're his half-brother's gloves," Tomlinson admitted. "But if Lucas wore them, his DNA might be on them."

"Did you check?"

"I'm not aware of a report on that so perhaps it was overlooked." The Crown Attorney looked disapprovingly at this admission of negligence.

"Well, I suggest you follow up to see whose they are and who wore them. Until then this charge is on hold." He put the file on his desk and escorted the officers out of his office.

***

"Inspector, the DNA tests on those gloves in Hummersdorf's car just came back. and Hummersdorf's is on the inside and the outside. Furthermore, the gloves show that they were used to pull wire that might fit the wire used to strangle Elisa."

"Let me just think for a moment," Tomlinson scratched his face. "O'Mallory admitted he went up and met her, and we have his print in the glove compartment, but denies he murdered Elisa and the gloves we found don't have Lucas O'Mallory's DNA. That would support his claim that he didn't murder her. Hummersdorf denies he went out that night, but his DNA is on the gloves which would suggest he was there. Who is lying?"

"Could they be working together?"

"Could be. Hummersdorf might have persuaded O'Mallory to commit the crime, but I don't see how, unless they went up there together. Did the constable who stopped the car say there were two people in it?"

"He was certain there was only one."

"OK. Go get Hummersdorf and let's question him again. Then let's talk to O'Mallory and perhaps we can find out what really happened."

348

"Should we charge Hummersdorf?"

"Not yet, unless we can show they worked as a team, or one of them confesses. Just bring him in for questioning."

Predictably, Hummersdorf did not change his story and had no answer why Elisa's DNA and the wire marks came to be on his gloves.

***

Mark van Vervoort was brought back to the interview room.

"Well, now. We've found O'Mallory's blood on your clothes. Want to tell us about it?" For the next hour, van Vervoort, other than blaming Lucas O'Mallory for the actual killing confirmed Lucas's description of events at the O'Mallory house.

"Let's go to another question. How do you know Lucas O'Mallory?"

"He and my dad are close friends."

"So, you knew that O'Mallory's father gave him gold from time to time."

"Yes."

"Did O'Mallory give you any of this gold?'

"Why should he?"

"Perhaps to sell for him?" van Vervoort just shrugged.

"Did you two often work together?" another shrug.

"Look, you come clean on everything, and we can think about reducing the charge."

"And if I don't?"

"You'll be facing a murder charge as well as a few others." There was no reply. "In fact, I doubt if you'll ever see the outside of a prison again."

van Vervoort started talking explaining many of the activities he and O'Mallory had engaged in. Among the activities was the sale of ingots that O'Mallory received from his father and which van Vervoort then sold on the black market. "But we always wore gloves to hide our prints."

"How do you mean?"

"I always gave Lucas surgical gloves and made sure he wore them."

***

"We just had an interview with Mark van Vervoort in which he admits he sold gold ingots for Lucas O'Mallory. They used surgical gloves to hide their prints in case any of the ingots somehow got back to the police."

"Can you repeat that last part?" Tomlinson asked and Watson did so. After the call, Tomlinson called in Alvarez and said, "Have forensics go over those gloves we found in Hummersdorf's car again, and this time in detail to see if there's anything that has been missed."

"Can I give them any specifics?"

"Yes, have them look both inside and out for particles of latex that could have come from surgical gloves."

50.

"Can I help you?" the secretary's voice floated down the line.

"I'd like to speak to Mr. O'Mallory, please."

"Who may I say is calling?"

"My name is Peter Holroyd."

"Just one moment please." Holroyd waited. "Are you there? I'm sorry Mr. Holroyd, Mr. O'Mallory is unavailable."

"Can I set up an appointment?"

"I'm afraid that will be impossible."

"Please tell Mr. O'Mallory I have something that belongs to the family, and I feel I should return it to him personally."

"Just a moment, please." He waited again. "Mr. O'Mallory thanks you and asks you give it the family lawyer who can then pass it on."

"Of course, if that is what Mr. O'Mallory wants. But he might wish to think about it a little more as I doubt he would it really want anyone else to see it. You may inform him that it concerns the whereabout of Koxinga's gold. And please call me when he decides to make an appointment."

"I will let him know." The call came sooner than he had expected. The conversation was brief and to the point.

"Holroyd? Simon O'Mallory here. I can make half an hour available tomorrow morning at 10."

"I'll be there."

On arrival he was ushered into the office and invited to sit.

"Well, sir?" O'Mallory did not look happy to see him.

"I came to return to you an item your father asked me to keep safe." O'Mallory sat silent before leaning forward.

"You will excuse me if I tell you that is hard to believe." He paused. "I have been informed my father's murderer or murderers have been arrested. However, I am given to understand, you are or were somehow involved in my father's death. Yet here you are claiming my father entrusted you with something that belongs to me or at least my family." O'Mallory made no attempt to hide his suspicion that somehow Holroyd was the cause of the murder.

Holroyd nodded, opened the briefcase he was carrying and took out a package that he placed on O'Mallory's desk. "This is yours." O'Mallory looked at it and then looked at Holroyd.

"And just what is it?"

"The diary, or perhaps the logbook of the captain or senior surviving officer of the Nuestra Señora de Vallodalid."

"I have no idea what you're talking about. Of what interest is that to me?"

"It explains the origins of your family's fortune."

"I think you had better explain that," O'Mallory showed his surprise.

Holroyd explained how he had become involved in the events after the discovery of the skeleton and how he had deduced the existence and probable location of Koxinga's gold.

"I see your point but not where you're going with this."

"Me? I'm not going anywhere with it. My interest was to solve the mystery as to why a Hong Kong businessman was searching for a ship that left China some 300 years ago. I believe I have answered that question."

"I see. And what is your answer?"

"The Hong Kong businessman believed the gold was his inheritance from an ancestor and so wanted to recover it."

"And why should that be of interest to me or my family?" O'Mallory looked closely at Holroyd.

"I believe one of your ancestors found the gold."

"And just where do you think this gold is now?" O'Mallory was not about to corroborate Holroyd's tale.

"I suspect it might be hidden somewhere under that massive structure your ancestor built here in Vancouver."

"What makes you think that?"

"I was curious why the building looks more like a fort or castle than a family dwelling. After all, Vancouver isn't a place where a building might be besieged unless, that is, it was thought to house something a great value." He stopped. "Given the history of the area, the most likely thing of value would be gold."

"But perhaps the gold was found during the gold rush."

"Yes, that is possible. But from what I saw in the museum, I believe the source of your family's gold is more likely to have been Koxinga's treasure. If so, its disposition would have to have been gradual and less open to scrutiny."

"I see." O'Mallory paused. "And what do you want?"

"Nothing."

"Did you come here thinking you would get some benefit from telling me all this? If so, you are sadly mistaken."

"No, Mr. O'Mallory. There is no benefit you could give me. I have solved to my satisfaction, the provenance of the treasure and the location of the gold. If any is left after all these years, it's none of my business."

"Well. Good. And don't even think that you can exert any pressures on me just because you think you know where the gold might be kept."

Holroyd looked at him. "You know, I find that a very mean remark. I wonder what your father would have thought of it." He stood up. "I came here to return to you an article that is of historical significance to you. Instead of expressing pleasure, I find you suspecting I had a hidden agenda of getting some benefit from you. Perhaps that is the world in which you live, but I don't. I hope you continue to enjoy it."

"Oh, don't act so innocent and pure. I've learned all about you from Joe."

"Have you indeed? You might want to re-valuate what you hear from your brother. But again, that is between you and him."

"Yes, it is! So now kindly leave and believe me, I will continue with my life."

"Yes, I believe you will. But I wonder what your siblings or Revenue Canada will think if they suspect you to be sitting on more treasure."

"And who is going to tell them that?"

"I have no idea, but it won't be me. I have no desire to become involved in what might turn out to be a very nasty family squabble."

"Then, sir, I believe our business is done." Holroyd nodded and left without waiting to complete the civilities of a friendly departure. *I won't be involving myself any further. What's that saying? Oh, yes! Uneasy lies the head that wears the crown or, in this case, holds the gold. As for Hummersdorf...* He did not complete the thought.

51

Lucas sat next to Shaughnessy in the interview room and watched the officers enter and sit on the opposite side of the table.

"Well, Mr. O'Mallory, would you take us over what happened when you met with Elisa?" Tomlinson asked.

"I told you before."

"Yes, you did. Please go over it again in detail." Lucas repeated to what he had admitted in the earlier interview. There were no significant discrepancies.

"You told us you wore gloves. Is that correct?"

"Yes."

"How many pairs did you wear?"

"That's a stupid question."

"Humour me. How many pairs did you wear?"

"Just one, obviously."

"Are you quite sure about that?"

"Yes, of course."

"And you did not wear any surgical gloves inside the outer pair?"

"That's dumb. Who would do that?"

"You did."

"Prove it," O'Mallory grinned smugly.

"We have. We re-examined the gloves in Hummers-dorf's car and what do you think we found?"

"I'll play your little game. What did you find?"

"Particles of latex." Tomlinson paused for dramatic effect. "Particles of latex with your DNA on them."

O'Mallory suddenly shifted nervously. "I don't believe you."

"You don't have to, as long as the Crown Attorney convinces a jury."

O'Mallory looked at his lawyer. "You're my lawyer, help me," he pleaded.

"Sorry, Lucas. I don't see how." Shaughnessy looked impassively at his client before turning to the officers. "May I have a few moments with my client?" The officers left and returned when Shaughnessy invited them back in.

"Mr. O'Mallory has something to say." For the next hour, the officers listened to how Lucas had long waited to do harm to Hummersdorf. He complained about how he and his mother had been denied the benefits that Hummersdorf and the other siblings had received. He went on to rail, how the family in contrast to their tolerance of Hummersdorf's lifestyle, had failed to stand by him when he was under investigation for his sexual misconducts. And finally, he confessed that when he met Elisa, she had recognised him. In a panic he had murdered Elisa and sought to get Hummersdorf blamed. He had indeed worn surgical gloves given to him by Mark van Vervoort not realising that modern forensics could discover the trick. At the end he signed his confession.

***

"Mr. Eddy, how nice of you to call." Holroyd answered the phone.

"So, it's all solved?" Eddy asked.

"It seems to be."

"And we get nothing for all our trouble?" Holroyd could hear the bitterness in Eddy's voice.

"If you mean, are you entitled to any of the treasure? I wouldn't think so, given that it was never buried on your lands. But I would not be surprised if you could claim against the university on the grounds that a faculty member, with the support of the university, started your troubles with his unfounded claims. But I'm not a lawyer. But at least the murderer has been arrested."

52.

Eddy sat on his usual rock and gazed over the calm waters of the cove and the bay beyond. The sealions and seagulls would soon be sunning themselves while squabbling over the best places to occupy. The totem poles clustered among the dark pines continued to fulfill their roles protecting the village and its heritage, and an occasional puff of wind whispered through the giant trees still acknowledging the homage these ancient growths were paying to the sanctity of the area.

As was his custom, he laid a fresh salmon on a nearby rock as an offering to his brother the Eagle and waited. Finally, he saw a movement near the entrance of the cove and a Sea Eagle flew to alight on a rock equidistant from man and fish. It stood there, ruffled its feathers, and looked at the man and the offering, and back again at the man. Neither of them moved until the eagle, satisfied that there was no danger or perhaps just driven by hunger took off, swooped over the morsel, and flew off with the fish in its talons.

Thank you, my brother.

53.

Holroyd opened the email from his contact in the Vatican. 'I was following up on your earlier inquiry and came across a report sent by a friar stationed in Acapulco following that city's establishment as a major Spanish port in the early 1530's. In it, he describes some exploratory wanderings up and down the coast. On one such trip, he came across what he describes as a stone monument with inscriptions that he knew were neither Aztec nor any other form he had seen in Mexico. He attached a sketch that I have scanned and included. I hope this is useful to you.' Holroyd looked at it.

He saw a pillar, or slab on a stone pedestal, that might have been carved to resemble something, perhaps a tortoise. The pillar was crowned by another carving that might have been of an animal that was a serpent, or dragon, or could have been part of Aztec culture. On the pillar the outlines of carvings looked vaguely familiar. But for a moment Holroyd could not place them. *I've seen something like this before. It reminds me of a photograph of a Chinese stele.* He opened up his computer and looked up Chinese stele.

As he scrolled down, he came across a report of the *Yongning* Temple stele erected near the Amur River. A sketch of the stele, by Ernst Georg Ravenstein was shown, and Holroyd went back to the scanned copy he had received and compared the two sketches. They were almost the same.

This Mexican object could be a Chinese stele! He examined the sketch again and focused on the characters carved on the pillar. After some thought, he recognised the outlines of a couple characters that might refer to, Zhou Man.

"Eureka! If I'm correct, this proves it*!" A Chinese stele put up during the Yongle Emperor's reign near the modern Acapulco means the Chinese did come here first. Put that in your hat van Vervoort and eat it.*

He sat back and luxuriated in the thought he had successfully proved his theory. But something nagged at him. *The Yongning stele and similar ones erected to commemorate an event were simple inscribed slabs or pillars on a stone pedestal. This one seemed to be crowned and mounted on the back of a tortoise which was a form reserved for noblemen and high mandarin officials, so what was the significance of this one? Was this one placed by such an official? I wonder if it still exists somewhere. I think I'd like to go check.*

Next, he called Merry.

"Well, old boy. Anything to report?"

"Oh yes! The enquiries into old ships sailing out of China to the East have nothing to do with modern proceeds of crime."

"Do tell."

For the next few minutes Holroyd gave a report on all that had happened.

"Bravo! Perhaps I should have mentioned this earlier, but we had reports of a great treasure on Canada's West Coast and that together with the search for an ancient ship is what really got us curious. What we wanted to know is whether this treasure was ancient or just a disguise for riches. So, we sent you find out."

"Dammit, Merry. Once again you ask me to do your work without giving me the full information."

"Yes, well, won't happen again," Merry managed to sound contrite.

"You're right. It won't."

"Too bad though you couldn't further your own research."

"Perhaps not quite." And he reported what he had just received from Rome.

"I say! That's wonderful! Are you going down there to check it out?"

"I think so, but I'll have to confirm it with the university and of course with Pearl."

***

Holroyd called Pearl and first enquired after her health. He felt a thrill of pleasure as she gushed how the baby was growing but expressed some irritation at interference from her mother who insisted she knew better than her daughter how to raise a baby.

"You must come home before I go crazy. Anyway, you have been gone long enough and you should have solved all the problems out there."

"Yes, dear. And you're right, we have solved the problems." He brought her up to date on all that had happened, omitting however, that he had spent time in jail as a suspect in a murder investigation. He congratulated her on her finding of the link between Wang Lin Fei and Wang Qu Ling. Pearl was ecstatic and almost purred with pleasure.

Then he told her about the email he had received from Rome and his thoughts on going down there to investigate. This latest piece of news was greeted in silence until "If you go there, don't come back."

With that, the line went dead.

Disclaimer

All persons named in this book, except for historical or publicly known individuals, are fictitious and in no way intended to reflect any living or dead person.

Acknowledgements

The author wishes to acknowledge the invaluable help of Lizy J Campbell, Lydia Gionet, Forest Maček, Paul Morisset, Richard Odey, and Eve Summerlee of Jericho Writers.

About the Author

Peter King was born in Scotland and grew up in Switzerland and England before coming to Canada to study civil engineering at McGill University. He obtained his MBA at Western University and his doctorate from the University of Phoenix at age seventy. He spent his career as a naval officer, a public servant, a consultant to First Nations, and as a professor at the University of Hearst. For fifteen years he was a professor at the Beijing University of Technology. He has competed and coached in fencing, rowing, and cross-country skiing. He was also an international umpire refereeing at the world rowing championships. He has been recognized by federal, provincial, and municipal governments in Canada and by the City of Beijing in China. He has published a history of rowing, several academic papers, and this is his second mystery thriller while rebuilding a model railway in his basement